The Dim Zone

CHRIS TURNER

CONTENTS

Chapter 1   5

Chapter 2   31

Chapter 3   57

Chapter 4   85

Chapter 5   105

Chapter 6   133

Chapter 7   151

Chapter 8   167

Chapter 9   183

I

The planet's horizon showed as a sepia smudge in the near distance. A small planet by most standards, lighter of atmosphere, half of Yul's home planet's gravity.

He stared over the drab terrain. His wrist brushed over the blaster at his hip and he felt sweat budding under his thermal suit. His faceplate misted with gray steam as his breath moved in easy rhythms. Tucked under an armpit he carried a bulky glass container for collecting plant samples. His sweat-slicked hair itched like the devil, plastered as it was to his neck. It was warm here, even by his standard. This alien planet, *Xeses*, was too close to the young sun that nourished it.

Brown shrubs and prickly thickets pocked the landscape. One could never be too sure what dangers lurked on these uncharted worlds. Various cases of mishaps on remote excursions were not uncommon. Equipment failure, oxygen-tank leaks, explosions, freak accidents, dangerous storms, wild critter attacks.

He flexed his shoulders, squatted to stretch his knees, studying what might be aquatic life in the shallow puddles that lay before him. Oddly his legs could already feel the stiffness from his long trek from the Lander VI spacecraft. Occasional pools of shimmering water glimmered jungle green in the distance. Bubbles oozed from the muck. He, Hurd and Regers could only safely venture a few miles distance from their parked vessel, the soft ground mushing more and more under his space boots. The ground was treacherous, too risky for a closer landing.

Brisk and wild-eyed, Regers peered back at him. He looked slightly off, bulkier now in his suit than in reality. He trudged to his right, holding a life sensor apparatus, a black box with sliders and dials. Hurd, who was in charge of ship's tactical, took up the rear, a lean no-nonsense type whose pale complexion seemed to mirror his mood. Three intense, dispossessed men, sent on a lonely mission far across the galaxy.

And yet, CEO Mathias, the smooth-talking industrialist who had approached them a few weeks earlier, had assured them that nothing dangerous existed on this remote world—the same man who ran a successful cybernetic company out of *Phallanor*, a few hundred light years away. "Bring back anything exotic or interesting," he said. "Especially plants." Those were his exact words. "The more you can carry, the more money you guys earn."

Provocative promises, thought Yul. But he couldn't refuse the impressive stipend the billionaire offered. Hundreds of thousands of yols to split among them, depending on the quality and amount of flora they brought back.

The details as to why this planet had been chosen, Mathias had not specified. Yul had not objected to this world or the region out in a far corner of space. *The Dim Zone*, as it was called, home to untold, unexplored planets and feral alien pirates, most notably the Zikri and the insectoid Mentera. Yul was getting paid handsomely. It was enough.

Some three miles from the lander, the trio halted to slog a bit further through knee-high ferns with broad green leaves bearing red and yellow stripes. The team's light silver suits swished in the alien foliage.

Regers stopped, a tinny buzzing emanating from his sensor. "Hold up. I got something." He knelt, lifted a tough frond and twisted off one of the peculiar pods that hung from its tip. Holding it up to his visor, he studied it like a chimp eyeing a banana.

Yul stooped to stroke one of the alien pods with his gloved hand. It seemed to quiver with a strange energy.

"Take these ones?" Hurd asked. He paused, squinting while the sensor continued to buzz.

Regers examined the pear-like pod with an air of distaste. The mottled patches on its surface seemed unwelcome intrusions. "What about these buds on the ends?"

Yul tipped back his head. "Throw them in. Mathias'll pay well for them."

"They're hardly buds," Hurd scoffed. "Some type of husk or pod." He wrinkled his nose and flicked his squirrel-like eyes over the specimens.

"Whatever. You carry them." Regers tossed the pods, which floated dream-like in the lower gravity to thud softly against Hurd's chest.

Hurd gathered them up, his teeth clenched. Yul carefully tucked three more pods into the corner of the covered bin he carried. He moved it closer to take the plants, soil and all.

The roots of these ferns, for lack of a better word, seemed stubbed with bulbs or nodules like small potatoes. Probably the low gravity had allowed them to survive with minimal root span. A plant such as this did not need huge stability. There didn't appear much wind on this planet either to blow it over or uproot it. No large water bodies either. Air, 38 degrees Celsius, saturated with excessive nitrogen, some carbon and argon, unbreathable for humans.

Yul toiled on while Hurd collected air samples in several canisters. This would keep the specimens alive on the ship. Let Mathias worry about keeping them alive after delivery.

The harsh daylight dimmed as the sun dipped behind some low-running clouds, or what looked like wispy, atmospheric moisture. The three had collected about thirty plants in all and as many pods. The few trees here, odd sculpted sentinels with yellow cones, looked out of place. Some were ragged and bushy with gel-like masses hanging from their ends, as if heavy with snow; others were stunted and bare of buds. The terrain was otherwise an empty shrubland, a barren moors with scattered pools. No movement showed of any kind. Windless wilds sheltering any number of mysteries. No sign of indigenous life forms graced the landscape. Again Yul asked himself why had Mathias chosen this particular desolate locale? No answer was forthcoming. The baking heat was diminishing as the sun crept towards the east in Xeses's retrograde rotation.

A sudden flicker caught Yul's eye. A large butterfly landed on one of the hanging pods. It began to extract juices with an extended proboscis. It was more a gray moth with four wings than a butterfly, about the length of his index finger.

He reached to grab a sample bottle from his kit. With an impulsive glint in his eye, Regers tore it from his grasp and blundered forward to capture the folded winged thing. Overshooting his mark, he stumbled headlong into the ferns and frightened the insect away.

"You bloody fool," Yul rasped. He snatched up the jar. "That bug could be worth a lot of money."

Regers scowled in sullen mood. He seemed antsy, as if eager to be done with this job and get back to the ship, almost as if he were high. The suit could not hide Yul's displeasure. His massive chest heaved. The accusing eyes and muscular arms lurking under that light protective outerwear, prompted Regers to back off.

Yul turned from Regers to watch the moth in rueful fascination. Its large, bulbous thorax twitched. Four wavy wings fluttered with back fin to guide it like a helicopter. It landed on another pod several feet away. Yul approached with stealthy steps. On a sudden downswing of his bottle, he closed the lid from underneath and secured the insect. He gusted a satisfied breath. The moth's proboscis dug into the plant leaf which had torn free. The moth happily sucked on the nourishment.

It had been a three-mile trudge through this treacherous terrain and not for nothing. This specimen would be worth a fortune.

He frowned. Easy to get lost here without landmarks. Fortunately the lander came equipped with a built-in homing beacon. He had programmed it to send out a short-range signal, in the event they got lost or separated.

Hurd peered at the few bins of plants, his blue eyes narrowed in skepticism. "Mathias will want more samples than this."

"We can't risk being down here for too long," Yul warned. "*Albatross* is crippled. I don't like leaving her in the hands of Frue and Greer. Besides, Mathias was specific about the planet. We got the plants he wanted—I think."

Regers raised a brisk hand. "If you'd listen to me, it'd be those two idiots, Frue and Greer, collecting odds and sods here instead of us."

Yul shook his head. "We argued about this already, deciding who was going planetside. Let's get on with it."

"Frue, the little baby, he whines like a—"

"Cut it, Regers! If we need to, we'll make a second trip down. For now, we've secured enough plant life, so Mathias can't squawk too loudly." Yul pursed his lips, pondering Mathias's cryptic remarks. There was much Yul wished he had asked the man earlier that he hadn't. Like why come all the way out here for some plants? Weren't there others on closer planets? They could have brought a team of scientists along to study the flora, eggheads more suited for collecting this stuff and codifying than them. He suspected Mathias had hired them more for their muscle than anything. Why?

A nagging suspicion tugged at him, one of those gut instincts foretelling that something was about to go strangely awry.

The three slogged their way back to the lander, Hurd slipping twice, almost into fermenting, slimy pools, earning Regers' laughter. But Yul could only curse out a few bleated warnings. Regers was out of line. The more they pushed him, the worse he got. Regers, normally efficient and cut-to-the-chase, was off. Something was wrong with him. Yul was more worried about damage to the samples than anything. Stupid to come all this way and have their investment spoiled. Already Hurd's ferns were wilting.

Yul paused.

Could the stems actually be moving? He shook his head. He must be imagining it. Hurd's jerky hops had the leaves quivering. Doubtless these plants experienced little to no change in their environment. It was important that the specimens survive until they got them back to Mathias's cybernetics lab on Phallanor, the far side of Arcturus.

Regers remained smug over the initial discovery, strutting and hopping with his shorter stride. He removed himself from the task of carrying the bulky containers and clutched the sensor box in a loose grip. His eyes were glazed as if he were stoned. The color in his face shone a waxy gray; beads of sweat dripped down his narrow cheeks.

In sour silence, Yul and Hurd carried the samples, eager to be relieved of this chore as soon as possible. It would be all over once they got back to the lander. Yul regretted that the electric cart that Mathias had supplied to transfer the samples had been insufficiently designed to handle this type of soggy, rough terrain.

Yul looked back. A new scowl creased his brow. Strange that there wasn't any larger animal life here. The atmosphere was near poisonous, but the flora seemed rich enough. What lurked in the pools, he daren't guess. One shimmered with a strange iridescence at his feet. He stooped to stir a twig in the muck, one fallen from one of the sparse and stunted bushes.

The cloud-shimmering water showed a faint ripple on its oily surface, leaving Hurd blinking as he crouched to collect one last sediment and water sample. Bubbles came up slowly from the water. The mud was soft and yielding. Hurd stoppered the glass containers and added it to his glass bin, then stared with suspicion at yet another ripple.

The ship's computers could check for microbes in the mixture. In the lower gravity it was easier to bear such weights, though it was difficult to adjust to the hopping gait necessary to keep from falling flat on their faces. They adopted a proverbial 'Moon Walk'—one energetic hop then another foot to spring off from the last. It could send a person flying six feet in the air, as Regers had learned the hard way while trying to move too quickly and vaulted over a pool, nearly smashing his faceplate into a trunk of one of the cone-shaped trees.

Yul wished the numbskull had. It would have taken him out and one less shit for brains to worry about on this mission. This seemed a different Regers than the one he had met back at the space hub orbiting Phallanor: the one who had shown no small amount of courage saving Yul's ass from the teeth of an eight-foot winged alien. It was all so puzzling.

As the gray octagonal hull of the lander came into sight, Yul breathed a sigh. He'd been wondering if the beacon had gone awry. Hurd triggered the landing hatch and the gray ramp lowered itself like a drawbridge between two metallic legs. Yul gripped the 80kg sample bins and lifted them one by one with effortless ease to Hurd who'd loped up the ramp and was now dragging them into the holding bay. The weight felt much less under Xeses' diminished gravity. Nevertheless, Yul shook off the heaviness in his prosthetic left arm.

The crew depressurized. The three stowed their gear in the side hatches and removed their helmets. Yul moved aft to start up the engines. The Vegas-U6 rumbled to life: a trim craft, cramped and cozy, but she did the job.

Regers lingered behind to pop some capsules in his mouth. Maybe the man was in pain and needed medication? Certainly he wasn't winning any friends. Regers adjusted his wine-colored cloak and gave it a twirl. "We're coming up, Frue." His voice sounded gritty in the ship-to-lander com. "Got us some real feisty ones here. Plants and a tiger moth. Get the *Albatross* ready." He croaked out a chuckle.

The engines roared. They took their seats for the short journey to the fast running Alpha-Explorer *Albatross* circling out in low orbit.

Yul did not laugh. An unpleasant feeling still clutched his gut. He often did not have such feelings. Old doubts returned to plague him. How had Mathias phrased it? *A unique task. You came up on our list ...a most suitable applicant.* He recalled the praise distinctly before he had landed on Phallanor, as he guided the U6 skyward.

What list? Yul had no answer. He tried to keep as low a profile as possible. Eccentric billionaires could afford to have their secrets. Mathias was no exception.

The dim rainbow hues of the Skull Nebula sprawled light years away out the viewport. The sleek mother ship *Albatross* came into view, a long, silver-gray Alpha retrofit of an earlier model with twin thrusters and cargo bays at stern and flared lander pads at midships. Frue, the pilot, guided them in.

Greer, the ship's engineer, greeted the three at the hatch, his face creased in an affable grin. He was a short, sallow-faced man with salt-and-pepper hair, expert with ship's functions. "Any luck?"

"We secured water and soil samples and some plants," Yul reported. "We didn't hang back too long. Oxygen levels were getting low. For whatever reasons, I'm not sure. Maybe Regers's been sucking on the tubes again." That earned Greer's laugh. "Night was coming on, and the barren planet didn't look that promising. I could skip the sightseeing."

"As long as we have the merchandise. Now we just have to get the *Albatross* fixed up."

"Any luck with our technical problem?"

"Nada."

Yul loosed a heavy breath. *What good was gathering all these samples, if we couldn't get Albatross out of here?* "The hyperthrust is not optional."

Greer chewed his lip.

No sooner had they dragged the bins down the ramp to the main level of the ship than the safety lights blinked green and the crew were hauling the samples to the midships bay adjoining the bridge. Yul's back muscles rippled as he manhandled the heavy weight of the primary bin on his shoulder. The bone'd been partially reconstructed after the surgery. Loose-limbed and square-jawed, the merc ran his keen eyes over the specimens. Regers, as usual, made no effort to assist. Hurd, the tallest of the three, took the lighter bin while Greer trailed behind with the key equipment: cutting tools, drills, monitoring devices and sterilized tubes. They decided, after a brief conference, to move the samples to the bridge to watch over them, considering they were their bread and butter. Greer and Yul busied themselves setting up the rectangular tanks at a place off to the side. Mathias had thoughtfully supplied air-tight glass containers for the samples, with three-inch tempered glass to withstand any contagion or assaults from within. Greer, anticipating the arrival of samples, had already readied the compressor to pump the planet's atmosphere from the sample tanks into the display cases. An upturned water reservoir on the upper glass panel was rigged with nozzle and gauge to drip-irrigate the soil.

Yul tested the drip to ensure it was working. He set down his drill and donned protective gloves and mask to transplant the ferns. Hurd took the remaining water to the ship's lab for analysis.

The animal container remained empty.

Yul and Greer dumped the extra soil into the plant containers. Each dug out some holes in the soil to admit the roots. Yul lowered the plants in and tamped the earth around the lower stems with his gloves. Pouring some of the water sample overtop for good measure, he gave a grunt of satisfaction. All seemed in order. The moth he put in last, watching it flutter about the plants with an effort of will. It dropped to crawl on the soil and climb up and settle on a broad, splayed leaf of a pod. The insect did not seem happy. "Sorry, buddy, but money is money." Yul sealed the circular opening at the top while Greer pumped in the rest of the oxygen.

Yul took off his mask and his eyes teared up as if a batch of raw onions had just been sliced. He caught a whiff of an exotic odor hovering in the air with a blend of burning peat and wet dog. *All that from the brief moments the plants were in contact with the cabin air?*

He stepped back to examine his handiwork and witnessed a depressing scene. The leaves had wilted, many lay supine on the yellowish soil, as if dead.

"Doesn't look too good, does it, flowerboy?" Regers jibed.

Yul pursed his lip. Though he had to agree. Even after they had taken such pains to gather and transplant the flora, they looked unlikely to maintain their upright posture. The ship's artificial gravity was likely the cause. Too high. The moth seemed unaffected.

"Well, live or die, I christen you *Kektus*—and *Graywing*," Yul said.

The moth, almost in answer, stuck in a proboscis and sucked instinctively on one of the yellow pods.

The other men flashed Yul blank stares.

"Kektus... cactus? You know, *Graywing*, as in butterfly," Yul explained.

Regers shook his head. He rolled his eyes and turned away.

"Want me to lower the artificial grav index for the plants?" Frue asked. "Stinks to high heaven in here. Might help the plants out. They're looking mighty sad."

Yul inclined his head. "Look."

The leaves had started to perk up. Small, buttress-like legs had formed at the base of every stalk to tilt the plants up to a 30 degree angle.

"Well, what do you know?" Frue mused. He scratched at his carroty-red hair and gestured in boyish surprise.

Yul's brows rose. "They're adjusting to the higher gravity. Even the moth's wings seem stronger. Look at her hovering over that leaf."

Regers ripped open one of the sustenance packs at the service counter and smoothed back his oily mullet. He punched some buttons on a microwave to the side to heat it up, only paying idle attention to the samples. Yul took a tentative pack of his own. He grimaced at the sawdusty taste of mash all too familiar after this two-week-long journey. Mashed potatoes with watery beef jerky. Mathias, for all his millions, had certainly cheaped out on food.

Hurd returned while Greer was cutting some of the plexiglas to make extra holders to house the pods. Entranced with the sight of the alien life, he accidentally cut his finger and gave a loud groan.

Regers sucked on his thumb to mimic Greer's pain.

Greer rounded on him. "Why don't you fuck off, Regers, and do some work around here for a change? Are you here to mock everybody? You and your ridiculous cape. Who do you think you are, Captain Wunderbar?"

"Watch your mouth, Greer. Or you might find you're wearing it up your ass."

Yul ignored the insults. Five men cooped up in a rabbit hutch was a recipe for disaster. Men of dubious compatibility and capabilities. Mercenaries who had been rounded up by Mathias at the last minute and prepped with only one hell-bent test mission. Cabin fever, a spaceman's worst nightmare. It could be their demise, Yul thought… and yet it had set in early. He didn't know much about these men's backgrounds, but he divined by certain hints that at least Regers and Hurd were ex-cons.

"One of us has to go out there and fix that rear ion-gun projection stabilizer," Yul announced. "The diagnostics' function is blown out, likely when we had that incident with the Mentera."

"Thanks to Frue here," Regers grumbled.

"What the hell were locust-aliens doing out here anyway?" Frue said. "Sure, our hyperdrive's screwed now. Worse yet, if we fix it, it could flake out on us again in the middle of light speed."

"I'm not going out there," Hurd said. "I did enough on Xeses. Get Greer or someone else to do the dirty work. Not so hard to sit in a pilot's chair, watching pretty pictures flash up on a screen."

"And who's been flying *Albatross* all this time?" Frue snapped. "Who's been evading marauders?"

"We're beyond the pale," said Yul. "It's to be expected."

"All's I know," Regers said, "is we've been up here for three days. On half impulse power. It'll take us two hundred years to make it back to the nearest hub at Fevenar with the weak impulse drive we got and I don't plan on playing circlejerk here with you guys till the end of time."

"As I said, get Greer to do it," grunted Hurd. "He just stayed back and twiddled his thumbs watching the lander take off."

"Screw you, Hurd!" cried Greer. "Don't think for a second that I—"

"Do it." Yul waved his cutting tool at Greer. "Either you or Hurd. We need Frue to watch the ship...and Regers's obviously too much of a princess to do anything."

"I don't see you volunteering," said Greer. He bared a set of yellow-stained teeth.

"No, I'm not. Nor were you volunteering to go down to Xeses."

Greer grumbled, but he made no efforts to squabble further. Perhaps he realized that to take on Yul was a losing game.

"We're getting no read from the diagnostic," Greer said. "I'm assuming the sensor's blown. I've rigged up something makeshift in the meantime."

"Good." Yul nodded. "A step forward at least."

"Yes, goody for you," jeered Regers. "Do something useful for a change."

"How 'bout instead of whining like a silly bitch, you get out here and help, Regers?" Greer snatched up a length of air hose. "Rather than criticizing everyone who doesn't live up to your standards—"

Regers leaped over and gave Greer a vicious shove that sent his head smacking into the glass housing the plants. Yul cursed and moved in like a cheetah to hold the seething Regers back from laying fists into Greer. "Easy, Regers! Don't be an ass."

"Shut the fuck up, Yul. Get your mitts off me or I'll rip them off. Wasn't Greer who got his hands dirty down there."

Regers' vulture-like face, greasy hair with receding hairline, and thick-soled black boots were a sorry sight. Even then he only stood nose to nose with Yul, who was at best 5'10". Regers' wine-colored cloak flared as Yul wrapped it around his neck and pulled. Regers rasped out monosyllables. He thrashed as he struggled in Yul's mechanized grip, wincing as the iron fingers dug deeper into his arms and caused him to flinch. Regers struggled harder but Yul only tightened his grip. Faces inches apart, it was at that moment that Yul figured out what was the matter with Regers. Those pills. The chalky gray face, the shaky hands, the sweat pouring down his brow and neck. He was jacked up on something. Devirol? Addicted to some filthy drug?

Greer picked himself up, wiped his bleeding scalp and growled threats. He looked ready to brain Regers with the end of a pipe wrench, but he contained his fury. He took up his repair kit and the makeshift diagnostic sensor and mumbled curses. Without a look back he marched down the hallway.

Yul loosed his grip on Regers and shoved him out of the way. "Stay back and don't do anything stupid. Damn Mathias for putting us together."

And damn Mathias for not naming a leader among this motley crew. He had just herded them all together like yard dogs and told them to work together and get the job done. A mistake. He caught up to Greer and helped him suit up in the midships utility hatch. "Forget Regers, he's zoned out and high."

"No kidding. I doubt my going out there'll help," Greer said. He held up the replacement part. "But I'm game and I'm beyond solutions at this point."

"Attaboy, Greer," Regers sneered from down the hall. He chewed the last of his synthetic, microwaved mutton and smacked his lips.

Greer ignored the jibe. He checked his magnetic boots, adjusted a few gauges on his suit, then stepped into the pressure hatch. Yul closed the inner hatch, watching him through the glass. The outer hatch opened and Greer was exposed to space.

Taking five decisive steps, Greer unraveled the umbilical cord from the command post at the hatch and plugged it into the life support system at his side. The cord, shielded with hypertensile alloys, served as an auxiliary air feed and fluid feed, a backup should his own systems fail.

Yul watched Greer through the port, as his magnetic heels clanked on the hull's surface and allowed him to walk safely. It gave Yul time to assess progress, and chills to watch Greer space-walk despite the safety mechanisms in place. A number of things could go wrong. It happened all the time when technicians went to repair systems on the fritz outside the safety of the hull.

It seemed Greer was making some progress at least. He could hear the dull clunk on the ship's outer shell: Greer squatting down to unscrew the housing and remove the palm-sized sensor from the projection gun jutting out from near the rear fin.

"Plate is ripped clean off," Greer reported. "Mentera fire, I'm assuming. The light-drive sensor is shredded. Small wonder. The projection cap looks clean. We could be lucky."

"Let's hope so," said Yul.

He watched as Greer unscrewed the capsule. From what he understood, the projection cap was a robust piece of hardware that could handle a lot of shock, but any skew in its central core could incapacitate the light drive. The projection beam scanned the physical makeup of the ship and created a physical 'disruptor' that moved the ship's mass to the frequency domain. Then it propelled it through the light highways. Even that layman's description did nothing to capture the atomic physics that worked to power the light drive.

Yul's earphone crackled. *Frue.*

"You'd better get over here. We have a problem."

"What now?" cried Yul. " Jesus! Keep an eye on Greer for me. He's out there alone."

"No kidding. There's something you should know—"

"Not now." Yul cut the channel. He left the hatch pad, hastening down the passage to the bridge.

He scrambled into the command area to hear Regers arguing with Hurd and aiming a fist at his head. "I told you not to fuck with the plants, and what do you do?"

"They were trying to get out," complained Hurd. "Figured they needed some water. Scratching on the glass. Now look, they're all agitated."

Yul stared as if Hurd had gone mad. *Trying to get out?* He saw that the moth was gone. Had Hurd killed it? No, the plant must have eaten it. Right, a Venus flytrap?... Damn! The moth was their greatest find. Could it have burrowed into the soil to hide? Yul saw no insect parts, legs or wings littered the damp soil. But eight of the thirty-odd plants had already perked up, adapted and grown fleshier. Fibrous tissue formed ribs along their stalks almost like muscle to support themselves.

Hurd sputtered in defense. "It's beyond me why Cyber Corp wants this plant shit anyway. I'm no botanist, or gardener."

Yul dismissed Hurd with a wave. "Who cares or knows what these CEO's want? As long as Mathias pays us, we do what we're told."

"We'd better—"

The ship's emergency klaxon rang.

"Oh, shit." Frue paled. "That's what I was telling you about earlier. A blip on the microchannel—It faded away, thought it was a sensor malfunction. But looks as if we do have company. A Mark IV on starboard."

All eyes turned to the viewscreen: a monster orb-like ship covered in iron spikes hurtled after them.

Yul swore.

Regers wheeled on Frue. "I thought you scrambled our cloaking frequency? Not even government cryptos could crack it."

"They decoded it, what do you think, Regers?" Frue said miserably. "Must have found a crack. Or some blind spot or loophole. What do I know? The Mentera must have tipped the Zikri off to our presence."

"Do something, you dumb fuck!" Regers yelled.

Frue gave a snarl. "What can I do, if we're reduced to half impulse?"

"Gun them down then!"

"Right, a Class B Orb?"

A shockwave ran to port. A bright flare bounced off their shields, nearly compromising the hull.

Yul raced for the weapons' console. Greer was down, hit by residuals from the heat wave. Hurd stood blinking dumbly. The whiffs of the alien air must have affected his brain.

Regers shook his head. "Move this ship!" He leaped to the console and jerked the control out of Frue's hand. Regers jammed the lever to an upright position and the ship lurched out of its smooth glide and its stable orbit.

Frue croaked in horror. Greer was ripped from his umbilical cord and went twirling out into space, toward the yellow planet.

"You fucking bastard," Frue cried. "What are you, some kind psycho? You just killed Greer."

"Right, I did your dirty work for you, Frue. Greer was already a goner. And your alternative was to get us all killed? Maybe check your logic, Frue."

"Screw you, Regers," said Frue. "How do you know we couldn't have got Greer in?"

Yul glared in disbelief. "You're a callous bastard, Regers. True, we could have been gunned down but—" He bounded two strides with aim to lay the man low. "We'll settle this after this is over. Battle stations!"

Clenching his fists, he let his anger subside. The strong metal in his left fist ached to pound Regers into the ground. But he desisted. They needed the cretin until the mission was over.

Though he hated to admit it, Yul knew Regers had saved their asses. If he hadn't taken action, they'd be targeted by Orb fire. But perhaps Frue could have dodged the Mark IV at sublight speed long enough to get Greer back in the hatch? Who knew? Then again, maybe he couldn't have.

Frue muttered under his breath while Regers stared grim-faced at the approaching enemy. "You think I'm going to trust your goody-goody evasions, Frue? Look at what happened to us last time with those locust freaks. You played cat and mouse and we almost got blown out of the sky. Remember?"

"Do something!" growled Hurd, now joggling the weapons console. He loosed bolts of ion-fire at the invading craft. The ion blasts glanced harmlessly off the attack Orb's shields.

"They're closing in." Yul's sharp eyes scrutinized the oncoming craft on the viewscreen.

The *Albatross* rocked to enemy fire. Reserve shields were low. Only a matter of time before they would fizzle out.

"Zikri!—I hate Zikri," Yul muttered.

"Yeah, who doesn't?" Frue wheezed. "Take our ship for parts, kill us or sell us to the bloody Mentera."

"Whatever. Let's get the fuck away from them," Regers growled. He cocked his blaster. His eyes darted every which way.

Frue stabbed out at the screen. "It's a mid-size scavenger vessel. Look! Class B, as I said. Likely a skeleton crew, but—"

"They're deadly, we know." Yul scanned the viewscreen and racked his brain for a solution. He saw no weakness in the massive Orb's plate defenses pocked with metal spikes that drove in on them like an undersea mine.

The *Albatross* weaved like a firefly. Zikri uro bombs lit up the space outside *Albatross's* rear fins. The hull caught scatterings of explosions. Red flames burned from starboard to port viewports. Frue threw up his hands in despair.

The *Albatross* decelerated to a standstill. The Orb loomed ever closer in the viewscreen.

A tractor beam had caught the ship. Yul could not mistake that faintly perceptible jar tugging at the ship and the backward drag of deceleration.

Silence. A low throb of ominous frequencies. Yul's gut plummeted like a deep sea mine. Light dimmed, as a shadow fell over the ship. Now *Albatross* began to move back toward the larger menace.

"Fuck." Frue jammed the thrusters to max. Nothing.

"Do something!" croaked Regers.

"There's nothing to do, Regers!"

Regers slapped his arms down with frustration.

Yul watched the rear viewport screen and caught twisted glimpses of strange metal walls spiked with barbs closing in on them. The Orb's tractor hatch closed; starless darkness wrapped around them, as black as a mummy's tomb.

The dull thud of clamps sounded on the outer hull. Then the scratching of probes, instruments and alien sensors grinding on the surrounding metal. Yul could count the times this had happened to him on one finger. Now it was happening again, though he had vowed never to be caught like a fish in a net.

"Christ!" He leaped to his feet, leaving the command post. "They're going to board us! Lower the outer visors!"

Frue hit a switch. A whir of machinery gave way to titanized plates sliding over the viewport glass around the ship's hull.

"Follow me," grunted Yul. "Grab as much gear as you can. Then haul ass back to the bridge." He raced to the midships bay. The others, fast on his heels, raided the weapon stores like thieves.

"Suit up!" Yul ordered. "Take extra adhesive in case your suits get breached. The Zikri'll hit us with everything they've got, nerve gas first—or a concussion blast."

"Both, if we're unlucky," grunted Regers.

Yul snatched at pieces of body armor. "We're going to need protection too if we're to stay alive."

His mind raced. His commando sense took over as he rummaged through the lockers for his suit. They'd be expecting panic-stricken crew members, not hardened, armed defenders.

He grimaced. He'd make sure they were caught unprepared. He focused on a battle plan. He grabbed whatever concussion bombs remained in the lower weapons' shelves.

Frue gaped at him. "Are you crazy? You'll blow us sky high."

"Ever hear of surprise? They won't expect it. We're already goners, Frue. Give them something to think about. That's the way. A gruesome welcome. I'm setting them for half stun. We'll shield ourselves behind the consoles."

"But the samples—"

"Screw the fucking samples, you idiot! We're dead if we don't do something." He shoved the others along the corridor and through the portal to the bridge. The plants stood curiously upright under their protective glass, oblivious to any imminent danger.

Hurd opted to take his chances wearing only a mask. "A full suit'll only hinder my mobility."

Regers sneered.

Yul ignored them. He planted one of the hand-sized bombs at the door's threshold. Quickly, he programmed the remote control of the detonator for a five second delay then positioned himself behind the master console in the bridge's center. Cocking his weapon, he sent a prayer upward.

"Seal the hatch," came his first murmur to Frue.

Frue hit the switch then ran beside Yul. The shielded metal door dropped down, plunging them all in silence. They waited, Regers to the left of the starboard console, Hurd, Yul and Frue behind the central stand. All aimed blasters at the door. Plunks and scratching noises sounded on the hull over their heads, tools digging and doing grisly work.

A dull reverberation echoed throughout the surrounding metal. The aliens had breached the hull. As an ominous silence ticked away, a deafening explosion rocked the ship. The central port hatch exploded in a spray of metal. Jagged shrapnel flew everywhere like poison darts.

Yul was thrown back. He hit his shoulder hard on the side wall. Regers howled as he opened a stream of fire on the yellowish smoke where the door had been. This was home now to an indistinct blur of shapes struggling through. Grotesque shapes. Neither squid, mollusk or mammal, but some gruesome parody of all—alien life from the most vivid nightmare, complete with stub legs and tail. Zikri surged forth in body armor like phantasms out of the dark nethers. Tentacles wavered, thick and slimy. Dark bodies pulsed with scintillating menace. Yul could see moving shapes in the smoke and thought to detect a sprawl of tubes and a diamond-shaped headpiece denoting air masks that covered the withered, ropy flesh.

His fingers clicked the timed release on the detonator. He crouched back, counted the seconds.

Kaboom! The scatter bomb went off like a Roman candle, blinding anything in sight. His armor caught the first wave of the concussion as flying debris slapped at him.

The plant aquarium went flying to smash against the nearest wall. Glass sizzled and melted. Yul could hear the crackling of burning leaves and pods. He could see nothing in the smoke. His faceplate was clogged with soot and alien blood. Only a roaring rush came in his ears, then a whistling noise, then the faraway whimpers of living organisms in pain.

Wiping at his faceplate, he squinted through the glass. The plant aquarium had rolled to a stop, overturned on its edge. The melting, liquid glass pooled and sizzled at his feet, a gaping hole left in its side.

Things crawled out. To his horror, the surviving alien ferns had sprouted new root-like legs and limped from their broken crib like crippled frogs. They skittered and curled around the shins of the Zikri invaders.

Yul's ears still rang, but he caught sight of other bizarre movements. Some of the pods had rolled, many half burned, others scorched but intact, rippling in multicolored confusion like certain chameleons camouflaging themselves in self defense.

Yul groped. His hand latched onto one while reaching for his blaster. He shook the thickening haze out of his skull. Staggering to his feet, he felt the pain in his right thigh arc in a red hot wave.

Faster than snakes, Zikri flanked him and Regers and Hurd, using smoke as a screen. One hauled Hurd back in a sea of tentacles. Hurd's mouth opened in a high, soundless cry. His back arched like a man whose bones were snapping, then he disappeared in a swarm of rank flesh. Regers, at the edge of the fray, briefly managed to avoid their attacks.

Yul opened fire into the blur of menacing shapes. Tentacles sprayed in thick ruin and black blood. Gutters of fetid liquid flesh pooled. Squeals and chitters rang out in mad waves as Zikri writhed and twisted in their death throes. The creatures had not expected any organized resistance. Hurd flopped in a bloody pool, groping and crawling his way along, gasping out what sounded like his last breaths.

Too many!

Yul sprang sideways. Arching away from the flesh-rending tentacles, he sprang back, trying to evade the gruesome clot.

It was ineffective.

Hurd's agonized wail shrilled over the com.

A dozen or more squids came streaming out of the yellow smog, savaging the fallen Hurd in a sea of glistening tentacles. Hurd was engulfed before Regers, he or Frue could do anything. A group of the first Zikri wave gripped him and hauled him into the hall.

Yul loosed more fire. With Hurd's wretched howls crackling into obscurity, the crawling plants jerked their brown stalks upright from under the Zikri's webbed feet. The plants hissed. They wrapped the longest of their leaves about the advancing squid's lower motilators and short swishing tails. The Zikri flung them off. They slapped against the wall with wet, sucking sounds.

"Christ, they're morphing!" Yul yelled at Frue. "Get away from them!"

The man, panic-stricken, floundered at his side, spraying blaster fire blindly at the tentacled monsters.

A crawling plant jumped like an enormous leech, wrapping its leaves around a Zikri's midsection.

Regers kicked away one of the curling leaves as it tried to climb up his leg. He screeched as one of the plants clambered on his back and wrapped around his neck.

Yul stared dumbfounded as he fired into the smoke. Through his squinting daze he could swear the ferns were trying to protect the defenseless pods from the tramping feet of the Zikri.

Regers choked as the ring of foliage tightened around his suit. Nearly strangled, he thrust up with his bowie knife. The tough plant tissue parted and fell with a thud to the floor. But more things sprouted from the viscous goo.

"Get out of here, you fools!" Yul could hear the whimper of the plant-like voices. Things which seemed immune to the nerve gas, or whatever toxic mix the Zikri pirates had pumped into the air.

Zikri cornered Regers who raged and fired as their tentacles bit into his suit. For all his erratic behavior, the man's grit could not be denied. He threw off his molesters, heaving and cursing, then ducked under one's whipping tentacle to twist away, blasting it with his sidearm.

Yul's body armor caught a sudden Zikri gun blast. The metal deflected the shot which would have punctured his suit and left him prey to the vapors. Yet the sizzle left a scorching mark smoking on his ribs. Had the ray hit his helmet...

Despite the dirty-yellow smoke drifting Yul's way, a sixth sense warned him of a sudden movement to his left. He lifted his blaster, caught a gliding Zikri square in the face. The alien face went all pudgy for an instant, green and angry with air mask and nozzle askew. Then the head exploded in a gelatinous mass.

The Zikri leader that had fired the shot surged through the mass at Yul's right. Rippling tentacles caught Yul in a grip that had his eyes bulging. He fell over in a heap, blaster thrown from his hand. Landing on his side, he groaned at the hard abrasive jab of pear-shaped pods under his ravaged ribs. The Zikri was all over him, suffocating him like an octopus. He could not break free. Clammy tentacles crushed his torso despite his body armor. His ribs began to cave. The creature emitted an electrical discharge that made his nerves tingle with fire.

He thrust up an arm, his left mechanized one, and ripped off the alien's facemask. To no avail. He couldn't reach far enough. His upper arms were pinned by the monster's strangling tentacles.

The whimperings of the plants, the frenzied chitter of Zikri—the tumult of madness, all crowded in on his brain. He thrashed with all his might, looking for any way to free himself, a weapon, any object. His questing fingers hooked onto a long shard of glass. With savage force, he plunged it into the Zikri's squishy skull. A splurting sound filled his earpiece. The repulsive grip loosened. He pulled free another of the pods under his back that was grinding into his vertebrae and smashed knuckles into the Zikri's faceplate, ramming the pod into the mouth of the creature that champed toward him.

The alien gave a slobbery moan. It convulsed in a pile of twitching flesh, face writhing.

The pod had cracked open. Something had slipped down the Zikri's throat—an insect with wings? At least they looked like wings. The Zikri twitched and gurgled, loosing a horrible, shrieking chitter. Yul had no time to see what emerged.

Another vengeful squid, larger than the others, lunged at him. The thing tried to wrap a slippery coil around his neck but with a savage wrench of his mechanized fingers, he pulled the thing forward. Its flesh tore at the shoulder. Blood spurted from the mangled limb.

More aliens rushed to avenge their fallen leader. Obscene things with hose and nozzled faces and rippling tentacles. They surged out of the smoke with fury. Electrical shocks flared through Yul's nerves as tentacles brushed his armor like jellyfish. He jerked in pain, but he reined in his strength, teeth gritted, and slashed out with his shard of glass. He tore away from the quivering mass of tentacles, snatched up his blaster, struggled toward Regers.

"Get away from them," he cried at Regers who tottered unsteadily. Frue was moaning and crouching monkey-like in the smoke, spraying fire every which way.

If not for the gripping strength of his prosthetic arm, Yul would have perished. His desperate urge for life and his unfailing body armor saved him from a horrible death.

Damn these filthy things! How many did he have to kill? Did they store a potential charge in their bodies? Hurd was wrong. If not for the suit the thing would have electrocuted him. Which meant that—

He thrust away the thought of Hurd. He plowed on, managing to break the slippery grip of his determined foe. Hearing Regers' howls of pain beside him, he lurched forward, knowing well the consequences of being pulled back into that ghastly clutch.

He raced for the blown exit hatch, shooting anything that moved.

Sweat poured down his spine. The back of his skull rang. Their only hope was to break through this rabble and reach the exit.

Dodging return fire, he saw a Zikri had curled a slimy tentacle a luminous weapon and was aiming it with deadly intent; the others had no weapons, only blood-splattered nozzles and hoses that passed over their mouths to protect them from the nerve gas.

"Move!" He pushed Frue away from the fray. In a fierce rush, he bolted for the exit, feeling the brush of tentacles snatching at his limbs and stray fire at his heels. Out through the blasted door, down the *Albatross's* hallway Yul fled. Regers and Frue clumped close at his heels. Through the smoking hole in the *Albatross's* hull they stumbled on into the alien ship.

Towering black walls of a massive hold arched around them. Ribbed like a whale's belly. Yul caught a glimpse of a human figure— Hurd struggling feebly in a mass of tentacles, pulled screaming into a side hall. Yul struggled to catch up with the three creatures that held Hurd, but the diamond-shaped portal closed and Yul stopped dead, his nose inches from the dark metal.

Two V-Zon lightfighters sat chained to the wall. Prime hardware, mostly intact, but fuselages charred from bomb blasts.

Where were all his enemies? Hopefully they had killed them all.

The sounds of heavy chittering echoed behind him. The scuttling of crab-like movement—Zikri out for revenge, hot for blood.

What Yul saw had his jaw dropping.

Some of the Zikri had yellow-red leaves banded around their torsos, their tentacles fighting to rid themselves of the invasive presence. They clung to them like leeches and seemed to burrow deeper into their scaly flesh.

The leaves that had survived the blasters had become broader, stronger and more spiked. They had adapted to their environment. To the enemy creatures that populated it.

Hurd was a dead man. But where were the squids taking him?

Yul rushed on with Frue at his heels. Regers limped behind.

All this coursed through Yul's brain in a blur as he caught glimpses of low, strangely-wrought benches and shelves along the sides with assorted metal tools of long, chilling design. Welding torches? Drill cutters? Yul's brain spun with the possibilities, but he was too dizzy to register a plan. The place was as much of a chop shop as a spaceyard for captured vessels.

Several arch-shaped exits or entries lined the near wall. Yul, Frue and Regers ducked into the nearest arch and staggered down a narrow corridor. Walls crowded in on them. Panels rich with motifs of writhing tentacles, malformed heads, Zikri faces, strange star patterns and backdrops of space. All monochrome, a black or charcoal gray wash. Yul guessed these walls were crafted of octagonal plates. But an otherworldly glow lit the interior. Bio-luminescence? He could only guess. Either way, it was from some source unknown.

Regers gave a rasping cry. He collapsed, holding his leg. Wheezing, spitting his own blood into his helmet, he groaned. "Damn it! I can hardly lift a leg."

Yul turned, paused. "Move, Regers, or you're snake bait." His voice was a hoarse whisper.

Regers held up a hand. "You know, old Mathias practically begged me to join this mission. Shuttled me about like some grand vizier to his lordship's mansion." He coughed. "I humored the old fool, levered him into tripling my wages."

"So?" Yul gave a sad mutter. "I was approached by him too. God knows how my name got on a list. Wouldn't have taken this job had I not so many damn debts to settle." He looked around, expecting Zikri to pounce on them any second.

None were in sight.

Regers threw up his hands. He coughed out a gob of blood. "All for this? Out in *The Dim Zone*, grubbing for daisies on filthy worlds, in a Zikri hold, lambs to the slaughter?"

"Come on! We've got to keep moving." Yul snatched at his arm, felt a trace of pity for the rogue, who had succumbed to an addiction and a plant parasite—even though that pity seemed ridiculous, given

Regers' part in killing Greer.

"Maybe, maybe not. We could run right into more of those squids up there. Where do you want to die, Yul, here or there?"

"Neither. How be we get to a safe place?"

Frue opened his mouth to speak but Regers cut him off.

"Shut it, Frue. You always were a gasbagger, you little fag. Let me die in peace."

"Let's go, then." Frue pulled Yul's arm.

Yul shook his head.

Chitters echoed up the ship's hallway ahead. Back the other way, snorts, bangs and the heavy clomp of metal and machinery rang. Another percussive blast echoed up the corridor.

Yul was knocked backward as a massive girder fell, nearly severing his leg. He stumbled to his knees, panting. The passage had been blocked—with a rain of falling debris. Frue and Regers were trapped on the other side.

Yul cursed. He rubbed his aching back. God help the bastards now. He pounded on the fallen mass. It would take a tank to move the rubble. Fuck it. With an exasperated grunt, he turned away. Little else to do. He left the others to fend for themselves and ran on undeterred.

Chapter 2

Yul moved ahead, blaster in hand. The cuts and bruises he suffered, less severe than on other occasions, did not impede his half-shambling pace...or quest to take down as many of these fiends as he could. He wondered if his companions fared as badly as he thought they did.

The wide corridor curved, shaped in a crude arch, rising mere inches above his helmet. His breath coursed in rasps, leaving a trail of gray vapor behind him. His eyes flicked over the oxygen meter on his left wrist. He had sixteen hours of air left. The helm and suit sensors showed breathable atmosphere in the Zikri ship.

Odd. Yet he would not discard his protective gear. Who knew what foreign elements floated in the air. He clutched his weapon with new resolve, assured of a measure of safety in this upside down world of life and death. The stabbing pain in his shoulder had spiked so he touched the pain inhibitor at his wrist. The resultant muscle relaxant released into his air mix took the edge off the worst of the throbbing.

Yul marveled at the twisted and demented designs that peppered the ship's walls. Glossy, veined ridges ribbed them like bones flayed of flesh. It was as if he walked the innards of a butchered whale. Those features were glazed with a patina of shellac gleaming with a hideous purpose. Zikri decor? Housings for power cables? Yul traced his gloved fingers across the irregular surface only to sense an impending doom.

The passage widened. If anything, it became more garish with incomprehensible designs—floating cities crafted of gargantuan blocks of translucent crystal with Zikri squid riding strange, gnat-shaped vehicles through the air highways. The images were always static, yet in the dimness, everything seemed to move with a life of its own.

The slithering rustle of scuttling feet came from somewhere ahead and had him halting, every muscle tensed. Zikri were on the lookout.

He darted across the metal-plated corridor, blaster in hand.

A large circuit box with three aerials sat near the wall. He hid behind it, crouching rodent-like in the shadows. He guessed it to be some artificial grav-generator. It emitted a low, barely-perceptible hum.

Dim designs of Zikri heads and loathsome tentacles loomed overhead. The pictography made Yul's flesh crawl, backlit as it was by an unknown source. Yet the eerie shadows could not hide him forever. Hopefully long enough for these fiends to pass.

Had they detected him? He did not think so, but he was still unsure of how keen their senses were. From close-quarter skirmishing he knew they sported some sort of crude nostrils and repulsive mouth, but he did not know how they worked.

The chittering echoed closer. Yul crouched lower. Three Zikri glided out of the murk to pass before the corridor in which he lay hidden. No mistaking those horrid polyps of mouth and tiny, yellow-green teeth. Nor the glistening gray tentacles that wavered as vocal organs warbled out some semblance of communication.

The trio rippled their stocky bulks and moved side by side, three tentacles to a side, torso to throat. Thick, webbed feet padded like lizards' feet and stubs of tails provided balance to facilitate the creatures' locomotion. It was almost reptilian.

It was the first he had observed them up close while not hunched in a frenzied bent-kneed run. The creatures were the most ghastly things he had ever seen. For years, the Zikri had been nothing but bogeymen in his mind, things of myth versus the space pirates they actually were. They relied on the constricting and electrifying strength of motilators to overcome opponents, rather than modern blasters. The reality was much worse than the myth.

Let them pass, Yul willed. With teeth clenched, he stared transfixed as it seemed they were returning to the hold.

Gripping his blaster, Yul resisted the urge to cut down the gruesome threesome. More would swarm, alerted by the blast—like rats to a feast. God help Regers and Frue, if they were still alive. He may have signed their death warrants by not killing these aliens, if in fact, the predators were heading in their direction. What was done, was done. He had to trust his instincts.

The noises faded and Yul loosed a relieved breath. Stealthily, he crawled from his hiding place and listening with both ears strained, he heard no spine-crawling chitters. With gentle force, he scratched the butt of his weapon on the glimmering wall protrusions as he crept on, in case he needed to retrace his steps. Cross-corridors ran rife here. A maze of passageways. Why so many built into their ship?

There must be a command center. If he could—

He paused, spellbound.

Rounding a corner, he discerned a greenish glow spilling across a gloomy corridor ahead. To his left rose an open archway.

Risking a peek, Yul took half steps to the entrance. He spied a dimly lit chamber spider-webbed with designs, depicting cruel torture instruments, spiked and barbed. More incomprehensible tendrils ran up and down the walls and across the ceiling like branches of a tree. The ceiling ran high into gloom. There was a wrongness to this chamber that raised the hairs on the back of Yul's neck. An inexplicable aura of subjugation and horror lurked in the shadows.

Perhaps the Zikri had replicated their halls with simulations of their primordial habitat? But then their cities, if that's what those depictions were that he'd seen scratched earlier on the walls, seemed crafted of geometric forms. Yul shook his head. The disparity perplexed him.

He advanced with caution. At once, his mind flashed on the skulking Zikri that had passed him, perhaps the very same that had been dragging Hurd to some doom. Where had they taken him?

Thirty tanks holding various lifeforms filled the hall. Some were human, or semi-human, with budding horns protruding from their temples. Others gave Yul pause.

He blanched with terror. Hurd hovered in a half curled position, floating upright in his tank like an embalmed puppet. He hung suspended in some foul pale green liquid with arms and legs akimbo, as if typing at a keyboard. His eyes were glazed over, dead for all appearances. The air mask dangled around his neck. His head lolled.

His crewmate must be dead. But wait! His eyes...had they blinked?...no, impossible..Yet those lips had moved with a soundless cry. A bubble popped out of the parted lips and rose to the surface. Could Hurd be alive?

Yul grimaced at the utter impossibility of it. His weapon sagged. He reared back, almost brushing against a larger tank behind him.

Enclosed within the glass loomed a grotesque leviathan of an earlier age. Great white tusks curled on its snoutless face, neither fish nor mammal, looking like some Zikri, but not. Baby tentacles sprouted on its thorax, as if they had just started budding in their process of maturation. The thing held itself suspended by triangular upper and lower fins of blue and white cartilage.

A cursory glance revealed some quarter of these disturbing tanks contained alien mammals or hybrid fish, but the rest were human or human-like. Open archways ran back of the chamber. From the greenish glimpses Yul snatched, there reposed more tanks of similar quality in those side rooms. An anger like no other stabbed him at the hideous implications.

He gave the monstrous, mammalian squid-like thing a wide berth. It had an incredibly hostile look to it. Who had created such a monstrous menagerie?

It must be the Mentera that Frue talked about so avidly. Those bloodsucking locust mutants.

A slithering sound echoed out of the shadows. Yul was roused out of his reverie.

More Zikri. Gliding on skulking feet, they moved like phantoms through a rear entrance, undulating tentacles extended. Why did they always travel in threes?

Yul ducked behind Hurd's tank. He scarcely dared to breathe, his blaster held on the ready. His dim outline was hopefully hidden behind Hurd's opaque shimmer, though he prayed his thin vapor trail had not been seen. He could hear their squashy movements as tentacles guided their gliding motion. He hunched lower. Like wraiths they slipped across the plated hall and Yul's flesh crawled. Those tentacles, thick as boas, could strangle a man in seconds, squeeze his liver right through his mouth. That fate not so long ago he had barely escaped.

Yul could hear the squids' incessant chittering, like the insect chatter in faraway jungles. How many more of these creatures must he kill, creatures that roved the ship down the many corridors meandering in gloom and eerie stillness?

No time to deal with Hurd. Yul lay in wait, weighing his options. If he startled them, they could storm him in a single swoop. Easy to spray them with a burst of fire, but what of the chance others were skulking nearby?

One of the brutes passed close, only to pause.

It lifted its polyped head as if to sniff the air like a stalking predator, its slimy, gray tentacles pausing from their writhing rhythm.

The Zikri's features were a smear of indistinct sense organs, pig-like eyes, flattened snout, warted, pudgy cheeks. The stuff of nightmares. Its sense orifices and protuberances were nothing more than chilling, gray-black blobs set against a slightly darker hide.

The thing had sniffed him out like some mutant bloodhound.

He opened fire. Dismembered pieces sprayed black blood. Its comrades whirled, tentacles rippling on robust torsos. More of the grotesques slid out of the shadows like serpents.

Yul slipped on the gore. The fiends were upon him in seconds. He flipped over on his back—just in time to blast the first grisly head and the eel-like appendages about to riddle him with electricity. Yul rolled away—no time to get to his feet—as he swatted off the ghastly flesh from his faceplate.

Two surged after him. More were gliding their way back from the hall where he had come.

He gained his feet and scrambled to an exit. He ran full tilt down an unknown corridor, to an unknown doom. He wheeled around to spray ion fire, a defiant cry on his lips in face of the futility of it all. There were too many of the fiends! Everywhere.

Ducking down a cross corridor, he raced on, then sped down another, panting with horror. To his left loomed a wide doorway. Beyond it, four Zikri wearing crude, spiked, metal headgear worked at the ship's helm. Holy shit, the control room! Two others to the side had turned to gaze back at the source of the ruckus. They lifted gray tentacles at the human that aimed a blaster at them. Their angry chitters reached out to send shivers up his spine.

Yul heard padding sounds at his back. Webbed enemy feet.

He whirled, blasted the first questing feelers that threatened to wrap around his throat. The Zikri sagged on his torso in twisting ropes of death.

The bridge door came a foot from sliding shut. Yul heaved and jammed the shredded Zikri in it.

More webbed feet pattered from the corridor.

A stray blast came hurtling out at him from the bridge, followed by excited Zikri chitters. Yul ducked back, grimacing. The reality of being caught in the crossfire between two grotesque and hostile forces was enough to make the most courageous man quail.

His back flush to the leftmost wall, he felt the alien squid motifs dig into his back. A live grisly head poked out its mottled face through the doorway. He blasted it from stem to stern. The lumpy body split open. He caught the sagging heap and used it as a shield and pushed the creature back into the control room. An angry knot of confusion raged on the bridge. He riddled the knot of Zikri at the controls with ion fire as they leapt from their stations. The last Zikri choked on its own blood and collapsed in a charred heap.

Yul heaved the dead creature out the door. The sliding mechanism was jammed, but an inner safety door served as backup, a heavy barrier with thick black iron, equipped with a metal ring of sorts.

Yul clamped the door shut, cranking the smooth iron ring with his strong fingers, sealing it.

He crept over to examine the bodies. Obscene things. He licked his lips with distaste. Nudging the first with his toe, he felt it give way with a sludgy, slopping sound. The dark blood pooled at its side with slick and heavy emphasis and stuck to his boot. Under its misshapen back and unnatural neck more blood pooled. More squids would be coming soon. To avenge their comrades' deaths. He turned with a jerk, examining the rest of his environment.

He had a slim sliver of opportunity to figure out the bridge controls, at best sabotage them, so they couldn't hyperdrive to their home base, or alert their own kind. No way to know whether these creatures had been aware of the cockup on the *Albatross* and had alerted backup yet or not.

His wide eyes blinked at an unwelcome sight. Another glass tank? Yul reeled. Slowly he walked over to the aquarium, his mouth sagging, like a man in a trance.

* * *

The sudden blast had sent Regers' air mix out of kilter. Now it was injecting stimulus chemicals into his helmet—the equivalent of a shot of heroin and a zap of speed. The suit's survival pack—with sensors tuned to track vitals: BP, heart rate, reflex rate—was designed for such emergencies should an occupant require a jolt to get him functioning again. In Regers' case, it gave him a new vigor to survive. His head felt buoyant; the drugged air was having its effect; pain had fled his battered limbs. With an ear-to-ear grin, Regers stroked his aching neck, feeling his gloved hand press on his silver suit. His eyes glazed.

Frue, the smarmy weasel, had abandoned him. He recalled the pilot's juvenile taunts...enough to make him want to jump up and break his face. "Get up, Regers, what are you, a little baby? Tough man, murdering crew mates but now he's so weak he can't even lift a toe? You're a fucking joke, Regers. Gonna die here?"

Regers recalled thrusting his aching body forward to take out the wretch in spite of his pain. He saw the ploy now; the little freak had only goaded him, knowing his only chance to save his own ass was to have Regers' gun on his side. Frue had written him off and stayed well out of reach, taunting him from a distance. When the heat had finally come, Frue had blundered down the passage like a madman, emboldened into gunning down the first wave of Zikri that came gliding out of the gloom like phantoms. More out of blind fear and adrenaline rush than skill. Frue had gone kamikaze and escaped. That said, the Zikri that had stumbled upon them had bled and died in as much agony as his own blaster could have dished out.

Frue's little moment had given him time to limp away down a murky side corridor while the chitters and gasps of horror raged on, of Zikri and human alike. Eight had emerged, and he'd blasted them head-on, a lethal enough squad to have taken out Frue in a flash had he not been there to protect him. Frue's gasps and heaves were music to his ears. Where Frue was now, alive or dead, he had no idea. Nor did he care. What was for sure, the little weasel had left him isolated here to die, at most hoping that he would be bait for Zikri creeping from the rear or side.

The walls around him seemed to waver. Cold metal shimmered and blurred. Like a man influenced by a hallucinogen, Regers stumbled on. Despite the gas mixture easing his pain, he pined for the Devirol caps in his waist belt pouch. When Choko and Biggs forced him to take the bam, given him his first taste for it, he'd gotten hooked on that daydreamy shit and now the craving was out of control. He couldn't think straight. Images were stretched and blurred at the edges. As if this life-and-death situation were nothing more than a kids' cartoon.

The ship's low, hypnotic throb penetrated the layers of his waking consciousness. It was almost subliminal. Black, squid-like figures sculpted like bas-reliefs into the metal plates littered the walls. To his drug-hazed mind, they had the semblance of the nest of some creepy-crawling creature. All seemed to swell in the glow of a slightly sepia tint. Regers shook his head, struggling to dispel the illusions.

His fingers reached out and touched the squidly engravings...the rib and coral-like formations. His lips pursed. Hard cold metal. Just a ship. Only a ship, Regers, don't crap your pants over it. What could a freaky, hypnotic thrum do—

He blinked. The wooziness took over again. This weird ship was getting to him. It was only a ship, but full of grotesque shapes and images that sent his brain reeling. The plant creatures they'd brought aboard had inconvenienced the Zikri, but if he had his choice, he'd have shredded the alien things and commandeered Mathias's ship.

Fuck Mathias. He'd have killed the sod too, then the others of his team if they didn't agree to his 'mutiny' to steal command of *Albatross*. Regers paused, alarmed even himself at the reckless intensity of his rant. It must be those mutant ferns had infected his blood with some toxin? Turned him crazy. Well, it was the least of his concern now. Where was that bastard Yul? He'd been thrown to the other side of the cave-in. He and Frue had fled down the corridor into endless murk. Frue'd turned chickenshit and tried to shanghai him. The weasel'd taken out the first wave, true, but then he saw him scrambling back, beetling into a cross corridor with squids on his tail. Hopefully he got his just reward. He'd blasted most of the freaks after that, given both of them an avenue of escape, at serious risk to his own life, but Frue had initially left him there to die. Then again, would he not have done the same?

Regers gave a contorted frown. It was a dog-eat-dog world. And this rat's maze of corridors wasn't helping. No chance of easily gaining an escape route. His earpiece communicator was dead. He rapped his helmet with a gloved hand. All he heard was crackling noise. Onward...where else to go?

Regers shivered at the memory of the slimy, squeezing flesh. That last Zikri had almost torn his head off. The thing had followed him like a hungry spider, some straggler from the pack creeping from the hold. But in the end it had received its just desserts, a faceful of blaster fire. Ha ha. Fucked up thing. What a horrid species, these Zikri. If he were a god, would he have created such cosmic deformities? No. Another reason that there was no god in this universe. Just a random, cruel universe, screwed up in every aspect, with alien things and sadistic opportunists and powers-that-be ready to mess up everybody and everything.

Calm down, Regers. You're a ranting pessimist.

He slapped his hand hard again against his helmet, rattling his skull. He could barely blame his cruddy team, or the Devirol, but why waste his breath? Hurd, the fool, had got what he deserved, snatched by those squids. Frue, he need say no more. Messed up the light drive field generator through his ignorant escape tactics. Greer, well, Greer was gone too, nothing to be done there. He grimaced, knowing the engineer had faced a kinder fate than Hurd, given what the Zikri would have done to him. For Yul he had a grudging respect, only because the man took charge and was something of a natural leader. The muscled merc's level-headedness in organizing the expedition to Xeses was proof, in face of all the arguments against, especially the risk of leaving the ship prey to new assaults by the Mentera. He had chuckled when Frue had refused to man the controls and sit exposed to possible attack. Yul had lost it and shaken him like a rag doll. Even then, the man was too soft-hearted. A lamb. He would have them turning the other cheek and saying nice things to one another, even if they were enemies. Yul's thinking was too tunnel-vision. Though his spur-of-the-moment plan of delayed detonation was effective and had set the Zikri on their heels, enabled them to flee.

Regers glanced down at his boots, frowning at the strange throbbing at his right ankle. He noticed one of the plant things had latched on with tenacious force. It had formed a ring around his leg, much like a coil of string, or a dance-whore's bracelet.

The thing would not let go. At first, it was too puny to detect, but now it had grown. His skin itched, also ached under the coiling pressure. Likely cutting off some circulation. Whether epiphyte or symbiotic growth, he did not know. He tried ripping the thing off with his gloved hands but no go. His bowie knife had failed to pierce it.

Fuck it.

It seemed whenever the plant's host was attacked, it fought back to protect itself and its host anchor. It had a remarkable tendency to adapt. A defensive versus aggressive lifeform. Christ, he was sounding like Yul. If it wanted to cut off the circulation in his foot, let it. At this point he cared less. His time was running out. These were the advantages of being higher than a kite to the death, on *Devirol* or *Bam*, whatever the hell it was.

Now he was lost. He hadn't a clue where Yul was, or if he had survived the explosion.

Frue? Who needed the little shit? If the idiot had dodged the Mentera faster and not screwed up the projector beam, none of this would have happened.

Regers took a deep breath. Anger would keep him alive longer. Keep him from succumbing to the dominance of these squids. So would contempt for general humanity, and aliens. All the wealthy industrialists who conned innocent men into risking their lives for a fool's errand. He never wanted to see another fishy creature, squid or plant again.

It had all gone wrong less than two months ago. He had never wanted any of this. *Mathias. The Dim Zone.* Exploring dangerous worlds. But life had thrown him a curve, snatched everything from him—that mattered.

Tooth for a tooth. An eye for an eye. Those were the maxims that made sense to him.

Olg, the gang leader, and his brutes had played a number on his loved one. He had wanted out of that twisted gang. Finding her body, or what was left of it, it had been...gruesome. *Olg*, the fucker. The memories spilled back to Regers in a bitter flood. That spidery script of Olg's, written in Salma's own blood on a note pinned to her mangled corpse. The still-warm blood that caked her glossy blond hair decked with flowers...

The note, rhyming on about 'betrayal', 'duty', and 'commitments' to the guild. Olg was always a sentimental bastard.

If he had any regret at this point, Regers admitted it was that he might not get to repay Olg for his brutal vendetta.

He lifted his head, his blaster raised in a clenched fist. A glow peeked to the left down the corridor. Some weird room lay beyond a U-shaped archway.

As he stumbled in to take a look, pale eyes gleamed back at him from the dimness.

What the—?

A weird medley of creatures glared at him from within those tanks. He recognized a man-like Jakru with horns curling out from its temples. He saw a few humans, several Daulks with their elephant-like ears...and lastly Hurd! Dear old Hurd.

Of course, these were victims of the Zikri hijackings. Stored here for a later date. For what? The slave markets at Mansrath? The vampirism of the Mentera?

Very beguiling and sinister...

Regers staggered over to the glass of Hurd's tank and blinked, tapping on the surface.

Hurd gazed back at him with sightless apathy. He was a shadow puppet bobbing in his liquid, like some drowned mannequin. His wounds looked grievous, but strangely healed. A bright gash stained his military grade spaceman's coat where the Zikri had maimed him.

"Hurd, my fine man—are you enjoying the vista?"

Regers pushed an ear to the tank. "Cat got your tongue?"

Regers shook his head in benign wonder. "Well, at least you'll never be thirsty, or lack a place to swim in."

Regers edged back with a scowl. Hurd looked alive, but surely he must be dead. Shouldn't he? No man could have withstood that extent of Zikri savagery. Still, the man's eyes were open. Regers could have sworn the tall figure blinked earlier. How did he stay alive in that liquid with his lungs full of water?

Unless he was the next Aquaman?

Regers laughed at his joke. He toyed with the idea of breaking the glass and releasing Hurd just to see what would happen. No, it was insane. But if Hurd were alive, he'd need every ally to escape this mess.

He lifted his blaster, risking the noise that it would raise if Zikri were lurking about. It was then that a particularly loathsome specimen caught his eye. The creature lurked two tanks down in the largest vat—a creature neither squid, nor epiphyte, fish nor mammal. It was a *heptadoria*, if he knew anything about alien species. What the Christ would Zikri want with one of those? Surely no slaver in the galaxy would buy such a disgusting thing? But then again, Mathias, the crazy git, had put a gilded carrot in front of their noses to have them haul ass half way around the galaxy to gather these freakish plants. Regers still recalled the sinister grip, the leaf furling around his leg back at the bridge. It was one of the same that had spawned the repulsive vine that currently held him.

Regers was contemplating such thoughts, tapping idly on his helmet, when the Zikri came out of nowhere. He saw it in time. Slashing with his knife, he hacked off a foot of writhing tentacle, then he blasted the thing's face off. Croaking with heedless satisfaction, he kicked the thing and stomped on its ooze-gushing guts. He was a fucking superman! Come out, come out, wherever you are and get a taste of my E1! But he had not seen the other rooms yet. And so, while he stomped, he missed the slinking shape that slid from behind him, out of the shadowy doorway.

Until it was too late.

With a flurry of tentacles, a fleet-footed thing pinned Regers' blaster to his side. His first shot went awry, the bright flare smacking into a nearby tank, releasing its human occupant. Cursing, Regers slipped on the greasy liquid, as did the Zikri, offering him an instant of opportunity to break free and tear away from the loathsome sting of its pulsing tentacle. He cut at it with his knife, swatting flapping chunks of bloody tentacles away from his faceplate.

Dark blood splashed everywhere. The Zikri chittered in an obscene fury, loosing an awful pandemonium. Regers laughed. He battered the thing with fists, knees, and knife. But such an injury which would have disemboweled any other assailant did not stay the thing's advance. It was larger and more resilient than the others. His attacks only served to anger the monster more. Now it lashed out, pulling Regers in closer with its repulsive tentacles until his ribs began to cave. His helmet cracked, his protective suit rippled to the abominable pressure, and the Zikri air flooded into his suit.

Regers gasped, unable to stop himself from gulping the foreign air, but it was neither toxic nor corrosive to his lungs, only riddled with a stagnant odor of dust, molder and neglected places.

The tentacles gripped tighter and Regers' spine began to buckle. His left ulna snapped, then two of his ribs. He howled in anguish. He could barely move in the crushing grip.

The ravaged Zikri dragged Regers' struggling body to one of the larger tanks. Flicking off the tank's cap, it heaved Regers up and over with a mighty toss into the ghoulish water.

Regers felt his body sinking like a stone. He stared, blinking with dismay, unable to stop himself, as he choked on the foul, briny, putrid water, paralyzed from toe to throat.

The massive shark-like creature that moved around in the greenish fluid was at first curious. Then its wavering fins dragging at the water pushed it closer to the strange human who sank and choked. Regers' lungs filled with water. Slowly he drowned...

But he was strangely alive.

The fish-mammal he had called a *heptadoria* nudged him with its beak, then curled its flexible body around him and wrestled with his limp form, until he could feel nothing but arching pain. Yet new life was coming, springing, surging through his limbs and nerves from the alien fluid. He felt the tug of mandibles, teeth tearing at his hand which hung limp as it gnawed at tendons and gristle, relishing its appetizer, not so much out of hunger as boredom.

The Zikri that had assaulted him, chittering in new interest, swayed like a serpent outside the tank, but then it jerked to a new stimulus. It ripped at one of the ferns that had curled about its lower tentacle. A small pod had formed there at the frond's end. The writhing, red-green plant twisted in the Zikri's slimy grip, trying to escape. To no avail.

Almost in mockery, the Zikri surged toward the glass and pulled off the tank's cap and tossed the angry pod inside, resealing the top. It sat back again on its rubbery haunches to watch the interplay.

The pod sank in a stream of bubbles. A miraculous thing indeed, and an even more miraculous thing occurred.

The pod cracked open, given new life in the warm greenish bath and the Zikri shuffled forward in sudden, new fascination.

Even as the mutant heptadoria snapped and gulped down the plant and pod, its single eye bulged and its mouth opened wide, as if retching. A remarkable life form had birthed in the Mentera witch water. A fantastic, grotesque creature, some iridescent butterfly with fins and tail, glided out of the monster's mouth and finned about, a new Lord of the tank, something of a cross between a butterfly and a fish.

The butterfly came to pause inches from Regers' goggling eyes, its eyeless face somehow peering with wonder, curiosity, and a sense of deep connectedness into Regers' own.

The hypnotic stare bore into Regers' soul. The insect's wings outspread like a tiny avatar.

A cosmic understanding passed between Regers and butterfly, beings from worlds apart, beings of vastly diverse physiology, and Regers drifted into some kind of surreal dream, his mind spinning through the kaleidoscope of misdeeds committed in his days, and for the first time in his life he entertained the thought that there might be a higher power that guided the universe.

* * *

Yul's scalp prickled at the gruesome sight in the tank before him. Some remotely humanoid creature with locust head was suspended in the greenish water. Perhaps Mathias would pay extra fare for this absurdity, he thought as a chill raced up his spine. And yet, somehow he thought he would not be seeing Mathias anytime soon...

He found it hard to tear his gaze away from the macabre thing. If the Mentera were the makers of these ghastly tanks, why trap one of their own kind in the foul water? Why here on the bridge? It made little sense.

The banging on the door, however, was real enough. It grew with each second. Yul's fingers twitched on his weapon.

In sudden fury, he tucked it away in his suit and dragged the dead Zikri over to the insect's tank. If these fiends were in cahoots and wanted to be bedfellows, then let them get better acquainted. He unstoppered the tank and hefted the dead hulk of the Zikri into the greenish soup. His mechanical grip was strong enough to punch holes into its squishy underbelly. Its vile blood stained the green water a murky umber. The locust thing within flapped about, trying to evade the newcomer's plunge. The squid promptly sank to the bottom.

Yul tore his attention away from the two freaks and studied the controls on the Zikri console. Three panels of tentacle-shaped dials rose before him; a viewscreen in the middle showed the blackness of space, the twinkling of stars, and the planet Xeses suspended below, a thin, yellow crescent dropping off at the bottom of the screen.

The banging stopped. Had the Zikri given up? Why? To fetch explosives to crack open the hatch?

He swallowed hard and stepped closer to the main console, his eyes refocused. He tried to make sense of the controls and gave up, eventually to stumble over to the viewscreen.

His sharp eyes took in the situation. He did not like what he saw. How to navigate this alien vessel? The controls and script were gobbledygook. He knew far less about piloting than combat and weaponry. Where was Frue when he needed him?

The tall panels rose over him in mockery. The reconnaissance of the enemy craft's bridge left him sullen and frustrated. The nagging question came again: why bring Mentera technology to the bridge?

The Zikri's eyes, what he thought were eyes, glinted with sinister life in the alien fluid. Yul's flesh crawled. The alien seemed animated. A flicker of tentacle caught his eye; no, it was merely settling to a stationary position in the water. Some stimulus reflex after death? The locust creature hovered a few inches above the bottom of the tank, a foot from the tentacled monster. Its unblinking eyes stared on in calm detachment, as if those crimson orbs were in never-ending observation of the bridge's affairs.

Two antennae sprouted from its plated crown. Pincers hung motionless out in front, zombie-like, with its heavy hind legs bent like a grasshopper's. A wire hose, attached from the crystalline cap on the tank's top and trailed down with a circular clamp on its end, the size of his fist. It appeared to have circuitry. Obviously not of Zikri design; the symbology inscribed on the outer edges and base of the tank were much different than that written on the bridge's consoles. The Zikri must have added Mentera technology to their ship... The Zikri—whose infamous piracy was notorious around the galaxy— must have even terrorized the Mentera for generations.

Yul was about to start touching dials randomly when his headset crackled.

"Yul, you alive?"

Yul paused, stunned. "Frue, I thought you were dead! Where are you? Am I dreaming?"

"Open this cock-eyed door."

Yul blinked. So, Frue apparently had managed to make his way to the bridge.

"There's a heap of bodies lying about. I'm outside the door. I'm sure it's your handiwork."

"Thought I'd never hear your whiny voice again." Yul gave a thin-lipped grin.

"My com blew out. I just managed to get it up and running now. Hurry! These squids are lurking everywhere. I killed some but—"

"Never mind, Frue. Knock three times. I want to be sure it's you."

Yul heard a series of clinking thuds against the metal, probably Frue's blaster banging the plates.

Yul pulled the circular ring inward. The Zikri could wrap their squidlike appendages around such a ring and pull it open with ease. Small wonder it took his full force to open the portal.

Frue tumbled in, panting. Yul quickly resealed the door.

The pilot looked a mess, his suit blooded and grimed. Sweat poured down his cheeks. His eyes darted everywhere. But he appeared unwounded, his blaster quivering in a bloody hand.

"Where's Regers?"

"I tried to get him out of his lethargy but the stupid bastard came at me with his blaster, as if he was going to pistol whip me."

"Sounds like Regers. What happened then?"

"Zikri. They all came in a blur. Squids everywhere. I blasted them. So did Regers. He managed to kill a horde and hobble away down some corridor. We got separated. I can't remember much else."

"Forget it, Frue. In Regers' state, he's probably lost. We've got to get this ship somewhere safe. I've a sick feeling that the Zikri have some nasty surprise waiting for us."

"No kidding. But—"

"There's at least three squids out there, I saw. Gliding down the hall."

Frue winced, shaking his head. "You should have killed them when you had the chance, Yul."

"Hindsight, Frue. I found Hurd. He was dunked in a tank of water in some chamber a few halls down."

Frue blinked, his breath caught in his throat. "And you didn't free him? What kind of a friend are you—?

"Relax—He's dead or drowned. Though he seems kind of alive. Like this freak with the antennae here." He clinked his blaster on the glass.

Frue turned and grimaced at the hateful, glaring eyes. The Zikri and its tentacles repulsed him. "You threw it in there?"

"It was starting to stink."

Frue's cheek quivered. "I've heard the Mentera feed off whatever's in these tanks. Never seen it before or technology like this. See those hoses at the top? They stick them in their bellies and suck the life out of the victim in the tanks. Or so I've heard."

Yul felt a chill crawl through his belly as he thought back to the corpse-like Hurd. "That's messed up." He herded him toward the console. "Later, Frue. We've got to get this Orb out of here. Or scramble its frequency so they can't track us." He motioned to the array of incomprehensible controls on the consoles. "Start working on these. Get this thing out to the free colonies."

Frue gaped at the daunting task and the rows of dials on panels. "I'm good at this, Yul, but not a magician."

"Start trying, for shit's sake. There's always a first time."

Frue uttered a curse. Cold steam fogged his helmet as the air outtake valve wheezed. He lightly touched some dials on the console and the panel zapped to life. His eyes gleamed with triumph as he fluttered his fingers over the knobs with a scientist's curiosity. "It's meant for their cursed squidly tentacles."

"No doubt. Work with it."

Frue adjusted some stem-like levers while Yul stalked more confidently about, examining everything in sight. He swept his eyes over the crypt-like surroundings. He avoided the eerie tank, remembering the other vessels in the last chilling room. Much he saw that he didn't understand—the heavy chains on the wall, the seats behind the command controls that contained what looked like manacles on the armrests, with multiple rings for tentacles. He had no idea the depth of Zikri sadism running deep in this ship, but he assumed it was profound. Things of suggestive savagery, torture and bondage which may have easily been but simple entertainment to them.

A strange node, a black globe rested on a sleek stalk at waist height in the center of the room. It disturbed him as much as the grisly tanks. The globe was like some freakish signpost, radiating invisible waves of unwelcome energy.

Yul suspected it emitted a harmful vibration, but of what he could not guess. He pressed an ear closer but could detect no hum or warble; the unit appeared to be 'off'. Good. A cryptic panel of buttons, like everything on this bridge, stood at the globe's base. He did not want to touch such a thing.

"What the hell is it?" he whispered aloud.

Frue cast it a frowning glance. "Looks like a mind disruptor of some kind."

"On the bridge?"

"To torture victims? Maybe to keep their own in check. Who knows what these freaks do?"

"Nice species. Christ, Frue, concentrate! How long's it going to take you to—?"

"Relax, Yul. I've almost figured it out. The navigation system they've outsourced to Rangenkro. I know Rangenkro hardware. I can recognize other aliens' technology in their systems. Makes sense, the squids are scavengers. See the motifs?" He pointed to a circle of glyphs that came up on the console when he pressed the squid-like controls. "The weapons' systems and tracking beacon. Forget it. They're in-house, protected. Under some crypto cipher. Likely fingerprint activated, or in the case of these squids, tentacle-driven."

Yul gave a restless shrug. "How long?"

"Where do you want to go?"

"Anywhere but here."

"How about Vraigon then? There's a NOA base somewhere in the outer peripheries, so I've heard. Winterule, I think it's called."

Hope surged in Yul's chest. Could there be a happy ending to this? *New Order Alliance*. It was a sound for sore ears.

Frue set a course for the Vraigon sector and looked about at the weapons' systems as Yul leaned in. "What now?"

"Can you get a secure channel to Mathias?"

"Are you serious? He'd rip off our heads."

Yul drew back. "Could it be any worse than what we're already in?" With the *Albatross* toast, Mathias's disgust would not a stretch. He moved broodingly toward the exit.

Frue perked his ears. "Where are you going?"

"I feel guilty about Hurd. There're no Zikri tapping at the door. I think I'm going to venture out, maybe free him, or put him out of his misery. Maybe something I should have done earlier."

Frue swallowed. "Are you sure? Yul, wait." He motioned to a small screen showing several red dots on a grid map of the Orb's layout. "See those moving blips? My guess is they're marks. Five Zikri left in that sector."

"You be my eyes and ears then. Warn me of anything untoward."

"It's your life." Frue shrugged. "We have a shipful here of captured vessels. I think we should take this Orb to the end of the galaxy and sell it for parts and the ships too and walk away from this and Mathias forever."

"It may come to that, Frue." Yul considered. Two V-Zon cruisers in good condition. Tempting. He shook his head. Deep down he knew he could never pull it off. He'd made a promise to deliver the goods, as few of them as there were, and by God, he'd keep it. A matter of personal integrity. His own prosthetic limb, ironically, had been manufactured by Cybernetics Corp.

"If we take this Orb anywhere near the free worlds, they'll blow us to bits."

Yul nodded, chewed his lip.

"How about Phebis then?" Frue suggested.

"Where the hell's that?"

"A small moon in the Delta sector. An impulse hop from Winterule."

"What's down there?"

"Nothing, as far as I know. Some abandoned ore projects."

"Do it then."

"You still going out there?"

Yul hitched himself forward, blaster raised. "I can't just sit here."

Frue stabbed out at the console. "Think twice, Yul. There are hostiles in the room, if that's where I'm guessing Hurd is. Unless you want to tango with those squidly monsters?"

Yul hissed out a curse. "Then we wait." He crouched, elbows on his thighs, lost in sullen silence. He glared about, while the crimson-eyed locust watched them with imperturbable patience through the glass of its watery prison.

He'd conserve his energy for now.

* * *

Some time passed and as the Orb came out of light drive, a small featureless moon, cold, gray-gold, moved in its eccentric orbit. The planet Iom and its sun Mra shone dimly on the left of the viewscreen. The planet and its satellite looked dead, judging from their pale colors.

The indicator blips of hostiles had moved off to a lower level of the ship and Yul was about to open the hatch and go out, when a spiked shape sheared across the starboard viewport.

Yul looked to the glass and groaned at the ominous sight of a silver-black war Orb come glowing out of hyperthrust. "You've got to be kidding me!"

Frue cried, "Fucking squids. They've shut down our light-drive systems! Remotely. System's locked."

"Now we're screwed," said Yul. "No way to outman or outrun that. Can you hail Mathias?"

Frue hesitated. "If these squids' technology can carry radio signals along the hyperthrust highways, maybe. I hope they haven't disabled that too."

"Then do it!"

Frue fiddled with the controls. Sweat greased his face; his cheeks were flushed. He punched in some coordinates which looked like numbers. Yul could not be sure. A strange series of garbled electronic sounds came over the com, Rangenkro make, fortunately, then some crackly voices.

Frue barked out a command. "Put me through to CEO Mathias. This is important! Code DZ56A."

A pause. A woman's voice sounded over the com. "I can relay the message to Mr. Mathias. What's your emergency, lieutenant Friscas?"

"Call me Frue. This is for Mathias's ears only. Repeat, for Mathias only!"

Another pause. Then the static frequency discharges dissipated and the high and low of Mathias's voice came over the com, calm and measured. "This is most awkward, Friscas. An insecure channel at the very least, not to mention the timing. Very inconvenient."

Yul dashed over to the panel and snarled into the console. "Listen, Mathias. This is Yul and it's important. Don't talk, we need backup."

"Where are you?"

"We're on Phebis, Phobos some fool place. Get the hell over here."

"Where the hell is Phebis?"

Yul flapped his hand. Frue brought up the data on the info set. "Moon of Iom, sector 6.1. Local coordinates: 300-100.A61 Orion sector. No, Delta sector."

"Well, fly the *Albatross* in. What am I, your little bloody valet?"

"Can't, it's complicated. Look, sir, do you want the stuff or not?"

"Do you have the samples?"

Yul paused. "We're sitting on them. You'll need backup to secure it. Lots of it. You may need artillery."

"Where's my ship?"

"In bad shape, I'm afraid. Best to forget about the ship."

There was an awkward pause and an angry curse on the other end. "Yul, you have the balls to call me demanding backup with the *Albatross* incapacitated? This will be deducted from our contract! I'm guessing there'll be little left of that when this is all over."

"Not a chance, Mathias, we had a deal."

"Listen, soldier, buddy, if you have the merchandise, I'll maybe make some concessions, but otherwise..." The threat hung like a wet rag.

Yul didn't trust what he was hearing. "What's to stop me from running to the competition?"

Mathias's icy curse burst over the com, a cold forewarning of what was to come. "You do that, Vrean, and you'll be pissing iron stars by the end of the day. I thought you needed backup. Where the hell are you going to run to?"

"Just letting you know I have options, sir. Hurry up, or you won't have any merchandise left. Bring as much firepower as you can." Yul cut the channel. He did not want to hear another one of Mathias's demeaning threats. "Stupid cretin." He gripped Frue's arm. "Frue, work for me, tell me some good news."

"The Orb is a class D midfighter. I'm guessing more a Recon or scout craft than a war vessel. With a minimal crew."

"Good." But then he scoffed. "That's what you said last time— minimal crew."

"Yeah, well, we may be able to con them into believing we're disabled, sidetracked on some side mission, technical failure or malfunction, shit like that."

"Sounds desperate."

"It is. Recall we have no weapons."

"You're not giving me anything, Frue."

Frue exploded. "What the hell are you giving me?"

"Land this piece of crap."

"What do you mean, land it?" Frue stared.

"You heard me. We can hide on the moon, fight on land if need be. Better yet—"

"Mathias will hang us out to dry. You don't just bilk billionaires."

"Mathias wants his stuff badly enough. We'll dodge these squids until he gets here."

"How do you propose we get to him what we don't have?"

"Don't worry. That's his problem."

"Why don't we just fly this thing somewhere else?" Frue wailed. "The Orb's a fortress."

"What part of 'impractical' don't you get? We can't keep flying this craft. They can track it. It's built into their systems."

Frue rubbed his temples.

"Can you get the tractor pad lowered?"

Frue closed his eyes. "Damn it, Yul. It's part of their weapons' systems. I've told you, I have no access! I can't decipher the weapons' systems. We're sitting ducks."

"Any chance of getting the *Albatross* online?"

"Are you kidding me? You saw it. It's a write-off."

"What about the lander?"

"Possible. The landing bay seemed intact when we scuttled by it. Unless the Zikri have fouled it up."

"Okay, work on getting the tractor port open. If you can't, I'll rig explosions from the *Albatross*. We can use *Lander* to get off this crate. It has minimal impulse boost and can put us into Vraigon in a few weeks."

Frue shook his head. "I still think we should fly to—"

Yul cut him off. "Shut up and listen. The Zikri'll follow us to the end of the universe. We have to ditch this heap."

He was about to open the hatch and go to the hold when Frue quavered. "We're gonna die, Yul. I feel it in my bones."

Yul snarled at him. "Quit being a pussy and guide me. You died hours ago when the Zikri tracked us here. Better yet, you died when you stepped in the *Albatross*. We both did."

Frue sucked in a dry mouthful of air.

"Watch the readout. If they get close, let me know."

"If I'd have only known... Okay, make your way down here—by this route, away from them." Frue motioned a trembling hand to the readout. "Five more moving blips are near the tanks. According to this layout there's another way in, longer, a better route. See those moving blips? Stay away from them."

Yul committed the map to memory. "If they get anywhere near

where I'm headed, Frue, scream bloody murder. I'll come back and get you and free Hurd. In the meantime, keep those vultures cruising out in space, not wandering these decks, or we're all dead."

"There'll be more Zikri lurking down there than you think."

"The hell with the Zikri! Dodge that war Orb. Use whatever impulse power we have, otherwise it won't matter."

Frue nodded vigorously.

Yul wrenched opened the door, his blaster aimed in quick sweeps left and right. Nothing. No squids were in sight. "I'm closing the door now. Tighten the ring as much as you can."

Yul exhaled, felt his rattled nerves prickling. Frue was losing it, bowing to the pressure. Yul cursed. He needed him to be on track.

Gritting teeth, he pushed failure out of his brain. Out in the hall, his senses tingled at the sense of eerie danger. Death and terror lurked in those shadows. He kicked at the coagulated body of the dead Zikri and pulled the door tight. Dull thuds. The sounds of Frue struggling to tighten the door. Damn him, not tight enough.

Nothing to do. He couldn't mess with the door at this time. He'd have to stay focused if he were to accomplish his mission. He coughed out a slurry gob of phlegm, clenched his fists. Every muscle in his body knotted like an oak's. God help Frue. If only the man could pull it off...

Chapter 3

Yul's new route took him well away from the tanks and Regers' horrific predicament. A shaky voice in his helmet informed him that Frue had no new enemy to report. Frue couldn't track where he was without a homer but he could detect Zikri enemies on his intercept path. Not ideal, but better than no early warning at all. He only hoped Frue could keep the enemy Orb at bay.

Yul snuck back along his circuitous route. One corridor left, three right, two straight ahead. He took care to notch a mark in the wall at each junction with the butt of his blaster. A risk, should wandering Zikri stumble upon the marks, but better to have an escape route marked than not.

He passed under a spidery-veined, diamond-shaped archway and into a spacious area. *The Zikri hold.* The dull cavernous thud of his booted feet echoed back in his ears, causing his heart to quicken. The *Albatross's* pilot light came to his view, a familiar beacon. The blue lamp was still functional after all the damage to her. He passed through the gaping hole in her side and crept up the companionway breasting the bridge, with the ship's faint blue glow permeating the dim murk. The unknown lurked here. So far, he had yet to encounter a single squid.

Slinking to the bridge, he saw the interior was in bad shape. Whole walls were blackened from blaster fire and explosions. A faint smell of decomposition prevailed. Like humus in a forest. His suit's compressor attempted to draw oxygen out of the surrounding air to preserve the stored resources. This enabled Yul to pick up the faint odor, or was it fresh? His blood chilled at the prospect of new developments. The weird, pear-like pods had popped open. Dozens of them, showing brown, skeletal, rib-like formations. What had hatched? Yul shuddered. A scuttling motion came from overhead.

He ducked, heart hammering, but he saw nothing. He was about to dip back into the hall when the muted roar of the Orb's engines jarred him, followed by the sudden thud of metal bracing against rock.

The Orb had landed. Good, Frue had come through; they were on Phebis.

Yul moved with speed down the hallway. He had heard no clunk of tractor pad door retracting so he assumed the task of opening the Zikri hold was beyond Frue. He hastened to the *Albatross's* armory to rummage for explosives.

Frue's panicked voice hissed over the com. "Get back here, Yul! The squids, they've blown the—"

"What the hell?" Just when he thought nothing else could go wrong. He groped deeper into the pile of hardware in the weapons' stores. Frue would have to cope with the Zikri himself. No way he could get back in time to save him. Snatching up two decent-sized explosives with detonators, he turned to look up. His eyes bulged at what he saw.

A colorful shape, a blurred winged thing, crashed into his forearm. He whipped it off him with a swipe. It chirped like a bug then flew off as fast as it had come.

Frue's voice was drowned in a peal of blaster fire...amid chittering shrieks, gasps of terror. At the same time, a shadowy movement brushed by the doorway, then a familiar slithering. Damn, Frue was in trouble, but why hadn't he warned him earlier?

The pilot's wails of panic rose to a crescendo. Yul heard the slap of tentacles and Frue's last agonized howl before the com went dead.

Yul cringed.

No time for remorse. He turned and a Zikri hit him like an

avalanche. He rolled on the ground, clawing at rubbery, strangling flesh. His blaster rained fire askew. His mechanized fingers tore at the slimy tentacles, creepers that wrapped tighter about his waist, his arms. A hideous, mottled face jerked closer to his faceplate. He caught a strange, crablike movement hovering over his shoulder.

A dragonfly thing, some winged crustacean, flung itself down from the ceiling and latched onto the Zikri's neck. It pricked pale barbs onto the lower part of its head and lifted and jammed a white, pulsing proboscis into the thing's brain.

The Zikri howled, slumped. Its short head stalk dangled while the butterfly pulsed, as if extracting fluids from the Zikri's brain.

Yul gasped, struggling wildly to extricate himself from the weakening Zikri's embrace. He staggered off, sickened by the sudden assault and the horror of it. He wiped off the sticky goo from his suit.

Mercifully no butterfly-dragonfly flew shrieking after him and seeking his flesh. Only a writhing mass of tentacles, confusion and horror. The Zikri tried to tear off the winged invader, but the thing only clung on tighter. In the space of twenty seconds, the Zikri's head cracked like an egg and it stiffened forever. Yul plowed on down the hallway with an instinct for preservation. Why had the creature crashed into him initially? To warn him? Unlike the Zikri, he had made no overt motions of aggression against the parent pods during the bridge attack. As for Regers, that was another matter... Under no circumstance must he allow a bulb-like proboscis to enter his brain.

A last look back confirmed his suspicion; he must be victim of some mad hallucination. The Zikri's head oozed vile fluids while the dragonfly, some magnificent avatar, sucked up the issuing ichor, its wings trembling. A hissing, gurgling chitter burbled impossibly from the Zikri's exposed throat. Yul winced. A metamorphosis. A butterfly, a quarter of the size of the original dragonfly, morphed out of the Zikri's shattered skull.

Yul staggered back in disbelief. Had his world gone completely apeshit? He tried to erase the image from his brain, but he could not.

He scrambled back through the *Albatross's* companionway, empty and eerie as was the darkened hold of the Zikri ship.

Tottering on drunken legs through the hold, he reached a dark wall of metal, the gate pad through which the Zikri dragged their victim ships. The spiked barrier rose impossibly high. An impenetrable rampart. As he guessed, there were no controls on the gate to draw it up or down or unlock it.

He armed his detonator, set the time sequence and clamped the magnetic casing at eye level. He stepped back. His mind could not help but postulate theories about the insect-plant aliens. He stumbled away in a dream-like horror... He had seen that flying insect in all its vivid, grotesque majesty.

It had formed crab-like legs as a springboard. Why? To jump like a spider? Perhaps a speedy adaptation to a dire situation? In the heavier gravity, wings could not support its mass. So, it seemed legs had been a necessity.

The detonator went off and the explosion rent the Orb's hold with tongues of red flame. A terrible concussion batted Yul forward with jarring force.

He shook his head, crumpled in a dazed heap by the far wall, in a tangle of overturned benches. The blast fortunately had not damaged or punctured his suit. Why the devil had he set it for only seven seconds? Stupid. He was not thinking. Shock? Shrieks raged in his ear as the thin Zikri air was sucked through the hold into the outside atmosphere which was even thinner there. It meant the Zikri on board, caught exposed, would die. Perfect! He ground his teeth in a satisfied leer.

But his body shook and his ears rang.

He staggered over to the brink of the shredded tractor pad, feeling the tug of air nudging at him and his suit. The ship depressurized. He looked upon a desolate landscape. Frue had landed them on a slight angle in the dusty soil that looked like snow. Boulders flanked the pliant Orb's side. Small dusty ridges rose distantly behind it. To his right, ran an endless plain of frosted soil that disappeared into a dark horizon. The time of day, if day it were, could have been early evening, perhaps approaching dusk. Mra, the distant sun, was setting. Long shadows spread across the lunar soil. The enemy Orb stalking them was nowhere in sight. A welcome circumstance. Perhaps the erstwhile Frue had taken care of it.

Somehow he thought not.

He looked at the digital readout on his helm's suit: -25 degrees Celsius, humidity 3%, Gravity 0.84. Air: 60% carbon dioxide, 9% oxygen, traces of sulfur 1% and Argon 0.7%. The rest was indeterminable. A weird mix, Yul thought, unsuitable for human organisms. Lucky that his suit had not been compromised. His only chance would be to board *Lander* and arm her.

He turned back to the Zikri hold, but his eyes caught a brisk movement on the moon's horizon.

A ship? Yul gaped. He squinted, saw a familiar, cylindrical Wren X, a Mark V design, skim the landscape. It emerged to face the Orb. Twin verimark torpedoes were mounted on its sleek underbelly and ion-blasters to the sides. It was a state-of-the art light-drive propulsion model. Heavy artillery its trademark. Fast. A deadly machine. Mathias did not scrimp. Yul imagined the Wren X contained only the most modern cloaking devices.

Yul's lips twisted in an ironic smile.

So Mathias had come—sooner than he expected. Those plant samples must have meant more to the industrialist than all the gold in the universe. Sad that the plant pods were either hatched or burned. Mathias would definitely not be pleased about it. The ferns? Who knew where the hell they were?

* * *

Crouching on his haunches, Yul let the daze wash out of his head. Nervous exhaustion crept over his limbs. He cast a furtive glance back to the shadowy spaces where *Albatross* sat, expecting one of the iridescent dragonfly horrors to come vaulting out at him. He doubted there was only one. But if any one of them had wanted to hatch something inside him, it would have done so earlier. It hadn't. For whatever reason, Yul did not feel the fear he should in his heart.

That was a good thing.

He sucked in a grateful gust of oxygen and struggled to his feet. A hailing frequency came over his headset. Then a staticky rasp.

"Yul Vrean? This is commander Goss of the Mercedes Arknot, Cybernetics Corp. Do you read?"

"Clear," croaked Yul.

"Any damage to report?"

"I'm clear."

"How many hostiles are left?"

"Not sure."

"We see you've cracked open the tractor pod. Good. We're coming in."

"Over." Nice timing, you morons, Yul thought. His whole team had been wiped out. But impeccable timing.

The Wren X hovered and landed in a safe area on the plain before the downed Orb. Twenty figures sprang out in gray-camo spacesuits, looking much like marines. The ship flew to a safe corridor in the hills while the figures moved ant-like toward the Orb. They seemed to be under the direction of a single leader. They reached the edge of the craft and used the spiked surface as handholds to scale the side. Yul paused to watch. It was only an eighteen-foot climb up the ship's hull to the tractor pad from spike to spike, which the team managed with apparent ease.

Yul reflected: the crew had hid the ship despite it being cloaked. They were taking no chances. But the Orb in the sky, where was it? Was it no longer a threat?

A suited man with waxen face and unblinking eyes struggled over the lip of shattered metal and faced Yul.

Yul stepped back to examine him with curiosity. A man of medium height wearing a commander's badge. High forehead. Shock of sandy hair. Another figure of similar appearance followed next and vaulted to his feet like a kangaroo. A rare dexterity for a man in a suit. Sixteen other men followed, of various builds, complexions, and races. All carried weapons, Master E1 assault rifles, sleek, black, ten-inch instruments of death. The commander sized up Yul with a flick of eyes, something he was apparently used to. "Where are the samples?"

"In the *Albatross*. There." Yul jerked a thumb back deeper in the hold.

"You lead. I'm Goss, this is lieutenant Xix. A synthetic, cybernot SC 34-6. You're going in there to get them. Mathias paid you to do a job, so this time, let's do it."

Yul stared awkwardly at Goss's flattened boxer's nose and his equally unglamorous synthetic minion. "Aren't you the man of charm?" he remarked dryly.

"Cut the quips. I get paid for my competence, Vrean, unlike other people. Not for my good looks."

Yul shrugged. "Greer is dead. Hurd may still be alive, near the ship's bridge. Frue and Regers?" Yul gave a sullen grimace. "I think are toast." A guilty feeling brushed Yul's guts. He hadn't left Hurd in any position to escape. In short, a toy for the Zikri.

Goss plied him for details then waved an impatient hand. "Dumb bastard was stupid enough to get caught without a suit, so I say let him die in a stew of his own making."

Yul gritted his teeth. "I'll take that as a no then, regarding rescue."

"Move on." Goss waved his weapon.

Yul didn't like Goss. The man was abrupt, devoid of feeling or the value of human life. This was going to be a difficult operation. Somebody was going to get killed and it sure as hell wasn't going to be him. "What about the Orb up there?"

"What Orb?" Goss's toothy smile gleamed through his faceplate like one of the undead.

Yul's jaw sagged. "You blasted them? Are you up for a war with the Zikri?"

"Whatever the cost," grumbled Goss. "Move along, Vrean. Your foolish questions are eating up time. Better we get out of here before more squids show up."

Yul clenched his fists. He stalked over to the *Albatross*, holding his tongue.

Goss grunted at what he saw, not liking the look of the charred holes in its outer hull, where the Zikri had forced their way in.

Entering the companionway, the commander frowned at the headless carcass of the Zikri splayed in death. Yul gave it a wide berth. A spray of flesh where the head had exploded had coagulated faster than what Yul thought normal. He darted glances here and there, but saw no sign of the dragonfly. Some men stayed to tear off samples of Zikri flesh, fragments of skull and its slime-drenched tentacles.

"What killed it?" asked Goss's lieutenant, Xix. "Doesn't look like blaster fire."

Goss waved him on. "Who cares? It's dead." The commander liked even less the state of the rest of the ship. He glared at the wreck of the bridge when Yul showed it to him.

Yul considered warning the zealous commander and the last eight stragglers of his team about the menace of plants and strange winged crab-like bugs, but thought it wouldn't matter much to these wordless robots. He knew men like these—soulless automatons, men who followed orders without questioning consequences, with fixed impressions in their tiny, programmed brains. No heart or soul.

They pushed by him one by one, shouldering him out of the way.

Yul grinned, his suspicions confirmed. A raging heat gathered in his chest.

"You did a number on the bridge," Goss said critically. He inclined his head. "I see the casing fragments of our own titanium bombs over there. You blow up our bridge?"

"Well, you know how it goes, Goss—better to go out with a bang when improvising."

"Clown," rasped Goss. "We'll see what Mathias thinks of all this, and how much grinning you're doing when he cuts off your balls."

Yul was somewhat surprised, even disappointed, that the dragonfly-crabs hadn't put in an appearance. But now he was ill at ease. Where was the bloody thing? There couldn't be just one. There was never just one. He'd rather know where they were, than discover them hidden somewhere, leaping out of some dark shadow and driving a white proboscis through his skull.

His fingers curled about his blaster. His dark eyes darted to the ceiling.

Goss caught the movement and his steel-blue eyes beetled up to follow Yul's gaze. "Something up there, Vrean? You got a story to tell us?"

Yul shook his head.

The men scooped up a few charred ribbed husks in their sample bags. They looked about the ruined bridge with unease. All aboard the bridge felt some deadly menace lurking about the blasted spaces.

Goss spoke in husky tones into his communicator. "The Orb is carrying two V-Z lightfighters. Saw them on the way into the hold. Also some charred, but charming exhibits here on the bridge which might spark your interest." If it was who Yul thought it was, Goss must be using the Cybernetics Corp ship's hyperdrive coils as a means to relay the message back through the light years. Goss droned in an impersonal voice, "A mutilated Zikri in the hall, dozens more in the bridge. Ship's taken a beating. Not skyworthy. Some of the corpses seem killed by blaster fire and explosions, others not. Vrean here, appears not to have taken much physical damage, or care of your plants."

Angry words sprayed through the receiver to which Yul was not privy. It seemed to cause Goss mild amusement.

The commander grinned, shook his head with solemn emphasis. "Not looking good for you, Vrean."

Yul looked around with cynical eyes. "Are you happy now? You got what you came for."

Goss sighed with impatience. "The samples are useless to us, Vrean. Charred and dead. Mathias wanted live ones. As explicitly stated in the contract."

"I don't give a damn about Mathias." Yul's fists knotted in fury.

"Tell him to come down here and get his samples himself."

"Tell him yourself, Vrean. Don't jerk me around, I'm warning you. You really don't want to go down that route. What the fuck has gone on here?"

Yul glared. The two eyed each other with menace, nose to nose, neither willing to back off.

"You're coming back with us. The others I could give a flying fuck about. Somebody has to answer for this mess. Looks like you're the lucky pick."

"Not until we get Hurd."

"The fuck with Hurd!" exploded Goss. "There's no time. This ship's a time bomb waiting to go off. Zikri will be all over us like flies on shit."

A cry issued from behind and Yul caught the sudden movement of a blurred shape—some crablike thing winging its way through the air. One of Goss's men tagged it with his E1 and it fell crumpling in a charred heap, clicking and rolling. Manta-ray like wings curled up like dried banana peels. Blue smoke coiled up.

Goss tramped over to investigate the creature and peered at the blackened husk with little interest. He trained his weapon. "Bag it, Xix. Don't kill any more of the things, for shit sakes. Mathias wants live specimens." His thin lips twisted in a frown. "Doesn't look like our plant, does it Vrean? What's going on here?"

Yul flashed him a sour grin.

The man who had shot it, eagerly tripped forward but accidentally stepped on a pod and cracked it open like an egg. In less than a second, another dragonfly thing flew down from the ceiling. It had been camouflaged, and buried its proboscis in the man's skull, piercing both helmet and bone.

The man dropped to his knees, clutching his helmet and ear through which the thing had bored. His anguished howl rang throughout the bridge. The sudden assault had spurred a chain reaction in the team. They started blasting anything in sight.

Yul sucked in a stunned breath. How had he missed the creature?

The dragonfly had splayed itself flat against the ceiling; its wings blended in masterfully. No wonder his eyes had glossed over it. He'd heard of butterflies and moths changing color, able to mimic a tree's mottled bark over a period of years, but never in such a short period. How long had it been? Only a few hours? It was incredible.

It seemed likewise true that once they had adapted, the creatures made efforts to preserve their environment in whatever state it was, as unnatural as that might be. Yul wondered where the plant-crab-butterflies would go from here. Their eerie environment was now in a stasis. Evidence supported the fact that species that remained static in their evolution would die off, unable to survive further catastrophes. But not these horrors. He hoped he was not about to find out.

"Stop, you fools!" cried Goss. "Vrean, you fucker!" Goss whirled on him as he made for the door. "Stop firing those guns, you idiots!" He slapped one of the men's weapons down.

Pretending submission, Yul put on a penitent scowl and casual droop of his shoulder. Without warning, he snatched at Goss's sidearm, wrenching it out of his grasp. He blasted Xix, Goss synthetic's goggling lieutenant, wires, head, android fluid and all, as it lifted its E1. Greasy liquid spewed everywhere.

"Are you insane, Yul?" Goss cried, staggering back, gasping.

Yul debated taking out Goss but he saw himself getting cut down in a line of fire. If he didn't die here, he saw Mathias hunting him down for the loss of his lieutenant. Living his life as an outlaw. Not knowing when the next civilian at the local space hub who had innocently asked him for directions might put a plasma shell between his eyes. "I'm no man's bitch, Goss," Yul roared as he fled for the exit. He tore down the companionway past the mutilated Zikri. Goss cursed after him, his men at his heels.

Blaster fire clipped by him. Stun shots, he surmised, by the sound, but enough to create enough deadly pain if they found their mark...and death if his suit were punctured. He scrambled on into the Zikri hold.

* * *

Subcommander Krin had always been larger than his peers. He had built developed muscle on his upper body, giving him massive strength that made him a fearsome enemy. He had been part of the bomb team that had extracted the first human specimen known as *Hurd* from the alien control deck. Now he stared unblinking down the corridor from the tank room through eyes like slits. Why were the humans being so exasperating? All they had to do was yield. The Mentera would take proper care of them.

Krin's polyped lip curled in a fleeting grin. It quickly faded to a stony grimace. By his calculation, only one rebel remained in the halls. But this one was a formidable specimen—full of piss and vinegar, a tricky, ruthless one. Three times the human had eluded their nets. By luck or circumstance, possibly skill, Krin still had not decided. He had caught a momentary glimpse of the human as the bridge door had slid shut, sealed by the protector ring. A stocky, suited creature managing the impossible. A fighting machine. He had a compact body, balanced weight and design which Krin respected grudgingly.

He remembered that offensive-defensive technique with vivid clarity, alternating with blaster, kicks and shoulder butts as he took out Gorge, the hall monitor. Before that wretched door had clamped shut, the thing's assaults had been assisted by the extraordinary strength of his left arm.

The other survivor, the weak, suited, freckle-faced human, had yielded without struggle.

The rebel would make a good slave. The tanks would be too good for him. He would personally see to the human's torture and breaking. The manacles and brain disruptor would come in handy in this regard.

Krin gave a snuffling grunt. The rebel could be sneaking around anywhere aboard his ship. He must stalk every corridor and flush him out. Krin's commanding officer, Druluk, and other Zikri had died in agony in the battle on the human bridge. Through no fault of his own, he had been blamed. Druluk had been stupid to underestimate the resourcefulness of the humans. Now he was a blood-caked carcass, host to those plants or whatever fiendish brood they were. Already, his superior, Zrake, had warned Krin of the death penalty for botch ups on these hijack missions. Two black marks were tagged to his name already. One on the primitive monkey world of Ygramex, the other during the gory Pzyon affair. His life hung in the balance.

First priority was to flush out the human with their limited crew, now that so many Zikri had been killed. A foolish and unnecessary waste. If only he had taken more Zikri warriors, more firepower, when they stormed the bridge, this mess could have been averted...

Hindsight. How could he have known the human demon would have fought with such ferocity? Never before had explosions been used against them on a boarding mission, especially coming moments after being tractored aboard. It was unheard of. Still, he had to admire the human's ingenuity.

The frail, freckle-faced survivor looked out from his tank with goggle-eyed surprise. Why hadn't his superior been on the bridge? He had left the weak one there to die? Krin gazed back upon the specimens in the tanks, staring out of their glassy prisons like helpless minnows.

Could the human thing be playing him?

No, the human was not that smart. He had made mistakes before: wandering the ship alone, leaving the human unguarded on the bridge. He was lucky to have pulled through this far.

With his two, blood-slimed comrades, Krin stalked the halls, looking for his quarry. His tentacles curled in a menacing expectation. He would find his quarry. When he did, the rebel would pay dearly.

* * *

Tottering on through the Zikri's spidery corridors, Yul desperately retraced his path back to the tank room. He avoided the dead-end corridor where fallen debris had blocked it off. Shouts and blaster fire raged behind, echoing like hail on metal. He crashed through the hallways, following the places where he had notched the creepy veins and motifs with his blaster.

Much of the corridor had lost its scary menace in contrast to all the horrors he had thus experienced: mutant crazed moths, bloodthirsty Zikri, explosions, murdered crew members...

Panting, despite the slightly lower gravity, he reached the familiar U-shaped archway that gained entry to the house of horrors he remembered so well. *Are you crazy, Yul? Why go to this length? Is Mathias going to let you off the hook after this bungled job? Why not put a blaster to your head and be done with it?*

Some crazy intuition drove his legs onward. But now he staggered to a halt.

The room was slightly different than he had remembered it. The floor was soaked with water and smashed glass glinted at the far end. Twelve human figures hung suspended in separate tanks, their heads below water level. Regers, lolling doll-like, hovered inside the largest tank, coated in some chalky white substance. A grotesque monstrosity gaped behind the glass, coral-eyed, comatose, sprawled in a corner with some strange, moth-like fish with fins and wings grown huge, flitting about the water. It paraded about like some lord of the manor.

Yul reeled back in disgust, his blaster sagging in his hand. "What the hell?"

Even Goss, storming through the arched gap, did a double take, seeing the room with all its unseemly lifeforms.

He caught up with Yul and bawled, "What in the blue flames of hell is this? He swung his arm in a hostile arc.

Yul had seen enough. Opening fire on the barriers of glass, he blew up Hurd's tank first. Then Frue's.

Glass shattered everywhere. Water slewed, releasing a torrent and their occupants.

Hurd tumbled out of his prison, sprawled in a ragdoll heap. He did not move. Frue struggled to his knees, gagging, coughing foul liquid out of his lungs. Miracle of miracles, the man was still alive.

Goss caught at Yul's arm. A stray blast from Yul's gun went wild, hitting the alien heptadoria's tank.

Water gushed out and Regers came with it, cracked helmet and all, falling forward on his knees in a pitiful, slimy rush. His pale lips, white as chalk, arched in a soundless cry. The man's right-hand fingers trembled. Yet all that was left of his left hand was a stump where it had been gnawed by the heptadoria.

The butterfly, moth, or whatever it was, flapped about the ground like a beached mackerel, confused at its new environment. Then in a burst of soggy adaptation, its iridescent wings took it high and wide about the room, soaring inches over the newcomers' heads. It dive-bombed them like an angry eagle.

The men crouched and aimed. Six lifted blasters, others cursed and backpedaled for the exit.

Yul ducked, lest one of those razor sharp wings cut at his throat in a low pass.

A marine's throat was laid open ear to ear as a wingtip sliced flesh like a machete. He fell back choking on his own blood.

Goss slapped another commando's arm away as he lifted a weapon. "Fool! Capture the thing! We have no live samples yet."

"Sir? Brenes back there, his neck—"

"Use your gear, man! Why'd you bring it all this way?" He snatched away the marine's E1, his fist shaking.

The man cringed. While his team-mates trained weapons, others extracted nets that worked with their guns and ejected clamp-ons. Two rummaged through their personal kits to shoot darts and stunners at the flying thing. They did this, but with unexpected results.

A marine who had knelt in the pooling liquid and fired clamp-ons, yelled triumph. A metal restraint hooked on the thing's wing. The butterfly teetered and dropped in midflight. Men moved in, scrambling forth to net it. But it flicked out its wing and sent the shiny clamp spinning away with surprising strength. It dove at the gunman, squirting an acrid, glistening liquid from its proboscis.

The man's faceplate melted in a wash of glass as acid sizzled on the flesh beyond. He slapped at his face, yowling like a whipshot hound, clawing at his burning face.

"Damn!.." Yul edged back from the tanks, his eyes goggling.

More marines rifled through their kits. Others crabbed back, spooked, shaken by the grisly deaths. Goss cursed them all and kneed the closest man. "Contain it, you asswipes. What are you waiting for?"

The butterfly's knife-edged wings tore through the net like paper. It swooped upon the offenders without mercy. Its wings drove it with pulsing purpose, shimmering with bright color as the thing's thorax bulged with new strength.

How fast could the thing adapt? Yul marveled. The eyeless head zoomed in on its perceived enemies by some extraordinary radar ability.

Oddly the pooling water did not freeze. Only a fine blue mist rose from the viscid puddles. Yul assumed this meant the liquid retained its normal temperature. How, he knew not. The components of this alien world were unknown.

Yul took in the evolving scene in a glance. He sucked in a sharp breath. The butterfly had grown in size, shy of three feet long, and was adapting by the minute. Perceiving the men as a threat, it began to spurt acid indiscriminately and rake its barbed legs and razor wings across men's suits. The captives who had been released from their tanks, choked out vile fluid. They gasped and moaned, weaving about like drunken sailors.

Yul glared around at the insanity of it all. Let him out of this loony bin. How could the men and women be alive, their lungs full of water?

He considered blasting the rest of the tanks. But he envisaged the remaining nine human figures flopping out in dizzy confusion without suits and dying in the alien atmosphere. Better to live as prisoners to the Zikri or Mentera. Or die here put out of their misery? A tough choice. One he would not decide for them.

Goss loosed a furious cry. He flung himself on Yul. The commander, it seemed, hated being defied... but he also knew

Mathias would flay him alive if Yul was terminated prematurely.

Yul scoffed at the man's rancor. He thrust him away, disliking the ugly grimacing face mere inches from his own faceplate. But he recognized the strength in those bulging limbs. The strength was characteristic of a Class A synthetic. This one was a full cyborg, as had been Xix, whereas Yul was only a partial.

The commander's eyes flared in determined purpose. With some surprise he balked at the ferocious strength of Yul's fingers which dug rivulets into his shoulder and ribs. Fingers not completely human, suddenly hurled Goss over his shoulder to land in a clumsy heap in a slimy green pool.

The synthetic was up in a flash, as if Yul's move were but child's play. "You'll pay for that, Vrean."

The commander lifted his E1. An explosion smote the hull, its thud echoing from above. The Zikri hull shook with resounding force. Goss's eyes narrowed.

Goss's communicator chimed. "Two war Orbs, sir! They've landed on Phebis. More are coming."

"Engage them!" cried Goss. "Keep those fucking squids away from this craft."

The commander motioned his weapon at his remaining men. He staggered aside. "Back to the ship! if you want to live, men. You too, Vrean."

The commandos scrambled to the exit like drowning rats. The dead they left behind.

Yul gingerly scrambled across the trail of bodies. Goss, perceiving insubordination, jerked his weapon to peg him off with stun fire, but the dragonfly, hovering like a predatory shadow, perceived it as a signal of aggression and swooped. A splatter of sickly orange fluid splashed across Goss's rifle arm. His weapon melted and Goss's suit and arm beneath with it. Goss gaped, eyes widening in horror as electrical sizzles flew from the prosthetic. He flapped the ruined stub uselessly. Cursing, he struggled with his good left hand to seal up the crack. Failing, he stumbled back in the direction of the fleeing men.

Yul saw Goss's features frosting up as cold penetrated his suit and bit into the artificial skin. His straggling team members blinked in wonder at their commander who, with the visibly sparking synthetic limb, revealed he had never been human.

"What's the matter? Never seen a prosthetic limb before?" he bawled. "Move!"

Yul checked Hurd's pulse. Nothing. The man wore only his air mask and was not breathing. Frue was shaking like a leaf, sprawled beside his crew mate, gagging and gibbering like a lunatic. Yul pulled the pilot to a sitting position, readjusted his helmet, which had jarred loose. The offensive water had drained from his suit but the air was freezing and Frue had gone into shock.

Quickly he knelt to tear strips of repair adhesive from his pouch and apply it to the punctures at knee and waist. The resilient polyethylene instantly bonded and would handle any kind of rough wear, having properties of industrial duct tape. Oxygen would fill the suit soon. Frue's suit was still functioning. The green pilot light on the helm was a steady glow. Yul slung the quivering man over his shoulder and stumbled toward the exit.

His journey took him close to Regers. Yul paused, his heart beating. He considered dragging the half-crawling man behind with his free, mechanized arm, but seeing the sorry state of Regers, mauled by the mutant fish in the tank, he reconsidered. There passed an intense lucid moment between the two that would haunt Yul for the rest of his days. Regers' bloodless lips formed words 'Fucking bastard' and 'Leave me here to die?' and his voiceless croak an echo at his back. Yul shivering, lurched back, empathetic to Regers' deplorable condition, as he bowed under Frue's weight, but not willing to do more about it. An image of Greer fleeted past his mind, wrenched from the *Albatross*, dying in space. Yul's scowl deepened. Regers would have to fend for himself.

He reached in his pouch and tossed one of the extra rolls of adhesive at Regers' side, sensing the man's suit was beyond repair. Regers was a dead man crawling.

Yul stepped back, nearly upending himself on one of the marine's remains. He hauled out of that chamber, happy to leave butterfly and fishy horrors lording over their pile of corpses behind.

Yul struggled to catch up with Goss. He hefted Frue as best he could. The man's suit had been breached. Seven hells, the man had drowned! It was inconceivable to believe that Frue was still alive, or Regers. But he could feel him twitching and the occasional racking cough jerking his lightweight frame. He would die of exposure unless he could get him to Goss's Wren X asap.

His mind thought of the oddest things during that mad dash. Like when he would get to take his next favorite meal of steak and eggs, his cool tankard of ale at the Earl House on Beringa. Staggering through the Zikri hold nearing the tractor port, he saw Goss's small clot of men frog-hopping their way in the lower gravity toward their ship that hovered at the ready over the lunar plain. The rough-hatched hull lit in a ghostly gray-white of fresh fallen snow before the low, slate-gray hills.

Yul turned his head. He saw Frue's lips shivering. The man was hyperventilating, his skin turning blue. The suit was not heating up his body fast enough.

"Almighty hell!" Yul swore. Frue would never make it out there to the plain on time. So what to do? Leave Frue behind and race after his peers? He made an instant decision. He turned back to the *Albatross*, only to catch out of the corner of his eye, a starburst of fire blossom on the armored turret of Goss's ship. Kaboom! An iron-spiked Orb, like some ball on the end of a mace, shimmered out of nothingness. It dominated the darkening sky.

Yul stopped dead. New stealth tech? How had the Wren been caught so unawares? A stab of hopelessness pierced his heart. The Zikri were not taking any prisoners.

The smoking Wren loosed counterfire on the Orb. The Orb trembled to its double torpedo assaults. The invader loosed its last devastating bombs and the Wren dipped and fell, a ship now doomed. Both crippled, smoldering vessels crashed to the surface, igniting like matchsticks on the desolate plain.

Survivors of the blasts, a few of Goss's team, raced back to the Orb they'd fled from. They clawed desperately up the sides.

Without hesitation, Yul hobbled back to the hold and hauled Frue aboard the *Albatross* and into the landing bay. *Lander* stood there intact, her octagonal fuselage gleaming dully under the halogen bay lamps. He triggered the loading ramp, shuttled Frue aboard.

Six of the survivors of Goss's team were soon clawing at *Lander's* hatch, Goss himself with his shorn forearm. Before Yul could seal it, the ramp descended and Goss came storming aboard. He spat curses and waved his E1. Two of his men forced their way up the ramp and crowded themselves into the depressurization chamber. There was only room for five. Goss jammed the hatch closed. The three other men in his team trapped on the other side gaped, the door slamming in their faces. Yul grunted in dislike at the synthetic's cold-bloodedness.

Through the port window he watched side blasts of Zikri fire lapping at the tractor port. Nevertheless he dragged Frue out of the air lock and struggled for the lander's controls. He booted up *Lander's* engines, reached for the ramp control to lower it again, then let the men in, but Goss, hot on his heels, slapped his hand away and nudged the blaster under his ribs. "Stand down, Vrean." Goss turned to his henchman. "Morag, get in there and fly this tub." He motioned him to work the controls while the other grinning marine disarmed Yul, who stood stunned, his jaw clenched. Morag edged the lander out above the *Albatross*, leaving the three screaming men behind.

Yul fumed, cursing himself that he had let himself be taken so easily. He had underestimated Goss's cunning. How he himself would have loved to leave them all behind—Goss, his feral foxes, the same as they would have done to him. Frue's life hung in the balance; he hadn't even had time to get his helmet off.

Goss stepped over the prone man and ordered his minion to watch over Yul.

Lander hovered like a bug, then sped out through the tractor port, her sides scraping past the twisted screen of metal that Yul had blasted earlier. Goss's man lifted the vessel skyward, with no small expertise. The roaring engines took it high up into the cloudless night sky, while Frue lay gasping at Yul's feet, shivering on the floor. Greenish ice still stuck to his suit.

A blip sounded on the console.

Yul's eyes widened. He saw the characteristic blue-gray signature of a Mark IV, emerging on the console. "Look now, Goss. Just what we need. I hope you're happy. I hope you have a plan."

The android just glared at him, roaring into his headpiece. "*Lander* to *Lesior*. Salvest, talk to me! We've got a Mark IV bearing down on us." He turned to his pilot. "Get us the fuck away from here, Morag. Why're you piloting this thing so slow? Going to take those idiots on *Lesior* minutes to get down here with all the heat they have."

Morag hit the controls with helpless frustration. "I can't. Where's the manual override? It should be here, right here, dammit. But the controls are reconfigured. It's as if Frue messed with it. I've got minimal thrust."

Yul knew *Lander*, being a short range craft engineered for planet-to-ship hops, was not designed for excessive speeds. Pushing the ship's capacity to dangerous levels wasted too much power. The override sequence was buried under layers of interfaces that perhaps only Frue knew.

Lander had no weapons. Whoever had built that 'feature' into the ship's design ought to be shot and pissed on.

A massive ship appeared out of nowhere, a spiked scout Orb shimmering into existence via its advance stealth tech. To the crew's horror, it reared up behind them like a predatory hawk.

Goss's pilot dodged the Orb fire, but one blast sent it tail-spinning. Klaxons shrilled and Yul heard the hiss of leaking air. "Bloody hell! Where's your backup, Goss?"

Goss roared into his headpiece. "What's going on up there, Salvest? *Albatross's* love bug is breached. She's losing air. *Lander* is going down!" He pushed up on the sliders, trying to max out *Lander's* power to her shields.

The move bought them precious seconds.

Frue, gasping out monosyllables, twitched a finger. He was somewhat cognizant of what was going on. Yul saw through his faceplate that he was trying to say something.

Yul clawed his way forward to reach for Frue's helmet.

"Back, you!" Goss lifted his weapon in his good hand. "I don't trust you one bit."

Yul snarled. "Do you want to die, Goss?" He crouched before Frue. Without hesitation, he tore off Frue's helmet.

Goss motioned his weapon at his man who was ready to knee Yul in the groin. "Let him be."

The ship rocked to a spray of a scatter bomb. Frue wheezed out some words. "Override sequence...A287....left monitor."

"Enter it!" Goss roared.

Goss's pilot punched the code into the monitor. Another blast hit the ship.

Yul's guard hitched forward, muttering, "Minimal shields. Another hit and we're done for."

"Thanks for the observation," growled Goss. "Get back there and watch those two monkeys."

The pilot pushed the thrust lever. The ship lurched into the planet's upper atmosphere.

Yul saw Orb fire go wide through the viewport. But one uro blast caught *Lander's* rear and the ship's thrusters died.

The world spun dizzily as they whirled out of control. All were buffeted around the bridge.

Goss's backup flagship, the *Lesior*, came roaring in on a sharp angle, its landing bay port opening wide. Shots came from the lateral rear cannon to strike the invading Orb dead center. Morag desperately struggled with the top-spinning ship. While it rolled and buffeted, clamps from *Lesior* shot out to latch onto the smoking hull.

Lander reeled. The cables wound them in and the hatch closed.

Goss screamed into his helm: "*Lesior*, finish off that shitball Orb!"

The captain of *Lesior* acknowledged the order. Zikri shields had saved it from the last blast, but the Orb was flaring red. *Lesior*, with her superior impulse maneuverability, drove toward the Orb, arched up and over it and sent two ion-cloud missiles firing from port.

The projectiles connected dead right, knocking out all transmission towers. A gigantic explosion filled the sky. The *Lesior* flew through the flames and wreckage. Super-charged debris shuddered off its electro-shields.

Yul squinted in the glare of *Lander's* viewscreen. Several tiny blips registered on the horizon. The *Lesior* lifted past Phebis's exosphere.

Then Yul's vision clouded. *A Zikri armada was out there.* A wave of dread seized him: an ungovernable fear that the Zikri would make them lab specimens in their tanks. And yet some consolation that the cursed samples would be lost forever under threat of such a vanguard.

"Engage hyperthrust," growled Goss. "Salvest, get us the fuck out of here!"

"Aye, Commander."

Salvest took the ship into a wash of trans-light haze. It disappeared in a flash of blue, just as the vanguard fleet of Orbs came pulsing out of light drive like digital wasps. Uro bombs loosed from their cannon bays like fireflies, only milliseconds from impact.

Goss banged his fist on the console. "They'll never catch us."

"You'd better hope they don't," Yul croaked.

* * *

An hour later Yul stood in the *Lesior's* detention room, stripped and sullen. Frue hunched beside him, shivering, his face a ghostly mask. He was weak as a kitten.

"Search their persons."

One of the guards covered them with blasters while the other ran harsh fingers over their torsos.

Goss examined the blackened, grime-faced men with distaste.

He leveled a look at Yul that would take down a bull. Walking over, he knuckled him across the face with his good fist.

Yul stared defiantly back at him, his lip bleeding. He wiped the trail of crimson away.

"Let's see. Destruction of an SC 34-6. Jeopardizing an important salvage and rescue operation. Failing to protect company property and the willful bombing of a state-of-the-art Vegas-U6 explorer, making unwise decisions leading to the ultimate loss of millions in hardware. Up to your neck, Vrean, I'd say." He nursed his stub of a forearm, hissing breath through his teeth.

Goss's communicator sounded. He snatched at it impatiently. "Yeah, Goss, here."

"Any indigenous life forms recovered?"

"Nada," replied Goss.

"Bring them in," growled the voice which Yul recognized as Mathias's. "They have much to answer for."

"Roger that." Goss scowled. "We have only this bulb we found cached in Vrean's suit. Think he was concealing it. Might be one of the pods of the creatures that attacked us on the bridge.

A pregnant silence pervaded the room. "Bring it to me with all possible speed." The connection went dead.

Yul ground his teeth. God help the world. That those damn pods had not stayed on the ship was a bad omen. Why were they on him? One must have inserted itself into his suit pocket when he was rolling about the *Albatross* floor fighting Zikri. He wished they'd all burned. The pods, Goss and his motley crew, all of Mathias's cursed expedition...they could go to hell.

* * *

Subcommander Krin, garbed in his air mask and nozzle, watched the lander take off with a mixture of disgust and frustration. His squid-like face rippled with apprehension, emotions too complex for even a Zikri to process. The events played through his mind in a savage blur. He struggled to pinpoint where he had gone wrong: his arrival just moments too late after his scouts had been scouring the lower levels searching for the intruder, following the incident in the main specimen room. His gliding in to investigate, only to find the place a shambles and the warning buzzer blaring.

A strange thing, all those tanks, and the bodies strewn about like kibble from a starving pup's maw...and that strange butterfly gliding about the air like some commandant. How it killed Rarl, his number one field officer, when he had reached up to apprehend it, was unexpected. The insect had carved razor-sharp wings through Rarl's probing tentacles like a butcher's knife, then it had doubled back to cut his throat, slicing a deep line through glottalus and epithermial... Poor fool's innards had spilled out like mash before he had a chance to catch them as another pass sliced a thin line along the abdomen. He and his squad had been unable to seal the chamber completely. Let the practiced forensic team take care of it. Explosions had sounded from above and they had been forced to move.

And yet, several more mysteries remained.

When the cold air had pushed in from outside, he and his soldiers had grabbed their masks. The freezing air had not affected them unduly. Zikri bodies were more resilient than those of humans. The four humans whom the retreating ship had left behind had been a serious error on the part of the invading team. But why had they left them? It seemed ridiculous.

How they squealed like young Zikri pups upon being caught in his scouts' tentacles! Two of them stared out from tanks in the torture room like dead fish. The others had died earlier, scrabbling for their weapons too late.

During the interrogations, a name had come up. A certain 'Mathias' of 'Cybernetics Corp'. The primitive translator module he had commandeered from the Orb's bridge had identified the human-speak as a business mogul on a world called 'Phallanor'. The human was owner of a galactic robotics firm, which partially explained the mission to the Dim Zone, certainly the financing, but not the purpose. What a cybernetics' mogul would want with plants still mystified Krin. Zrake, his superior, had put ships on high alert for this 'Mathias' and he had little doubt Zikri intelligence would track the suspects before long.

Krin paused, considering another thread of events: stealth Orbs landing on the moon, laden with welcome reinforcements and murderous intentions. The Orb, deemed 'unsafe', to be thoroughly investigated in due time. The hull breached and all breathable air sucked out. Systems might have been damaged with the onrush of cold air and the resultant temperature drop. The ship would remain where it was, not considered space-worthy. But Zrake had ordered a contingent of guards to ensure the Orb was not pillaged by scavengers. Without a doubt, the Zikri were masters of the art.

Meanwhile, the Zikri fleet was in the air, ready to execute Zrake's plan. Zrake and his superiors were in savage moods. The humans had slipped away—but they would not escape for long. Zrake had made it sufficiently clear to Krin that there would be no rest for him until all the humans had been apprehended.

Krin mused upon the aforementioned details and the last blunt statement. The human they referred to as *Yul* would not escape. He had his honor to uphold. Zikri code demanded an exact reckoning. So would it be, even if it went badly for Krin.

He scratched the blue-gray scar on his neck, a large oval gash, which always throbbed in moments of stress or panic. The wound was the size of a tentacle width. He recalled the mark ever since the coming of age ceremony when he'd had to prove himself against another young pup. The event was co loured with triumph rather than pain, him suffering terribly, but so had the other, bearing grievous wounds.

His impressive musculature rippled as he shifted position, the tissue extending from shoulder to mid tentacles. Another distinguishing mark on his lower scaly leg, denoted an old wound that had never completely healed, gray-scarred now. It ran several inches from what would be considered knee downward. If he had any weakness, it was that, which limited his speed and dexterity. But coupled with his training on the harsh, Zikri-conquered world *Vyan-Ry* from an early age, it was relatively insignificant.

Krin shook his head and resolved himself to a course of simple vengeance upon the human. To dwell upon the matter was a waste of time. Other pressing concerns lingered. He would punish the desecrators of the Orb, or would die in the attempt.

The alien plant ring that had gripped his minion Dax earlier was still an enigma. Another specimen with similar red and yellow bands had latched onto Rok's left motilator and the tentacle was raw and rosy with constriction. Nothing could get it off, even after he had rigged winches and applied manacles taken from the bridge to pry it off. Short of amputating the whole tentacle, which Rok was loath to allow, it seemed hopeless. In fact, the thing had struck back with an acidic spray from jets in its fern-like outerbody that blinded any Zikri attempting to excise it. Also severely burned their skin. It seemed the ring considered Rok its 'host' and did not want to relinquish its perceived stable habitat. Barbed suckers pried into Rok's flesh and fed off it in some bio-chemical way. If it were a symbiotic relationship, Rok certainly did not appear to enjoy the experience. Should anyone try to attack the ring or even menace its victim, like pulling his tentacle to get the ring off, the thing would fight back with a vengeance, lash out with caustic fluids or inflict undue woe upon Rok. It had been most interesting to watch, though grisly. An odd, almost intriguing arrangement, yet death was Rok's fate unless there was some way he could get that parasite off.

Nothing would end well for any of them, especially if, as the surviving officer in charge of the *Mzigji* Orb, he did not punish the offending humans.

Krin's mouth curled in an ugly leer. The other human, wandering about, had fought wildly yet stupidly in the Mentera tank room. In the end to join the predatory *hedrax* en route to the Ring Station. A vicious creature, this whale-like beast, at best a grisly showpiece, not to be trifled with. Let the Mentera do what they would with such grotesques.

Krin snapped out of his dark reverie at the sound of Zrake's brittle voice. He was back again in the dark conference hall aboard the *Wikrik*, Zrake's warrior Orb, the Spike-Runner, heading toward the Zikri-Mentera alliance space hub orbiting *Kraetoria*. A number of Zikri were present, including Zrake's closest aides and his superior, Mrupuk, the old butcherer.

Zrake looked down with contempt upon Krin, after claiming Krin's human prisoners as his own.

"Because you have failed to protect our customs and ships, you should be put to death. But since you have brought me these humans, I have reconsidered the death penalty. I will give you a ship and one last chance to exact revenge. Do not fail me, subcommander." Zrake chittered the last words with a sneer in front of his senior Mrupuk. "I give you the task of bringing me back a hundred human prisoners or more during your assigned mission."

Krin bowed, stunned at his good fortune. Even before the Orb had come to pick them up on the moon *Urknu*, he thought he had been as good as dead.

"You will be under Vngbrug's supervision, of course. A trusted *gurkuk* of mine. If there is any difference of opinion, the *gurkuk*, my eyes and ears, will prevail. Vngbrug kills on the spot anyone who exhibits disobedience."

Vngbrug quivered, bowing slightly with a twitch of his fore-tentacle. Smaller of frame, he sported a white splotch on the left side of his wizened face, similar to the color of his top left tentacle, completely albino, which Krin presumed was a congenital defect.

Krin bowed.

"At ease, Krin." Zrake made a conciliatory movement. "Continue where you left off. Use Vngbrug's talents. Round up these *druk* who have cost us dearly and remain alive."

Krin gave a chitter of brisk acknowledgment. At once he sped down the hall with a fresh lease on life. Vngbrug matched his stride, polyp-ridden head bobbing at his side. Krin's newly assigned crew members, Kral, Vryk, Dax, Bral and six others were close behind.

Krin was back in his element. His features twisted in a vengeful grin.

Chapter 4

Phallanor, a hub among the free colonies as far as planetary commercial centers went, came up fast on the *Lesior's* sensors. The most influential and powerful galactic companies set up shop there, or at least held a presence. The city center shone like an emerald circuitboard over the rolling landscape as the ship streamed down toward her skyline. With her bustling air highways, a population of 23 million, and a network of junctions to outlying communities, traffic was not as diverse as could have been: air taxis, long and short range shuttles, cargo vessels offworld and domestic, from the sleek and daring retro-fit to the rustbuckets of earlier generations that were the mark of the space explorer age. Noticeably, the tall super towers pushed high their steel and chrome pinnacles into the cumulus clouds. Phallanor City was the super metropolis of this sector of the galactic worlds.

Banking low, the *Lesior* finally docked on top of the Cybernetics Tower #1. No sooner had the engines died than Goss shuttled Yul and Frue out at gunpoint, down the landing pad into the reception bay where a detail of marines took the prisoners into custody. Goss conveyed the precious 'pod' to Mathias while the marines forced Yul and Frue to cool their heels in the White Room, as Goss called it—a windowless, padded detention hall.

Yul was in a sour mood as he paced the spartan confines. His body ached and his guts growled with hunger. When was the last time he had eaten? Aboard the *Albatross*, synthetic mash with the late Regers.

* * *

Yul looked up from his stiff crouch a day and a half later to see Goss's pug-nosed visage emerge through the locked door with three of his marines. All bore arms. Arguing with the cyborg was useless; Yul did not waste his breath. He opted for a surly silence.

Goss's mangled stub was repaired. He wore a broad grin as he escorted them down in an elevator of the glass tower. They were still many storeys up.

The synthetic herded them into a plush room furnished with velvet divans, a wall of windows from tile floor to ceiling overlooking the city's busy highways. The splendor of the artificial parks and spire-like towers sprawling before him did nothing for Yul. High ceilings, marble and chrome decorative art, gold-trimmed doors—the place was an immaculate palace, not a piece out of place, nor a speck of dust unaccounted for. Goss motioned to a tall wine jug on a glass table stocked with a tray of crystal goblets and plates of expensive foods. Here were chilled local caviar, assorted roasted meats, warm loaves, rich casseroles, poultry, poached fish. Needing no further invitation, Yul and Frue ate wordlessly. They devoured the food, paying no heed to etiquette or Goss who glared nearby.

Goss went to stand by the window with his back to them while Frue mouthed words in monosyllables as if he were still in a state of shock. Goss spoke some unrecognizable words into his com as he looked down upon the city. Yul followed his gaze, feeling the blood returning to his cheeks, registering no emotion over his present predicament or the abundance of multi-windowed buildings clustered below. Pale sunlight streamed down from a nearly cloudless sky on their shiny summits—this world was so different from the murk of the Orb where he had scrambled for his life.

It was yet another hour before Mathias appeared. The CEO strode purposefully through a door better suited for a cathedral. A short wait by Mathias's standards, an imposition which he inflicted by dint of his executive-privilege.

Yul had never liked the man. And now he regretted having been propositioned at the last minute by a messenger of his, for the faraway mission to Xeses.

"Well, gentlemen, it appears we meet under less than happy circumstances." Mathias's long face, high cheekbones and gray, owl-like eyes were part of the imposing mystique of the man. They did not mask the hard, arrogant exterior, though, that Yul had come to expect. Mathias was of middle years, clean cut, wearing an expensive camel-hair suit, a chocolate-brown tie that highlighted the straight hair and gold cufflinks, but there was something odd about him, something that at first impression did not ring true. Yul had felt much the same upon meeting Goss—always considered himself a good judge of character. A synthetic? Could Mathias be owner of a large galactic company, and a synthetic? It seemed a stretch. And the idea was repugnant.

He took Mathias's outstretched hand, more out of necessity than any respect for the man—the grip was strong—a trademark of a cyborg.

"I'm sure we can come to a resolution of this little problem of ours," Mathias said in a disarming voice.

Frue did not get up; the pilot sat sprawled on the nearest divan, his eyes staring listlessly past Yul and the CEO. Frue, returned from the dead, his face haggard, scratched and pale as a ghost, looked as if he had aged ten years.

Mathias raked Frue a cursory glance, lifting a finger to indicate that he should stand. Frue paid no heed to the request.

"He was in one of the tanks," explained Goss.

The word 'tank' seemed to snap Frue out of his daze. "I feel like it broke every bone in my body," his quavering voice rasped. "Then it tossed me into the water. Scab-faced squid horror."

Yul recalled scenes from that grisly episode back in the Orb's tank room: the pale greenish water, the lolling form of Frue.

Mathias motioned to two of the marines that they might go.

Goss frowned but said nothing.

"Mr. Frue, what to do?" Mathias mused, tapping his chin. "I have other missions for you. Take him to the briefing room—with Axle." Goss's nearest minion saw to it and escorted the pilot away.

Yul did not have a good feeling about what was to come next.

Greer dead. Hurd too. Regers... He twitched in unease, a snitch of dissatisfaction piking his veins. Regers' death still disturbed him. What could he have done? He had tried to help him, but had been insulted, Regers responding with violence as his usual custom.

Yul pushed the unpleasant memories out of his mind.

Mathias glared at Goss. "You drag me into a war with the Zikri? Flub the job and lose another of my ships?"

Goss shrugged. "Couldn't be helped, sir. You wanted the samples."

Mathias's teeth flashed in anger. "You left men down there."

"They have nothing to tie them to you."

"Bullshit! The Zikri aren't fools. What's the first thing they are going to do when they round up the strays?"

"The bodies and suits had no markings."

"What about my Wren X?"

"Destroyed completely."

Mathias scowled, looking as if he trusted neither Goss nor Yul. "Not the *Albatross*, though. Just the Wren."

Mathias pierced Yul with an invasive stare, as if studying a disobedient attack dog. "That you survived this fiasco is a testament to your skill. Or perhaps your tenacity, as I see it."

Goss trembled with anger. "The man's a menace, Mathias. He's not to be trusted."

"My captain doesn't agree with me," Mathias laughed, jerking a thumb at his fuming commando. "I've another mission for you."

Yul's mouth twisted in defiance.

Mathias held up his hand. "Don't say a word. Regers and Hurd didn't make it. Frue only lived because of your efforts. The facts speak for themselves."

"Get somebody else to do your dirty work," Yul hissed.

Mathias balled a fist. "I don't think so. You'll do as I say. As I see it, you pay back the ship you owe me, until then, you're mine."

"You mean the ship that Frue, Regers and the others owe you too."

"If dead men could pay, sure."

"What do you want from me?"

Mathias glowered. "Two years ago my chief scientist, Hresh, started building something. The bastard could have made me millions with his breakthrough. But he took off with everything: designs, schematics, formulae, for the next generation of AI that could have shocked the galactic worlds. If I ever find him, I'll hang him out to dry. They were legally the property of Cybernetics Corp."

"So?" Yul shrugged. "I've heard this sob story before. I'm sure your man Hresh thought differently."

"I don't give a shit what Hresh thinks!" roared Mathias. "I want the man buried and the plans to the tech back in my hands. He's a mild-mannered genius, but a deadly viper. It's revolutionary technology worth 80 million credits and possibly billions in the future. Reports indicate he has formed his own company, or umbrella firm in direct competition to my own."

"So, what do I care? What does this have to do with those plants?"

Mathias looked off into the air, as if trying to control his frustration. "Where should I begin? I dug up a ship's log in the archives a while back, written by some biologists searching for alien life on Xeses. 'A set of rare, most extraordinary creatures' wrote the chief biologist, 'exhibiting remarkable intelligence in their ability to adapt to sudden pressures. We subjected them to all sorts of tests before the *accident* happened. The plants seem to have no ambition, other than to protect their environment, stasis and habitat, to an obsessive degree.'" Mathias fixed his eyes on Yul. "It seems you witnessed the phenomenon, or were privileged to see first-hand the aliens in action."

Yul set his jaw.

"The tragedy is that the *Ventura Explorer* never returned from out in the Dim Zone to report its full findings or accumulate workable data or samples. If they did make it off the planet, they were either horribly attacked or waylaid by outer-zone pirates before reaching safe haven at Pzison gate. It's the *Dim Zone* after all."

Yul twitched. That explained the expedition to Xeses. "But why the fuss about acquiring the plants?"

"Xeses was a planet of only moderate interest to explorers, colonists, or a few curious scientists, even miners, owing to its large deposits of selenium. I'm thinking that's what gave the plants their innate intelligence."

Recalling the strength and instant adaptive morphing, somehow Yul thought not.

"Consider their super-adaptive abilities—it's a trait embedded in their DNA. Lucky for you, you secured a small sample for us, or I'd have terminated you. Goss, here, says more by accident than generosity did you deliver us the sample. We want to channel these capabilities into a new line of mechnobots."

Yul's mind flashed on the butterfly and he gave a cold shudder. The insect was content to sit in its contained environment biding its time, even though it had the ability to wrest itself out of its prison. But it chose not to.

An advanced form of life, unknown to anything on the earth-like worlds. What could the thing not do or become in the hands of some ambitious madman like Mathias...? Yul stifled his mounting anxiety. It was unproductive at this time. "I've given you your sample. My work is done."

"You've only just begun, Vrean."

"If I refuse?"

"Things could get very ugly for you."

Yul grinned sourly. Both men—Mathias and Hresh, ruthless technocrats, were unpredictable, and he was caught in the middle. The little voice in his head that he should have heeded, and didn't, was speaking again—

Sensing hesitation, Mathias nodded to Goss. Before Yul could act, Goss drew a star-shaped weapon from his hip. A blue flare shot out blasting Yul with nanoparticles. Yul felt two pinpricks enter his upper shoulder. He staggered back, reeling. "Ow! What'd you do?"

A wave of fire seeped into his blood. Bastards! They had impaled him with some kind of drug. As it spread throughout his body, it jolted him with a deep searing pain.

"Should you try to remove those particles—" Mathias's face assumed a dark grin "—the effect would be like a long time addict trying to come down off of cocaine. Only worse."

"Son of a bitch!" A creeping itch moved along his nerves as whatever it was, nanoparticles or microscopic dye, suffused his blood stream.

"Your final instructions will come soon enough. Don't defy me, Vrean." Mathias's eyes bored into him like daggers.

Yul hunched, eyes darting around for options. He had to get out of here.

"The beauty, simplicity of the implant—is that it is undetectable by modern instruments—MRI, surveillance scanners, probing extractors—the dye could be in any part of your body. We experimented with it on synthetics, pure cyborgs, until we found a compound mix effective on humans. The mixture which cycles in your blood now."

"Spare me the technobabble."

"Why? This is too much fun. The gun uses light highways for tracking, relaying your coordinates and body signature back from any open local carrier, via radio towers. So, if you wander afield in any way, in some zone, on a ship, near a transmitter, communicator, anything, we will know where you are and can transmit a signal of horrendous pain to your nerve centers. You don't believe me?" He motioned to Goss.

Goss depressed a button on the star-shaped weapon in his hand and it clicked.

Yul felt searing pain crawl over his skin. It went into his bones, forcing him to his knees.

Mathias chuckled. A wolf's grin suffused his face. "That gun is worth 10 million credits. The only one of its kind. I hope this suffices as an adequate demonstration?"

Yul snarled. Bright resentment shone in his tearing eyes.

"You wonder now why I chose you. You were survivors, commissioned to go out in alien territory, with proven skills to survive and deliver the goods. I didn't care how you secured them or the details. I just wanted the job done and the samples in my hands. Which I got. At least one. But I didn't expect half of you dead and my ship destroyed. I believe Goss quoted you as saying, 'I'm nobody's bitch.' Well, guess what, you're mine."

Yul staggered to his feet, clutching for balance. He had only one advantage—that they still underestimated him.

"Come, I want to show you something. You can be part of something big, Vrean, knowing that with your efforts, you will be participating in forging a new techno-empire." Mathias waved a hand and the massive door opened. He swept through like a prince, his swagger confident, his spirits high. Yul limped after, goaded by Goss's pain dispenser, feeling the aching tingling in his nerves as his spine seized up after the nanoparticle invasion.

Mathias took them through a high-ceilinged chamber, then down a ramp into a luminous glass elevator which descended several storeys below ground. Goss kept his weapon trained.

The elevator slid open and Yul gazed into a spacious hall full of robotic exhibits.

"The Cybernetics Museum," Mathias declared proudly. "Some of our earliest models are here." Mathias spread an arm. "The A3-Remnot, for example". He motioned to a knee-high white cube with rounded edges. It rolled on small wheels and three green lights glowed on its frontal turret which could have been eyes, but were most likely sensors.

Mathias's conceited smirk irritated Yul for reasons that were only too evident. The industrialist continued to look affectionately upon the bot, as if it were a favorite pet of his.

"A household pick. The model could vacuum, dust, answer the door. Rudimentary intelligence permeated its thinking and limited voice modulation, with voice recognition systems that kept it as a faddish impulse buy, but otherwise serviceable. Over here, we have the Bizbell M9."

Yul stared at a larger, more human-like shape, with legs for walking. Mathias hit a switch on the command post and the synthetic quivered to life, jerked over with its head bobbing like a parrot, neck swiveling.

"We expanded our reach to sell a whole line of these. They could take the roles of business people, valets, chauffeurs, clerks, you name it. They can cook, clean, answer portable devices, serve as general servants, factotums, or consorts."

Yul saw a whole series of them in ranked rows. They looked starkly identical: gray-black, elasti-plast steel and porcelain with gaping eye sockets, o's for mouth holes fixed in an expression of surprised elation. "Color, height and sex are modifiable," Mathias's grin was smug as he glimpsed Yul's critical look. "Why don't we step back over here?"

"Why not?" Yul muttered sardonically. He yearned to get his mechanical fingers around Mathias's neck and squeeze the life out of him. He leaned forward, but Goss, reading his intent, took a step forward. "Back off."

"Those are more advanced models. Though still quite antiquated," remarked Mathias, "if not obsolete as little as a generation ago."

Yul saw a more intriguing series of synthetics standing by the wall that wore clothes and looked more human-like than any thus far.

One of them approached with jerky steps. "Can I take your coat, sir?"

Yul stiffened, unimpressed. The machine stepped back.

"Quaint," Yul rasped.

Mathias gave a wry chuckle. "That one's a bit overzealous. We have advanced quite a ways to produce models like Goss here."

Mathias took them down an elevator to a lower floor. They entered a large lab while Yul simmered with hostility. Goss trailed behind, his fingers brushing at the trigger of his blaster, owner of an anxious frown.

The noise of machine parts and computer sounds greeted them, mixed with a babel of voices. Yul glared at the many shifty-eyed technicians garbed in white lab coats. Others monitored tall, multi-dialed instruments while some bent over crowded tables working on artificial limbs, not dissimilar to his own. A few tinkered with unusual, if not weird, hybrids of limbs and appendages, many of which defied Yul's understanding.

Scientists, engineers, technicians, all wore protective glassware and soldered wires, or welded machine parts. More of them milled about, figures with dark eyes, serious looks. Social misfits, Yul guessed, by the look of their bird-like movements. He did not doubt they were mechanical and electrical geniuses.

A man with wispy, straw-colored hair controlled a shin-high spider-like bot with a remote device. Several consoles and monitors ranged on his desk, flashing wire-frame diagrams of force fields and impetus vectors as the mechnobot moved. The bot jumped up the wall, trained laser eyes on a dark form, a blot or target which smoked and fell on the tiles in a smoking heap.

Was it a prototype weapon? Yul blinked in amazement.

Mathias turned back to the spider, now chasing a similar mechanical beetle-like shape along the floor. "An experimental model only, created for my own amusement. Charming, I know. Yes, the military have much more deadly mechanisms than this, but perhaps with some innovations of my own, it will be a precursor to a future weapon."

The man in the lab coat laughed. "Dream on, Mathias. It was my idea, and a dumb one at that."

Mathias motioned. "This is Dezmin, our most prolific engineer.

He has a fecund imagination even beyond my own. Currently he is ranked highest on the payroll. This is his other 'brainchild'...or was Hresh's before he ran off, which I specifically wanted to show you." He led him along to a low steel table on which rested a glass case, connected with many wires and panels hooked to a central computer. "Perhaps you would care to look?"

Yul stumped forward. Behind the glass, he saw none other than the pod Goss had snatched from his suit.

"A sight perhaps to encourage you on your upcoming mission...and ferret out Hresh."

"It's just one of those wretched pods," grunted Yul.

"It's much more than that."

Yul glowered.

"Any progress so far, Dez? I see you're picking up where Hresh left off."

The engineer shrugged. "The pod shows unusual signs of integration. But sees us as no hostile threat. I'm reluctant to prod it further."

"Good. Exercise caution. I trust you have a sure-fire method in mind with our only sample at stake. We will return to gather more when the heat is off Xeses."

Dez nodded. "We may need more samples, sir. My experiments will run roughshod pretty soon." With protective gloves, the engineer and one of his assistants transported the pod to a smaller glass case and hooked it up with wires and attempted to stimulate it to action with electric shock.

Mathias intoned, "My hope is that we can backengineer a large enough neural net mimicking the alien intelligence's behavior which may help us design better robots in the future. Dez, our senior analyst, is confident. Any movement on that, Dez?"

The engineer beamed. "We currently have two streams of innovation in motion: one by simulation, mimicking intelligent behavior in software via neural nets, the other by direct implant, splicing biological elements with machine parts. Just as Hresh started with his device called *Biogron*. One way to train the network is to provoke it, prod the intelligence under various situations. Like now, as I stimulate it with forceps and electric current. We observe the results, see how it deals with benign and irritating stimuli, then program the new synthetic to act accordingly, so the AI has a huge repository of ways to deal with tough situations."

Yul scowled. "It sounds like a shotgun approach. To an impossible problem. What are you going to do, program every possible scenario?"

"Not necessarily. We provide the synthetic with comprehensive classes of reactions weighted with highest priority, according to the 'personality' under which it is operating. An aggressive personality would respond to a stimulus with violence, a feral one utter carnage, whereas a diplomatic one would pause to weigh and analyze its options and negotiate."

Yul chose not to answer. It was interesting, but he didn't like the idea of anything of flesh and blood being a complete cyborg. He didn't trust synthetics, like that brute Goss. But then he didn't trust real men either—like Mathias, if he actually was human.

The pod under the glass seemed to make cracking noises to some stress Dez currently applied. Yul drew back.

Mathias squinted at him in amusement. "Are you that much afraid of it, Vrean?"

Yul muttered a curse under his breath.

"What's that?"

"You haven't seen what I've seen."

"From what Goss has told me, they're just a bunch of charred plants. It was the Zikri horrors in the Mentera tanks that got the better of you."

Let the man believe what he wanted, Yul thought. He owed Mathias nothing. The bastard would get his just desserts soon enough. Slapping nanobot particles in his blood was the line drawn in the sand. For now, he'd appease the tyrant, answer their questions, appear to comply. Then he'd strike back when they least expected it.

He peered slit-eyed at the pod, glad that he was suited when he had handled the things.

Dez continued to prod the pear-shaped shell with a metal fork, dangling his gloved hand through a flush, tight-sealed opening at the top of the case. The man grinned while he worked, making small whistling noises with his mouth. The outer surface of the pod seemed to absorb the prods with stoic forbearance and change color from green to yellow to deepening red.

Mathias turned to Yul. "If what you say is true about this 'hatched' creature you and Goss describe colorfully as a dragonfly, we hope to capture and use its adaptive qualities to drive our next line of cyborgs. So far, I haven't seen anything 'dragonfly-ish'."

Yul had not told Mathias about the remarkable adaptive power of the chameleon creature back in the *Albatross*. Let the sod find out for himself. If it morphed into something else—he did not want to be around.

Yul's muscles tensed as the pod grew visibly larger. His brows rose with unease. Crimson barbs sprouted like spikes, a means to protect itself from foreign invasion and now, menacing, mottled spots of color undulated over its surface. It seemed to quiver with a super-charged energy, as if on high alert to ward off some new threat.

Dez mused aloud. "This is a second pod. The original seems to have split again in two. We've isolated the others in a separate container. Interesting and provocative, but not telling us much."

"Why split in two?" Mathias demanded.

"Why not?" Dez shrugged. "Why change from green to yellow? A diversion, I believe. It increases its chance of survival. One pod may survive and the victim will go into fight-or-flight mode. A predator may go for one color, leave the other alone. Let's assume I'm the predator, one white-coated predator. The plant obfuscates its enemy. Clever. It's a marvelous display of self preservation. Whatever the case, it's awesome."

"Knock off the maudlin adjectives," Mathias griped.

Yul twisted with impatience. "I still don't see what fiddling around with alien plants has to do with building a new line of cyborgs?"

Mathias's eyes blazed. "It's beyond your pay grade, Vrean. I don't really have time to explain it. I just wanted to show you the apparatus you're to be looking for. Some mock-up of Hresh's black box, a *Biogron.*"

"Wait," interrupted Dez, "if he's curious about the science and wants to know—" He pushed himself forward with importance, away from the protective screen of the case. "Our neural network is recording all the behaviors, successes and failures of the pod and creating a vast output matrix while firing neurons at will: the input being predicament, the output being solution. I must say, so far, the pod has been remarkably successful in evading minor attacks and absorbing stresses."

Yul stared blankly. "And so? It's gobbledygook to me."

Mathias's patience was running thin. "What he's saying, Vrean, is that we can create anything we want. Something you don't understand. I have unlimited funds and resources. If an intrepid Cybernetics Corp explorer bot on, say, alien planet X is attacked, it goes into pod form, forms a protective dome, and when it's ingested say by some giant lizard, it morphs into an eagle-taloned dragon, ripping apart its attacker's innards. I can program anything I want. Better yet, I can have the bot figure out what to do on its own. So, instead of a shape-changing alien species out in Timbuktu lying dormant, doing nothing, we can exploit and harness it for our own use in the lab. We can make a fortune."

Yul sneered, "As much as I dislike Goss, he's more human-like and sympathetic than what you intend to do with your defensive, passive pod."

"Goss has a complete human interface. He can pass as a human, but lacks an adaptive process like our Xeses' friend. Lacks an arsenal of powers and the knowledge how to use them. I want to incorporate these adaptive features in our next wave of products. To specialized buyers, of course."

Yul flinched, remembering the feral handiwork of the dragonfly. "How are you going to control such an entity?"

"We have inhibitors—in software and hardware. That's the least of our concerns."

"It'll never work. The alien is too adaptable."

Mathias smirked.

As much as he hated to admit it, Yul began to understand Mathias's scheme, yet he shuddered at the implications.

Mathias gestured. "Imagine a whole army of these things powering the next generation of cyborgs." He gazed with rapture upon the pod, his eyes traveling to faraway worlds.

Dez's eyes gleamed no less intently. "We scanned and took bio samples of the pod, identified a liquid substance, various nucleotides and polymers inside, but unexpected ones too—sulfur-carbon and silicon-hydrogen, something vaguely resembling a fetus but as of yet an unknown. As for fertilization—" He shook his head. "My guess is it seems to auto-fertilize upon stimulus from the environment. On its own, in a contained sphere, it lies dormant, so we have to subject it to stresses, like this one." He zapped it with 50V of electricity. It bounced off the sand, rolling a few centimeters.

Yul shook his head, not seeing any parallel. Was Dez some sort of whack job? Mathias too? A billionaire psycho? A quack who used electro-shock therapy on exotic plants to make a name for himself like certain barbaric doctors from Earth's dim past?

"Because it looked like an egg, it gave me an idea," Dez said with excitement. "We put the second pod in a vat with some ants and an anaconda. The ants, well, they crawled over it and the pod reacted, oozing some foul yellow secretion that sent the ants reeling. I doubt the plant had secreted that stuff already, so it must have created it on the fly—miraculous... which tells us much."

"As for the snake, nothing has happened—yet. Betsy has just lain there, eyeing our subject without much interest. It's typical behavior. But wait... I am about to coat the pod with some bait, some chicken-egg yolk." He reached in with his gloved hand through the protective screen and using a delicate brush-like tool, painted a yellow slime on the pod which rested on the sanded bottom immobile.

The coiled snake uncoiled, darting its forked tongue in and out, poking its yellow and brown wedge-shaped head up curiously. In a flash, its mouth stretched wide, absorbed the egg in a single gulp. A vague lump passed down the snake's middle.

Yul stared.

"Look," Dez cried. "Our pod is consumed. Oh, well, back to the drawing board." His eyes glinted with a sick fascination.

Mathias pointed. "Look, again."

The snake's glistening middle suddenly swelled, its fanged mouth opening in a wide 'O'.

Yul drew back, horrified.

The reptile writhed, then thrashed. Its tail whipped against the glass as if it were having a seizure.

Dezmin breathed out a gasp of astonishment, sweat beading his flushed cheeks.

Mathias's lips parted.

Dezmin's young assistant hunched closer, pushing up his horn-rimmed glasses...to better observe the phenomenon.

The lump enlarged, then a writhing pulse rippled down the snake's body.

It ripped in two and a blood-gored shape tore out of the snake's tail to flap about the bloody sand, flicking bits of flesh off its wings.

Yul and the others moved back reflexively. What looked like a lizard's body with six prehensile legs squirmed and flailed, its four wings fluttering in synchrony, propelling it forward to smash against the glass.

Two quick successive strikes caused the glass to shatter; the assistant's face blossomed with glass fragments. Caustic fluid dripped from his eyes and nose, which the moth-lizard had spurted out of its proboscis. The faceless youth collapsed in a scream of agony.

Yul jerked away. So much for a neural network. He bolted for the exit, hearing the harsh ringing of an alarm. Goss activated the pain dispenser and he fell writhing to his knees.

Three security men seized him, hauled him to his feet, then dragged him out the exit.

More poured in the doorway. Technicians scattered about in confusion. Goss lifted a hand, gripped his blaster. The moth, winging about the room, shot acid right in the synthetic's face as if recognizing an immediate foe. Goss leaped back, his burnt face pooling liquid.

Mathias stumbled for the exitway, cursing Goss and Dez. "Control your experiment! Lock this place down!"

Mother of God, thought Yul, as the guards hauled him into the fire escape. Whatever the moth-lizard was, it seemed to absorb the qualities of whatever it morphed into. As had that thing in Regers' tank. The alien lifeform drew on what was around it, in its environment, adapting like an artist's imagination to some new stimulus or predicament.

Mathias's moth-and-snake became a flying komodo dragon.

Yul's brain registered the connection in an instant. It made sense! The essence of the pod was a *moth*, indigenous to Xeses. But upon coming in contact with something else, like the *snake*, it became some new hybrid horror, in this case, a winged lizard.

The shrieks reached an apex as Mathias's men died. Folly to have pushed the life form too far. Yul caught glimpses of the freak moth-lizard before he was pulled out of range of its sight. The thing spun out of control as stun fire caught it broadside and sent it thudding to the floor. It adapted. Jerking upright, like the sinister plants that had spawned it. Then it sent clicking sounds from its crazy, whirring wings. Those wings folded, then it fluttered uselessly on its black, prehensile legs, and scuttled across the tiles under men's feet under the protection of an overturned table, dodging fire...

* * *

It was a distraught Mathias who stood before Yul in the debriefing room. An icy grimace lay pasted on his face. Two of his aides stood by, hard, lean-muscled men, one holding the star-shaped pain dispenser with itchy fingers, the other peering on with hostile glances.

Yul took pleasure in Mathias's discomfort. He glared at him like a sullen wolf. "Having fun mopping up your mess, Mathias? What of your new bug friend?"

"You leave tomorrow for Namith," Mathias grunted briskly. "Goss will take you there personally."

"Goss? Odd. He looked rather preoccupied of late."

Mathias waved a clenched fist. "Nothing our technicians can't fix."

Yul glanced at his own injuries. Mathias waved that off too. "My team down in med bay will fix you up."

"The wonders of modern science."

"You are to spy on Hresh's operation. Fill me in on any details I request. Sybcore Labs, he calls it. Sybcore is a blatant front. I suspect the embezzler has a secret operation running from there. Find out as much as you can. What's Hresh doing there? Where are his real research labs? How is he funding his operation? It galls me to think he has used my resources to promote his own enterprise. My intelligence network reports nothing more."

"If he's thwarted you thus far, he'll continue to do so."

"If you're caught, you reveal nothing. Not of me. Of anything. No link to tie you to me. I will deny your every claim. I accept no culpability for your mistakes. If you fail this recon mission, expect pain beyond your wildest dreams."

"Naturally," said Yul through pursed lips.

"We've traced Hresh's supply ships going from Namith to remote worlds like Vegron in the Dim Zone. You're going out again."

"No fucking way!"

Mathias ignored the outburst. "Relax. I didn't say out 'there', as in the Dim Zone specifically. Namith, for starters. That you survived the encounter with the Zikri is nothing less than extraordinary. Almost as extraordinary as the presence of these remarkable pods.

We may have all we need for this operation, with that bulb you kindly donated to us. It has spawned other potentialities."

Yul jeered. "Why don't you get Goss or one of your cyborgs to go down and play spy?"

"Full synthetics are detectable by surveillance equipment. Minimal hybrids like yourself, do slip under the radar. Rarely are they on watch lists. We need trained muscle down there. Experienced men." He watched Yul, eyeing him like a fresh fish. "A man like you."

A thousand thoughts raced through Yul's mind. When would he be free of this man's ploys?

"Hresh was experimenting with splicing alien biology into the mechnobot technology. We still have some of his original schematics before he turned traitor. We've been trying to implement some of his edgy science, as you saw—with marginal success. Hresh got wind of our little expedition out to Xeses. I think he had planned his own excursions to dredge up life out in the Dim Zone—which leads me to believe that at this moment he's attempting nothing less than to mimic our own research here."

Yul chewed his lip as vengeance brewed in his heart.

Mathias thought for some time. "I think it's adequate recompense for the botched mission and the destruction of my ships." He would have thought no differently if he were in Mathias's shoes.

Mathias gestured as he gazed out the window on the multicolored lights of the darkening city. "Should you fail to report in..." Pain drove into Yul's side as one of the marines thumbed a switch. Yul doubled over. He sagged, clutching at his gut. "I may have to send out regular pain reminders for you, just for the fun of it. I've a key code sequence to give you, that my hackers managed to flesh together. It'll get you into the main installation at Sybcore; from there, you're on your own. Use your imagination."

It was painfully clear he'd need more than that.

* * *

Massaging his temples, Mathias spoke to Goss in his private

chamber. "Vrean's a proud, sullen man. He may need some 'coaxing' on this job, I fear."

"Even with the implants?"

"I've seen men like him." Mathias fingered his chin. "Rabid dogs, like crazed beasts, fight to the end, even if it kills them."

"I know the exact person you need—*Miss Cloye.*"

"Is she good?"

Goss grinned. "The best. Better, because I know her so well."

Mathias turned to him, his eyes glinting. "Summon her then. Orders are to terminate Vrean, if he becomes unruly. Otherwise keep an eye on him and see that he does his job."

"Roger that."

Chapter 5

Goss piloted the *Prosaic*, a light, weapons-heavy craft, toward the Pegasus station orbiting the world of Namith. He docked the ship in the designated bay near the passenger transhub then motioned to the craft's exit hatch which would grant Yul entry to the heavily trafficked platform. The trip to the warehouse outside Paranith City was only a short jaunt.

Yul blinked. "Aren't you going to drop me off?"

"Find your own way," growled Goss. "I'm not your chauffeur. Here's 200 credits to book passage to the city—to be added to your indenture." He tossed four luminous coins to Yul. "Don't screw this up. Remember the pain inducer. If it was me, I'd have killed you, Mathias be damned."

Yul ducked through the hatch to the passenger depot, his black bag of gear slung over a shoulder. He disappeared amid the throng down the main moving conveyor. A wall of sound hit him and he turned to watch Goss's ship's thrusters flare and the ship head off back to Phallanor. Goss hadn't taken him down directly because Mathias wanted nothing to do with him. Or perhaps Goss was just being a prick. Yul's back muscles stiffened.

As the babel of voices settled within his consciousness, he loosed a breath. How long had it been since he'd been among a crowd of free people? The transfer boards lit up with names, the destinations to far and domestic worlds: Virgas, Proplian, Zane's star. Pegasus station was a huge complex: a hub to many in the Geriah sector, of which it was the center, named after its legendary explorer, Tond Geriah, the colonizer who'd charted many of this sector's suns and planets. Easier to launch crafts from this floating airport than from Namith, or neighboring worlds. A way of avoiding the gravity and excess fuel needed to escape the planet. It was one of the newer innovations of this century.

Perhaps he would enjoy himself in Paranith. Goss had given him some throwaway money. He could lose himself in a few gambling games and the pleasure of a few women. Casinos and night life would be a welcome release from this predicament.

With a grim smile, Yul rejected the plan. The sooner he concluded this dull chore, the better.

He would have thought Mathias could have provided at least a shuttle to take him down to the planet's surface. Once again, Yul thought of bucking Mathias. An inner intuition told him it was the wrong move. Implants or no, one day his enforcers would catch up with him. It would take only a single slip.

First things first: when he finished this job, his number one priority would be to excise the wretched nano-implants, no matter what the pain or cost.

Mathias's words at the debrief echoed hollowly in his head. "Remember, try to run and we will fry you, Vrean, and deal with the consequences later. Anywhere you go, near a radio tower or some light drive system, we will track you. Unless you wish to steer clear of every civilization completely?"

It was an option, but not a pleasant one. He could always take refuge on some uncharted planet.

Yul bit his lip with moody unease. It was not a recourse that he was willing to take at this time.

Aboard the transfer shuttle that slowly edged away from the space station, he watched the blue-gray world of Namith materialize in a wash of bright color. The surface blossomed in a surreal rush—

an underpopulated world, one of the more recent human colonies, terraformed by the financing of a few ultra-rich investors. Tall oxygen convection pumps, noisy behemoths, installed at strategic places on the surface, comprised the main workhorses, running 24-7 to pump oxygen into the atmosphere. Similarly, flora transplanted from Earth and like worlds made it possible for whole towns and cities, assembled from bottom to top, to bloom overnight. Three mining companies had lent engineering input and raw materials from what he had gleaned; lumber and coal had been transferred at mega costs, all absorbed by investors. An ideal place for a man such as Hresh to set up shop, Yul suspected, if Mathias were to be believed. Namith was approaching a fully terraformed world providing low costs for avid business entrepreneurs.

Yul considered hiring a surface car to take him to the designated warehouse, but he discarded the idea. He wanted to leave no obvious trail. Instead he decided to hunker down in the city at Parson's Pub, waiting for dusk to arrive. His boots plodded along the oily streets slick with rain. The air, warm, scented and humid, soothed his lungs, richer in oxygen than what he was used to. Low buildings peered down at him. The pedestrians, moving shiftily, were mostly a multi-racial mix of itinerant workers. Near the bar, a lone keyboardist played a modern techno beat, entertaining the regular mix of barflies whom Yul expected in such a lowbrow spaceport town. It seemed the space station Pegasus had more action than the city planetside. Yul didn't mind. The chronograph on the wall showed mid-evening. Time to go. He quaffed his ale, took the air tram from the city terminal to the farthest line east, preparing to walk the remaining five miles to the warehouse that blinked clearly on his GPS.

* * *

Aboard his private N-Juen, Mathias sped to the world Rdelnar for a deal-closer with ambassador Chagin of the Upper Colonies, member of the World Planetary Society. The merger between Cyscox Machine Exports and Cybernetics Corp. would increase his profits by 30%, also facilitate the flow of wholesale machine parts and AI systems needed for his new line of bots, to his own labs. How he relished this deal! Of course, he had ruthlessly squeezed the Rdelnarian bureaucrats to smooth the way for a speedy resolution of all legalities and paperwork crucial to pulling off such a coup. Threats to Chagin's family and a veiled hint to courier his kidnapped daughter's finger to him had been the final convincer. He disliked resorting to such tactics, but they proved unavoidable to prevent an exorbitant personal payout and a serious loss of business to widespread, competitive markets. Business was business. How else had he survived thus far?

Kaymis, his financial advisor, sauntered into the ship's briefing room with an officious air. "The Rdelnarian representatives are ready to sign, sir, offering a not insignificant token of their good faith. An extra thousand Rangenkro-cloned circuits and as many robot-lens eyes. Chagin personally gift-wrapped these extra containers for you."

"Just what I want to hear, Kaymis. The Rdelnarians are wise to humor me."

Kaymis's hands peaked under his chin. "There's another matter you should consider. The Zikri have been busy. My sources indicate that they've been launching intelligence probes on you."

Mathias grew thoughtful, his eyes flicking over the lemon wax gleam on the polished mahogany of the bar in his private space yacht. "I'll broach that matter when the threat becomes real. I've had many threats in my day. I still blame Goss for that loose end. Idiot."

"Well, the problem does not go away by blaming Goss."

Mathias stirred. He pulled at his nose in anger, an indication that the topic was closed. Already his mind was fast-forwarding to the next problem. How to requisition torso parts as cheaply as possible and undercut the opposition. Parts, including Rangenkro, must come in under the 100 million credit mark or heads would roll. Luckily his insider Aragius had seen to the blackmail of certain key figures who managed the slave labor on the world Haigon out on the fringe of Vega. That included child-labor assembly-line workers who put together the basic shins and forearms and mechanical joints, all components he used in his synthetics.

Mathias smiled. "Bring the extra supplies aboard, Kaymis. Alert Goss regarding the usual security protocols. The shipment will be put to good use swiftly—it must reach my labs by tomorrow. We have room for it here." Mathias chewed his lip. It would take several days for his ships to get out here and transport the main cargo back to Phallanor to his main labs. Work must be underway asap.

Kaymis nodded. He left Mathias's private chamber on brisk feet.

* * *

Well-cloaked in his stealth Orb, thousands of miles away from Mathias's yacht, subcommander Krin intercepted Mathias's private transmissions and with a console-mounted device translated the alien words into something he could understand.

He turned to Bral, his assistant who had been with him since the Orb fiasco. "Be sure to give 'ambassador' Chagin a warm welcome. Let's prepare a little surprise for our *druk*, Mathias."

Bral emitted a sardonic chitter. "Overseer Vngbrug requests to be part of the ops."

Krin twitched, unnerved at mention of Vngbrug's name. "On second thought, I will go down personally to be part of this mission." A devious plan was already forming in Krin's mind.

Vngbrug arrived not moments later, overhearing plans of the operation. His upper motilator reached out to call in the new development.

Krin stayed the overseer's tentacle. "We can handle this with our own resources."

"I think not," growled Vngbrug, twisting free from Krin's grip. "We call in backup. I demand it."

A moment of deadly silence passed between the two. Krin's tentacles writhed. "Your call, overseer."

So did Krin contain his rage. The *gurkuk* was hovering on the border of becoming a serious nuisance, one that would have to be curtailed sooner rather than later.

* * *

For Yul, the roads quickly became dirt tracks through drab unwooded countryside. Weeds abounded in the shallow ditches, crudely trenched. Dark, derelict buildings loomed behind steel fences on large, mostly deserted lots. A noisy, battered vehicle clattered closer and Yul quickly hopped the ditch. He crouched in the weedy shadows. A flatbed truck carrying cylindrical objects, coils wrapped in clear plastic and rolls of packaged cables, passed, spewing noxious fumes. An old hybrid vehicle. No other traffic came. The area was unnaturally quiet.

Namith's moonless sky was dark but for a scattering of stars. Yul could see the lights of a fenced service yard ahead—must be Hresh's, if the coordinate readings were accurate. Assorted vehicles sat parked: transport trucks and low-backed pickups, the halogen glow of lamps reflecting off their sleek, gunmetal sides. Some were badly dented and others had odd-sized wheels, the rubber cracked on their edges. A front? He observed other buildings behind the main octagonal one with flat roofs. Large ones. He could not tell how far back they went in the murk. Possibly some underground operations going on there.

Yul checked his gear: his ion blaster AV9, his long bowie knife, circle-vision collar and mini camera, also a small pistol for good measure—more a trank gun with two settings, stun and full sting. It could prove fatal if it struck vitals. His weapon of choice was the ionblaster, minted 4035, loaded and locked.

He snapped the circle-vision about his neck, an extra set of electronic eyes, allowing the bastard Mathias to see what he saw in 360 degree vision. The edges rested on his collarbones, exerting a light pressure. He pressed the 'live' button. A switch on the other side turned off video and allowed him to take stills of whatever was in range. He also checked the key code card Mathias had given him at the last minute. It seemed sound; if it tripped an alarm, things could get ugly. The circle-vision's cam eyes were sending feeds back to Mathias in real-time so he could see what was going on from all angles...that is, provided the trans-light network was open, operating and active.

He tugged his black cap down over his brow and donned his night-vision glasses. He wore dark padding underneath a Kevlar vest, effective for grazing fire and minimal force, but no deterrent for serious blasts. Nighttime insects chirped away, of which he took little notice. He scaled the wired fence, his army-issue clothing protecting him from any electric shock.

The patter of claws on tarmac alerted him. He turned to the baying of hounds. He held his breath, lifted his trank gun as the first of the salivating beasts came charging at him. All fell in writhing heaps, then lay still. He walked over, nudged one with his toe. Its red tongue lolled from a fang-filled maw. They'd be out for 3-6 hours. Not enough time to raise suspicion. He hoped. Plenty of time for him to do his sleuthing and be back out over the fence before anyone detected his presence. Get in, get the footage, get out...

He crept up to the side entrance across the weed-cracked asphalt, casually inserting Mathias's card in the reader. He'd be on camera, but with his black cap and dark glasses, the security system's monitor would be hard-pressed to ID him. The door opened slowly inward. Yul slipped inside.

A twitching unease grew in his gut. Bad things could be in the works. It would be worse, he knew, to oppose Mathias.

He blinked in the half-lift corridor that gave way to a spacious depot. Nothing but old junk here. Sybcore was a company that prided itself in stocking ancient androids for replacement parts. He smeared his cheeks with charcoal and moved forward on the balls of his feet. There was something distinctly sinister about Hresh's warehouse. It had an unwholesome, abandoned feel. Eerie parts of 'mekkies' and bots of ages past, lurked in the gloom. The vacant, unanimated faces of the mekkies on display, chilled him. Or perhaps it was their complete lack of features. Whereas Mathias's display at Tower 1 had been well-lit, systematically organized and tagged, Hresh's depot was a hodgepodge of clutter, machine parts and broken or dismantled mekkies, most not on display.

In their heyday they were collectively called *mechnots*. Later he knew them as 'mekkies'. Would he be rightly classified as a 'mekkie'? Yul shook his head. Why was he pondering such inane questions?

He moved forward, bridling his impatience.

So far nothing significant stood out. Whether it was a lab, a front or depot, Yul did not know. He just wanted this contrived indenture over. What did Mathias want him to find here? That wretched Biogron-thing encased in glass? The machine gave him the creeps. He shrugged, continued his search

The echo of booted feet brought him to a halt. A security guard on regular rounds? He glimpsed a solitary figure edge out of the shadows, extending a stun gun. Just some night watchman, half asleep on the job. He could hear him mumbling about his ill luck at drawing the night shift.

Yul ducked into the shadows. To get discovered this early in his recon wouldn't pay. Get in, get out, take some video to show around Mathias's coffee room gang—Goss and his ugly boxer face, the CEO, and the rest of the bloodsuckers.

He turned his attention back to the disorganized scatter. These bots looked very old—parts of models no longer in existence. Who would want to buy such trash? Why no new ones?

Another sound caught his attention. He turned, raising his blaster.

A flitting, human-size feline shape moving on all fours skirted the shadows beyond the stacks. Christ, a live mechnobot? Surely not here?

He watched, waited.

Nothing.

If he took the bot out, security would be alerted.

Warily he advanced to investigate, his blaster clutched in a tight fist. The figure had pulled back into the gloom behind a large stack of robot parts.

He peered down the space between two rows of crates. Nothing. He squinted in the gloom. If it had been real, it was gone. He hadn't time to chase ghosts.

No new development of synthetics, no lab of any kind. Maybe he wasn't looking in the right place? Perhaps this place was a conduit to some other hidden research lab? He had the itchy feeling this was an undermanned facility. A feeling that important events were happening elsewhere. But where?

There was nothing of interest ahead, just some trolleys and carts to transport cargo from the service bay's double doors, now closed to this junk yard. Likely not the place Mathias wanted him to spy on, but there were several accesses, or tunnels at the back that led elsewhere, perhaps to the outbuildings that he had glimpsed earlier in the darkness of the service yard.

Yul turned off his video. He snapped only a few photos to spite the man. He knew these shots of broken, derelict bots would interest Mathias. It would keep the heat off him for now. The man seemed to get enough of a hard on over robotic parts as it was. Damn the bastard! He would feed Mathias his balls one of these days.

Shooting photos here was a waste of time.

He stepped into one of the tunnels, ducking below the grimy windows that overlooked the service yard. No use being seen by a wandering sentry who might be prowling about.

The tunnel dipped like a ramp and the windows disappeared. He moved on down a dim-lit corridor, halogen lamps glowing every 20 feet, figuring he had descended quite far underground.

At the passage's end appeared another depot three times larger. Something of interest showed itself here: bundled canvas cargoes, steel crates, hundreds of stacked wooden boxes. He heard the whir of front-end loaders and the scuffling of men loading cargo aboard what he saw to be a ship.

A ship? It must have been there for a while, for he had seen or heard no ship land in the time it had taken him to get to the warehouse on foot.

The thump of running footfalls came at him from behind. He pressed himself flush to a crate, in behind a compact forklift.

Shit...trouble.

Just in time. A breathless man came running toward the loading crew. His weapon was raised.

"Security breach! You guys see anything?"

"Nothing."

The guard frowned, tapping his monitor. "Could be an equipment failure. If you see anything—alert me. Keep your eyes open!"

"Yes, sirree, Eugene," one of the men snorted with amusement. He flicked an exaggerated salute, noting the nameplate.

The security man's lips twisted. "Let's make that commitment a little more serious, shall we, 'Guido'?"

The worker shook his head, ducking back to his work. "Whatever you say, Eugene."

His colleagues chuckled, resumed their crude talk and coarse banter which revolved around certain adventures at Dolly's strip joint at Paranith.

Yul quietly snapped more photos of crew and cargo. So, there was a ship in active range. Which meant that Mathias's pics would arrive on his desk instantaneously across the light years, as would his circle-vision feed. The device would upload the digital info to Mathias's computers, streaming along the light-drive highways.

Yul knelt and using his knife, pried up a crate's lid. He slit open a wrapped package lying within. These were not old bits of junk as in the last section. New robot parts: gleaming limbs, pristine headpieces, faceplates, masks, perfected skulls, helmets, circuitry, modules, power packs. The circuit boards were packed neatly in cellophane, sawdust lining them for protection. Ion power packs, bulging with Fe-Al boosters. Here was enough evidence to pique Mathias's interest. He turned his circle-vision back on.

Everything looked as it should for a robotics part distributor, but Yul felt there was something not quite right about this place. Why use a junk storage depot as a front? Were such components illegal tech? Where were they taking them?

One last recon for bastard Mathias, an exploration of the ship, then he'd make himself scarce.

Skirting crates, Yul looked up to see the gunmetal gray ship towering over him. He'd seen ships like this before, bulky, toad-like cargo-carriers with huge freight-hauling capacity. Older models which he couldn't quite name.

Overhead, the ceiling ran up over a hundred feet. He needed to move fast and with caution. One quick run-through the ship and he'd quit this scene. Nothing more of significance to see. Too risky for in-depth reconnaissance. Also his cover was blown. Not to mention there were guard dogs patrolling the yard.

He skulked around the ship's hull, using some parked loaders as shields. He dipped into a ship's service entryway. The cramped corridor connected to the open cargo bay where he'd have to be on guard for hostiles.

Dim amber light streamed down from a source within the corridor. Navigating by the light, he saw a steel bulkhead ahead—a dead end. Heavy cables ran along the walls where they met the ceiling, along with electrical equipment and scanners.

Yul peered back. The adjoining cargo bay within the ship was huge. More crates hauled by loaders, mechno-drays, and men wielding trolleys, were stacked against the far wall. Yul snuck forth, using his knife to jimmy open the lids of certain crates, discovered electrical tools, expensive lab equipment, weapons, oxygen tanks.

He made a wide sweep with his circlevision so that Mathias could get a better look at what was being loaded into the hold. As he was about to backtrack to the depot, a deep voice boomed out. "Hold up! Where you think you're going, boss?" The man trained his weapon on him from the shadows, a sleek 6-inch Obviator.

Yul shrugged. "Eugene sent me to check."

"Who the fuck's Eugene? Check on what? I'm the watchman here."

"Eugene from security. Somebody's breached the warehouse, didn't you hear?"

The man's brows rose. In that split second it gave Yul opportunity to lurch forward, elbow the man in the guts and twist the weapon out of his grasp, breaking the wrist. Bones snapped. The man squawked, but was silenced as a steel fist pounded on his back and sent him sprawling face first on the metal floor.

Yul's heart pounded. He crouched low, hoping no one had heard. No footsteps or voices.

One slip and he would have been rat bait.

The man lay at his feet, a limp rag. He listened for followup activity. None. Apparently nobody had heard the man's cry. He hurried back down the ship's companionway, wanting to get out of this tin can.

Yul winced. The workers and draysmen were moving closer, blocking his exit. Dumb bastards. No easy way to sneak past them without being seen. He could try to make a break for it, but at considerable risk to his health. For the moment, he was trapped.

Yul turned back toward the dim companionway. The glow cast a gleam on his steel fingers. Hearing the sound of men's muffled laughter ahead, he paused. It was clear that if he moved forward, he'd bump into some other nosy shiphand. Yet he couldn't backtrack and risk the loading men seeing him either. Gritting his teeth, he crouched on the balls of his feet beside a ventilation shaft. There were some lockers nearby. The sprawled body was visible and a liability so he dragged the slack figure into one of them.

Now the workers were coming into the bays. Six men loading foodstuffs down the companionway. Yul tucked himself into an adjoining locker. He pulled the door shut.

No sooner had the door clicked shut when the tramp of feet came closer. An authoritative voice snapped, "Denga, where's Hagran?"

"Haven't seen him."

Another said, "He's probably stepped out for a swig."

"We leave at 0100 for Remus in the Dim Zone," the first man declared. "If he's not back, we leave without him and he's fired."

"Roger that."

Yul gnawed the knuckles of his good hand. He squeezed deeper into his hiding place. Dim-fucking-Zone? Could this be for real? Mathias was not joking about Hresh having liaisons out there.

But why?

There was no bloody way he'd be forced back to that no-man's land.

The footsteps stopped with the clink of the bulkhead door closing and the whoosh of air.

Yul waited some time before he eased open the locker's door, just enough to glimpse a stealthy figure creeping up toward the bulkhead. This was no patrolman. Neither the garb nor the poise for one. He burst out, caught the figure around the waist in his grip and disarmed her of her weapon. His knife flashed millimeters from her throat.

"Who the fuck are you?"

She gazed at him with curious surprise. "Cloye. Backup, in case you fail."

He sized her up: her intent, cougarish gaze. Her black, skin-tight assassin's garb so easily blended into the shadows. "Yeah, like my ass you are. You're Mathias's goon, here to watch me and kill me, if he feels the need."

She shrugged. Her face, picture-perfect, deadpan. Her amber hair fell loosely over her broad-cheeked features. Her face was now a growing sullen knot...Skin tight, anti-ion garb did not discredit her figure.

She twisted away from his grip as fast and easily as a snake. The movement showed the perfect contours of her cleavage, her breasts heaving.

Yul grinned unpleasantly. At least the woman was honest, but quick. And dangerous. He motioned her to the locker. "Quick! Hide in here. I don't want you giving me away. You'll be lucky if they don't kill you on sight."

"I can take care of myself."

"Like the way you did a few seconds ago. I could have gutted you with my knife."

Her mouth drew tight, lips ruby red, closing over perfect teeth.

Yul took a quick look around. He dragged the corpse out of the locker, stripped it down and donned the dead man's gray uniform. He stuffed the limp form back into the locker. Cloye seemed startled at Yul's impressive physique and muscled body. He remained entirely oblivious to her scrutiny of his near nudity.

He crouched, thinking furiously. What to do now?

Capture the bridge, take over the ship? No, too messy. Too risky. He doubted he could make it safely back outside and past the fence. Better to stay put. When they were docked at their destination, he would make his move. If it came to that... As for what that move would be... it would depend on what was there. The risk of staying here was high. Huddled in the dim murk like a rat, he squeezed his temples in thought. The female... He looked over at her.

"How did you get in?"

"Same as you. You were easy to follow. I came in with a fake ID, no different than yours. I could track you with a device Mathias gave me."

"Let me see it," Yul growled, thrusting out his hand. "I wasn't expecting tails."

She reached into a slit at her spandexed hip, a barely perceptible smirk on her face as she handed it over to him: a flat blue triangle, no larger than an oversized Namith coin.

"It must work off local frequencies," Yul mused.

She swung her pale-blue cat's eyes left without comment. A movement in the shadows? Yul ventured a glance. No, just the instinctual reflexes of a seasoned spy assessing the situation.

He could not help but feel physically attracted to this assassin. She had a lithe, feral energy to her. She was more than a shapely bit of eye candy: muscular, but feminine, curvy in all the right places, just the way he liked them. But the eyes. Something mysterious, bewitching about them. This was an extremely unpredictable vixen.

He couldn't stay alert every second or watch the woman constantly while foes roamed the ship. Sometime, somewhere he would falter and she would pounce. A minion of Mathias he couldn't kill. He tossed her gun back to her. She snatched it out of the air with a look of surprise.

Yul's reasoning: she would need the weapon to get off this ship.

A heavy tramping of steel-toed boots rung off metal.

Cloye's eyes widened. In reflex, she threw her arms around the startled mercenary who couldn't see the figure coming up behind.

"Here, what the hell is that?" called a voice behind Yul. "Is that you, Lequin? What the hell are you doing stowing a broad here for? Stifford will have your balls for that."

While the man's attention was diverted, Cloye moved from her embrace and brained the man with her pistol.

A take-down in seconds. He fell like a log.

Yul stared, blinking at the motionless man. "Good thinking, girl. I mean with the amorous advance." He turned toward her, his face wary.

"Don't mention it."

He did not like the edge of insolence in her tone. But he didn't have time to complain. A sudden spasm ripped through his spine and he sagged, arching in pain, falling to his knees.

Cloye blinked, weapon moving in an arc.

The ship's light drive function. Yul clenched his fists in agony. Of course—it was the carrier that had allowed Mathias to send him pain across the light years. One of the bastard's little reminders he was not keeping his mind on the job. Yul gasped, staggering for the wall, trying to catch his breath.

"What is it? Mathias?" she hissed.

"Who else?" With effort he regained his balance.

She gave a disapproving scowl and reached out a hand to him.

"Just hope you don't fall on the snake's wrong side, like me," Yul croaked. "It's easy to do."

"Let's just focus on staying alive." She peered up the corridor, ignoring his outburst. "If we get Mathias the info he wants, then we both get paid."

"Maybe you do," Yul wheezed, "but I'm getting nothing out of this deal. The man says I owe him a debt."

She paused, toying with her blaster. "Then that's your problem, not mine, Yul."

He swayed on his feet. "What do you know of this *Biogron* we're looking for?"

"Some glass container hooked up to some electronic gizmos and computers."

"You saw it?" he rasped.

"When I was in the lab and Mathias was explaining this mission, the top was open enough to take a peek inside. I saw some ferns growing in the sand which Mathias's lab monkey Dez, claimed had grown from some pod. A moth flew out and landed on my arm." She gave a humorless laugh. "Gray-winged thing with red spots on it. Cutest little thing."

Yul felt a cold shudder run up his spine. "No more talk of Mathias and his bugs." He winced as he staggered down the hall, jerking open the companionway door. His nerve ends pulsed to the torment of aching joints. His mechanical fingers flexed, ready to take his wrath out on somebody. The ship's towering outer cargo door clanged shut somewhere behind them. Yul turned, glaring, hearing an annoying buzzer as the ship was finally sealed. A female countdown voice announced, *"Departure in T minus 5 minutes"*.

The headset of the prostrate man on the floor crackled. "Captain Lorde here. What the hell is going on down there, Rourke? You high or something?"

Yul cursed. He scrambled back, snatched up the receiver, his fingers itching to crush it. The man was out cold, maybe with a cracked skull. Cloye had hit him hard, perhaps too hard. He spoke into the com as unruffled as he could. "No, sir. Checking for stowaways."

"And?"

"False alarm. Falling crate near took my head off. Some fool piled it too—"

"Spare me the details. Take care of it, and be seated and strapped in within five minutes. Hresh is a stickler for orderliness. You know that."

"Yes, sir."

"And hurry up and get back to the bridge. Departure is at 0-15."

"Roger."

"By the way, what's duty Sergeant Lequin's status? He hasn't reported in."

Yul hesitated. "Don't know, sir."

"That's Captain Lorde to you."

"Yes Cap'n, I mean Captain Lorde, sir."

"Rourke, anything wrong with you? You impaired? And what do you mean you don't know? He was down there with you in bay L3, wasn't he?"

Yul winced. Things were going sour. "Hard to hear you, sir. This headset seems to be breaking up. Com must be malfunctioning. Crappy thing." He whacked it hard against the wall.

The captain's angry voice surged through the com. "Rourke, you dumb ass, what the hell's wrong with you? Are you gassed again? I'm sending someone down there."

Yul heard some more expletives and mumbling about the shipment being too important to tolerate mistakes.

"Now what in hell are we going to do?" Yul stared at her.

Cloye shrugged. "It was you who decided to hop this ship."

Yul balled a fist. He looked away in exasperation. "I have to think."

"I could kill our sleeping beauty, solve our problem."

"Wouldn't help." He held up a hand. His mind fled over several possibilities. If the captain found Rourke passed out, he'd assume he was intoxicated, had maybe slipped and banged his head. He would order him taken to sick ward before slapping his wrists and taking disciplinary action. End of story. But if he found a dead man, or no man...

No, better to leave him alive. "Discovery of a murder victim's only going to complicate things. We'll have to risk it." He shook his head. This was very sloppy work.

"Suit yourself, ace, you're in charge."

Yul scowled, resenting the woman's sarcasm. "Rourke'll be out for a couple of hours, if he even wakes. Gives us a chance to come up with a plan."

Cloye opened her mouth to argue but Yul shoved her up the companionway. "Move!" He recalled that she would have standing orders from Mathias to terminate him at will. But neither of them could finish the job alone, and he'd have a bitch of a time dealing with an assassin while he was in investigative mode. An uneasy truce was the only option... He had to reason with this Albatross. Manhandling her throughout the ship would only get her pissed off. Make his job that much harder.

A wave of heat surged through him. Her provocative curves in such close quarters were impossible to ignore. Rarely was he affected by a woman so blatantly. There was an electricity about her. Or maybe he'd been out in the hinterlands too long. Likely both. Things were never easy on a mission, especially with a woman of such attraction in the equation.

He felt the tug and otherworldly lift-off course through his bones. The ship was entering the lightstream to another place in the universe: Hresh's world and the completion of his mission. If they got lucky and weren't caught.

He moved forward about the deserted halls like a hound tracking a quarry. No question of sitting still. He had to look for some place to ride out the search for the errant duty sergeant. He kept Cloye ahead of him. She seemed reasonable but she might try something stupid even under their dodgy circumstances. At least until this mission was over, at which time they could get to know each other or kill each other; he wasn't sure which. Too many variables surfaced for his brain to distill—too much beyond his control.

But it was clear to him that if they loitered too long where Rourke got clubbed, they'd be discovered.

As he moved down the corridor, his eyes scanned the ship's layout. The ventilation system was noisy and gave out a clunking rattle. No secret it was an older model. Very old. The artificial grav was archaic and out of whack—his gait felt ever sluggish and his frame slightly heavier than normal as he trudged down the corridors deeper into the ship. A particular rectangular unit was suspended from the ceiling and he cocked his head, leaned in to hear the unit buzzing with an electrical hum. Boosted too high. He scowled. Maybe he should lodge a complaint with Captain Lorde...? Sardonic thoughts like these did little to help them.

He scratched at his shoulders where the skin itched something fierce. The coarse material of the shiphand's uniform reeked of sweat and rot-gut booze. Combined with his own sweat, the greasy stickiness felt as if he hadn't washed in a week.

He did not know how long they would be in light drive. If they were heading for the Dim Zone, it would be at least six, maybe eight hours.

It turned out to be seven.

He ducked back at a sudden noise, pulling Cloye down with him. A gray-uniformed officer clumped by a cross-corridor. This was the second time they had almost been discovered.

"Only a matter of time before we get sighted and ID'd," Yul hissed.

"Do you know this rustbucket well enough to navigate it?"

"There're three levels in ships like this, as I recall: cargo on lower tier, ships' engineering and weapons at stern, the bridge above, the toad-shaped belvedere seen from outside. We could go—"

"Elevators?"

"Maybe, or just a series of emergency stairwells at both ends."

"Let me go ahead to scout out the ship for you," Cloye suggested. "You hang back here and find some locker to duck into and play handsies with yourself. I'm better at this sleuthing than you."

"Too risky. We go together." Yul shook his head. Did she think he was that stupid?

"Have it your way," she grumbled, staring at him, her dark eyes focusing languorously. "What do you suggest?" She contrived to reach out a hand behind her head, arching her chest, twisting close enough to brush against him.

"Certainly not what you're thinking," Yul muttered.

"Oh, come on now! You playing the prude on me? I'm sure we can get to know each other better, have a few moments of fun. We both get lonely on the job, far away from home. We can find a locker big enough for the two of us. Unless you want to jerk off there on your own."

"As much as my animal instinct urges me to take up the offer, I'll pass."

"Oh, Vrean, such a gentleman! Charming one too. Didn't anyone tell you a woman hates to be turned down?"

Yul struggled to get inside her head. "So what's your story, Cloye? Daddy lean on you a little too hard when you were a schoolgirl?"

"Father? No," said Cloye sullenly. "Uncle. Introduced me to the spy world too early on. Recognized in me the manipulative streak I had. Plus, I was a hot piece of ass." She chuckled. "He used me." Her lip downturned in a moody scowl.

Yul said nothing.

"Irony is, I used him in the end. To get big contracts."

Yul pointed ahead. "Look over there, by those bulkheads, some storage areas. Maybe I should lock you in there while I go ahead and scout out the terrain?"

She sighed in irritation. "Why don't we just storm the bridge and take over this ship? Better than being a bunch of pansies waiting to be plucked."

Yul laughed at her brazenness. "Bad idea, think harder, Cloye. Let's say we take the bridge. You want Sybcore security after us?

They'll send attack ships out to intercept us. I've already been in this situation before and not about to do it again. If Hresh is half as ruthless as Mathias...we're dead."

"Meaning, if they catch us creeping about like rats, it's better? The result seems about the same."

She had a point. He did not want to give her the benefit of a doubt. Neither did he want to give in to her manipulations nor reveal his admiration for her cleverness.

More voices echoed down the hall. They traded knowing glances. "Shit," each swore and in unison jumped into an ungrated service duct at ankle level. They lay still as mice, listening to the footfalls tramp by inches from their bodies.

Inching their way along the cramped, dusty space, Yul stifled the urge to sneeze.

A metallic odor lingered in the air, likely of past cargoes. Almost as if this had been an ore ship a lifetime ago. Silver-Ferro-Umex mix? Used in lightship manufacture? Terraformers were known to bring back ample raw materials on the return trip after dropping off their planetary equipment payload.

The duct widened with Cloye low crawling not far ahead. Yul prodded her toward what looked like a forward hatch. His mind was awhirl. When they reached a dead end, he forced open the access grate above their heads. They crouched there for a few seconds, peering down the hall for signs of danger. They crawled out of the shaft at last and Yul wondered if Lorde and his brigade had come to ream out Rourke yet or had discovered his limp body.

He suddenly doubled over in pain.

Cloye watched in curiosity. "Get a grip, Vrean," she said. "They're going to hear you whimpering like a baby."

"Screw it...you should know, it's because I turned off their bloody circle-vision that you're still in the game. Otherwise, you'd have been made. Mathias would have seen how you failed to take me out and bungled your cover and reputation."

She blinked, licking her lower lip. "Really? You did that for me?

Why?"

Yul grunted, suppressing an involuntary groan. He hated to seem like a pushover. "Let's just say I'm not immune to the wiles of an alluring woman."

"Humph. So you say. So many would have thrown me to the dogs. You didn't. Then again, maybe you had an ulterior motive. Like for some sex later on." She bent down and kissed him lightly on the cheek.

He felt a thrill tickle his loins. "There's that, but I wouldn't have given Mathias the satisfaction of torturing another human being."

"At least you're honest." It seemed to be something she could understand and she let down her guard with a shake of her shiny hair.

Although he sensed a change, he had more pressing matters to attend to. Like why would Hresh need these supplies going out to the Dim Zone? Seemed odd, and a weird place to transport them. Easy prey to Zikri pirates. Especially in a rustbucket like this. Definitely an old terraforming ship of the last century. The ship didn't appear as if it could defend herself from an attack. Whole fleets of them were made to haul metals, soil, water, liquids, anything useful to seed new worlds, he recalled.

Yul had smelled the rank, musty odor in the ship's air: of soil and decay...and it still lingered in his nostrils. His boots crunched on some old gravel still left from ages past as he made woozy steps forward. Cracked tiled bins arrayed on the corridors' sides were laden with dust and fine dark loam, a testament to their age and disuse. Hresh, probably on a low budget, had bought the vessel cheap to service his outlets elsewhere. But the Dim Zone? What market was there to be had out there?

At last they came to a main hatch. Probably one that granted entrance to the heart of the ship. The ship was so big, he doubted if they had made it past the cargo bay section yet. The double-doors to the main were sealed; he did not know how to work the mechanism. "I don't want to risk failure, or try this key card and be flagged on their security screens. Nowhere else to go. You got any ideas?" Blank stare. "No? So we head back."

They made their way back to the cargo bay. Rourke's body was gone, as he expected. No one else was present. The ship would be landing before long. Yul's mind was formulating a plan of action, as he stared at a stray crate tucked over by the far wall.

About four feet square. About the right size. He tested it with his knife. He pried up the lid.

"What are you doing?" Cloye grunted at him. "You up for another robot arm?"

"Get inside."

She smirked. "What's the plan? You going to drop me in the box, do me like a filly?" Her husky laugh echoed in the hall. "I like the idea, though I'm not that kinky, just warning you."

"Very amusing, Cloye, now get in."

"No. Why should I? Why don't you get some other bimbo for your sports?"

"Because I have a fucking uniform and can fake my way through these dimwit shiphands, while you can't."

"I could have gotten Rourke's uniform, for shit's sake," she said, "but you stopped me from—"

"Right, and have them discover a naked corpse, and put the ship on hold for a red alert. Brilliant plan."

"That wasn't what I meant—"

"Get in!" he rasped.

Teeth clenched, she drew her long legs over the rim and hunched down, arms wrapped around her sides, fuming.

Yul grunted, somehow liking the look of her in that cramped bin. But he shook off the image and put the corrugated cardboard sheet over her, followed by circuit boards and some robot parts, not too heavy, over her head. "Keep still, and don't say anything," he hissed. "I'll ensure there are some air holes, so you won't suffocate."

"Very thoughtful of you."

"I thought so. Now, shh."

He resealed the tape. A bit of a hack job, but without tools, he couldn't do much better.

The ship came out of light drive. Yul felt a backward jar. The faintest echoes of human activity came from the companionway along with the clomp of feet. He slid back behind the crate, listening. He waited, churning over loopholes in his plan. A creaking at the hatch alerted him to the opening of the bulkhead. Three crewmen filtered in, bantering.

Yul crouched behind a larger crate, his muscles tensed, poised to attack. He waited until six of them had gathered before he slowly slipped in behind their backs to join the group. Rubbing his temples, he wiped off the rest of the camouflage from his face on his shirtsleeve. The crew started hauling the crates forward toward the exit hatch in preparation for the transfer. The ship's engines powered down. He assumed they had landed—on Remus.

The landing had been so smooth there had been no need to grasp the hand straps on the wall.

The ship's cargo bay doors slid open. Yul saw a huge, dimly-lit, high-domed depot illuminated by fluorescent lamps. Massive front-end loaders and hydraulic lifters sprawled off to the sides. Several terraformer ships lay docked at the far end, very similar to the starship he was in. Hresh had certainly been busy in the past two years since he had left Mathias's employ.

"Lorde was furious with Rourke," one of the cargo men bantered. "Didn't believe the sot's bogus story about being attacked by some female stowaway. Figures one of us played a number on him, revenge for some past deed."

"Yeah, well, it's not implausible. Rourke was a bit of a jerk. If it was anybody, probably was Tonkin, if you ask me. Always had it in for Rourke."

Yul's lips quirked in a mirthless grin. That's it, boys, keep the rumors flying...

Lorde, a tall, meaty man with a walrus-style mustache appeared at the cargo bay door to ensure that the operation was going smoothly. He was decked in full uniform with badges and knee-high leather boots. He peered around with officious disapproval. He gave some orders, then headed back to the exit.

Yul let out a slow breath. He had kept his face turned away, as unlikely as it was the captain would recognize all his men by sight. No sense in giving the man anything to arouse his suspicion.

Yul took up an electro loader with forks on the end and wheeled Cloye out of range of earshot while nobody was looking. He kept moving along, his eyes trained ahead, darting around a stack of thick cables beside two parked loaders. Sounds echoed here as in a large cave—the clomp of boots, the clink of tools, the murmur of men's voices. All merged into a background chatter of white noise. The smell of machine oil and fuel hung in the air. Also an unfamiliar odor not describable—the scent of an alien world. He wondered how inhospitable this planet was. He had no visual of the world as of yet.

When he was far enough away from the main crew, he bumped up his pace.

Cloye banged on the wood.

"Sh!" he rasped. "Don't blow your cover."

She stopped her noise-making. He turned to push her on, when all of a sudden, out rolled a monitor: a silver, insect-like, mechanical thing with long neck, beady eyes.

"State your mission," it bleated. A stalk of a neck extended. Twin blue laser eyes glared down imperially at him.

Yul blinked. Was this for real? One of the archaic droids from generations ago? Right down to the tinny robotic voice? In fact, he had seen one very much like it in Mathias's eerie collection on Phallanor. A Brille E3?

"State your mission!" it repeated.

"I request access to—" he gazed at the luminous number over the exitway "—Bay 6."

The thing beeped in rapid succession. "Request denied. Illegal transfer. All cargoes are to be processed at duty check counter 9-16C. Report there immediately."

Yul cleared his throat. "It's a special requisition. For Hresh's eyes only." He said it with as much authority as he could. But he doubted such tactics would work. "Have you been informed?"

The thing processed the information with fastidious effort. Its eyes blinked dizzily. "No such request has crossed my databanks. Duty roster is incomplete. You have cited a case without a file number."

Databanks? What kind of a cheesy outfit was Hresh running?

"Proceed to security officer Hanson—at once."

"Oh, for shit sakes." He pulled out his blaster and blew the thing's head off. The smoking head lolled, sparking blue. Yul grabbed it and stuffed it behind two parked loaders to the side. Then he dragged the sparking body off into the shadows, snatching glances left and right. Yul grimaced as he moved the electro loader hastily past the burning droid, darting a last look over his shoulder, hoping nobody had witnessed the act.

None that he could see.

When he was at the far end of the depot, he drew a relieved breath. He was far enough away from the unloading stations and main activity. Heavy equipment and giant cranes loomed over him, tractors with lift loaders at their fronts with interchangeable scoops, forks and tool grips on the ends. They arched out of the cold fluorescent light, looking like prehistoric stalking insects. There was a bustle of movement behind, as knots of workers moved to and fro. The activity caused Yul's heart to spike, but he was safe for the moment in his anonymity.

He pulled Cloye's crate into the shadows of a dim exitway, then started to remove the tape from the top. He hesitated. A voice in his head debated whether to keep her in the box, let her cool her heels.

She'd just try to break herself out. She'd make a lot of noise and tip off the workers. He might need the woman in the near future.

With a curt nod he ripped at the tape and pulled her out. Her hair was askew; cheeks and brow bathed with sweat.

"Took your sweet time, didn't you?" she grumbled.

"I could have waited longer."

Stumbling out of her hidey-hole, she refused his help, scratching at her left arm. "Damn sawdust must have dripped down. Itches like the devil."

Yul grunted. "My heart bleeds. Let's move away from the cargo hold. If our boys are diligent, they'll be dragging some crates down one of these service corridors any minute." He looked about, searching for some place to stash the evidence. "First we need to conceal this crate. We can't leave it in the middle of the hall."

"Let's hope they don't miss it."

"One measly container, I doubt it." Yul poked up ahead, looking for a side room. "We'll sneak back later to jump a ship on one of the terraformers when the heat's died down. For now, let's stay out of harm's way."

Cloye roamed the area with sharp eyes. She sidled down around the immaculate corridor, both sides granting glimpses through small windows of what looked like laboratories. It was a combo of med bays and robot assembly research manufacture stations. "A covert research warehouse is my guess. See those macroscopes and state-of-the-art scanners?"

"I do. And heavy tools. Both fine and coarse wares. I'm guessing a lot of intense work is done here. But where is everybody?"

She rubbed her itchy arm. "We're in Hresh's base. Hired hands could be anywhere. Bonus points if we can glean some information about his research and that Biogron thing of his. Let's do a quick recon while we have the chance." She hurried up the hall, lit with dim fluorescent bulbs.

Yul scowled. He had expected another zap from Mathias for neglecting to re-engage the circle-vision. He was puzzled by the absence of any shock. As much as he disliked giving Mathias what he wanted, he could see no harm in nosing around a bit until they could get back to the landing bay then hop a ship out of here. After dumping the crate and trolley in one of the empty lab rooms, he took leery steps after her.

A portal of steel showed at the end of a cross-hall. Red bars banded across it, denying access.

"There," she pointed. "Looks promising."

Efforting to pull the bars up, she grunted, to no avail. The mechanism was jammed. Without warning, she blasted it.

Yul gaped. "What the hell are you doing?"

The bars melted and Cloye kicked it with her foot, scratching at her forearm, as if some shrapnel had rebounded back at her.

"You want to alert everybody?"

"Got to take some risks, Vrean. We've living on borrowed time as it is."

He shook his head, questioning her impulsiveness. He pushed through what was left of the smoking door before plunging after her down a dim-lit corridor.

Chapter 6

In Mathias's private quarters aboard his N-Juen, he enjoyed the plush luxury of leather divans, rich carpet, imported mahogany, the exotic views of space, easy access to liquor, gourmet food, female company, anything he desired. A signal came up on Vrean's homing device, one that brought distinct pleasure to Mathias's face.

Better yet, Vrean had come through faster than expected. The beeper traced an image on the console to a world just within the Dim Zone. If Vrean could lead him to Hresh's secret headquarters then...

Yes, he could control the *Biogron*... He called in Goss.

"Set a course for Remus in the Dim Zone."

Goss hesitated. "Why Remus? Is that wise, sir?"

Mathias's fingers hovered over the button that would zap Vrean with more pain. No, let Vrean have his little reprieve. There would be other occasions more timely to administer pain whenever the oaf erred or double-crossed him. For now, he would give him the benefit of doubt, that Vrean was doing his job.

Mathias frowned. Why no visual? Was Vrean jerking him around? Bastard! A sudden surge of anger had his fingers pressing hard on the control. He did not release for several seconds. A vindictive smirk crawled across his face.

A momentary blip came back on the mercenary's circlevision 360 receiver as if, in a moment of lucidity, Vrean had turned the device on. An image showed Vrean staggering in the corridor of some space station, or base or starship with the female assassin Cloye beside him, steadying him with her soothing hands.

Mathias's cheeks crinkled in anger as he turned on Goss. "There, you see that, you stupid fucking synthetic?"

Goss peered at the visual.

"You recommended her, now you take her out."

Goss frowned. "She could just be playing him."

"Right, with her hand practically on his cock. The deal was no contact with the mark. If she was made, she was off this mission."

Goss glowered, his face an unreadable mask. "As you wish, sir." He fingered his weapon, spoke several quiet words into his command set. He listened to the response and grew attentive.

Mathias gazed off into space.

Goss turned to his employer. "Sir?"

"Yes, Commander! Do I need to babysit you through this? Go ahead. Do it. I'm not going to backtrack now."

Goss gave a curt nod. "Just a reminder of pirates. Zikri abound in those regions. No doubt the Mentera, the bugs, too."

"Standard security procedure." Mathias waved a hand. "Get alpha wing team to escort us."

Goss blinked. "Will that be enough?"

Mathias stared at him, as if he were talking to a brick. "They're an elite corp, cream of the crop."

Goss flinched, as if hesitating to tell him something. "The armada we saw at Phebis—it was non-trivial, sir."

Mathias sucked in a draft of air. "We'll risk it, Goss. We can't always be padding around like mice in granny's cupboard. We can always warp out if things go sour."

"Suit yourself." Goss jerked his head toward the door. "As a matter of routine, I would feel better shuttling aboard the *Draxen* and briefing Captain Adlis and his team personally about the dangers."

Mathias made a gesture of dismissal. Tedious cyborg. He watched the synthetic's back as he retreated down to the command bridge.

Goss was a useful commodity, logical, practical, a clever imitation of a human, but without passion and the instinct to take risks. It was doubtful that even his research lab could ever produce the perfect model. Unless the plant-insectoid-butterfly they hooked up to Hresh's machine accomplished the impossible. He hoped the alien creature could come through. His obsession for finding a true AI brought out the Hyde in him. It would never let him rest: discovering a true AI that could feel, and was instinctively driven and that operated from raw instinct to execute with passion and precision. It was a roboticist's wet dream. He thought back to the feral butterfly as his security men floundered about the lab, at last managing to trap it in a stoppered flask. There would be increased security surveillance from now on to prevent more 'accidents'. Dez was working night and day to incorporate the creature into one of the Biogron vats Hresh had sketchily engineered in his last months at the company. Time was of the essence. No telling how far along Hresh was in his research. If Vrean failed...

He would push Dez too to the limit on this one. Already 200 top scientists and engineers were working on the project. The rest of Cybernetics' operations would be put on indefinite hold. This breakthrough must be given absolute priority.

Mathias's lips curled in a cunning sneer as he envisaged the final goal—a superior AI, one the galaxy would gaze upon in awe...

* * *

Mathias woke up from a doze, rubbing his bleary eyes. He coughed, wincing at the fermented taste of liquor in the back of his throat. A sinister feeling ran up his spine. His sixth sense was alerted. He hit the wall switch and poked his head down the hall. The corridor was empty, eerily quiet. Where was Goss?...Janson, his security officer?

Surely Goss, the officious sod, must be back from his mission on the Scorpion ships? He called out on his communicator. Nothing. Mathias threw the device down on his divan in a sulk. Goss probably was dodging him, afraid to put out the order to kill the bitch who had betrayed him.

A flicker appeared at the edge of his vision: a dark form gliding down the hall, glistening with moisture over its squid-like body.

Mathias blinked. He grabbed for his holstered weapon and fired off a round. The shot deflected harmlessly off the thing's body, which was armored. Squids! How the fuck did they get aboard? Mathias's heart jumped. The frightening realization of what must have happened almost popped him out of his skin. The Rdelnarian shipment! For shit sakes! Goss must not have opened and inspected it. How many times had he warned the dumbass to beware of bombs, assassins, the like?

Mathias's last conscious thoughts were of desperation as he was wrenched from his standing position. A thick mass of tentacles coiled around his body...with force enough to crush the life out of him.

* * *

Goss winced aboard the Scorpion flagship *Draxen*, realizing how unprepared and ill-informed the crew were. "What do you mean Captain Adlis isn't even here? Is it vacation time for every nitwit here, including captains? And what do you mean we only have half arsenal?" He shook his fist at Bis, the new security leader who blanched under the android's glare.

"We were not informed of any offensive maneuvers, sir, just a routine escort. For Christ sakes, it's Rdelnar we're talking about here!"

"Goss, you better look at this," muttered the helmsman. "Two Mark IV's bearing down at heading 350."

Goss dashed over to the console. "You've got to be kidding me—Mathias, the bastard, said there'd be no—"

"They're coming in fast, sir."

"Engage them then, fools." Goss shrieked into his headset, "Alert all backups. Scorpions 6 and 7. Where are you? I repeat. Code red!"

"We'd better warn Mathias."

"Do it!"

"I can't, sir, signals jammed. It's like he's in hyperthrust limbo. Ship's offline. What the—? We can't even light drive out of here ourselves."

"What the hell does that mean, Lieutenant? Never mind! Get the targets locked—"

A blast came to forward port. A uro bomb. It knocked out their central visual. Goss and his men lay sprawled on the ground. The navigator leaped up, his hands clawing for the console. It sparked, klaxons blared all round, emergency lights flashing. A trail of smoke rose from the starboard panel. "They're hammering us!"

"Where's the rest of our team?" croaked Goss, dismayed.

"They got Mark IV's all over them!" Bis yelled.

A war eagle came rocketing in on a killing vector. Helmsman Jordan jerked the controls in time to launch an ion blast out of starboard with enough precision to transform the war Orb into a crimson inferno. Two more came zooming in from above to take its place. Jordan swore; he sent heat locks on the two. Bis clutched the controls, looking for more marks to lock onto.

"Weasels, prepare to die!" Jordan's triumphant shout rasped over the com. Both Orbs reddened, flattened, then flared into oblivion.

Goss pounded a fist into the central controls. "How did this happen?"

"I don't know, sir," said Bis. "Unheard of for Zikri to attack so close to secured Rdelnar space."

They must be desperate, thought Goss. He remembered the firepower of the Orbs on Phebis. His human-attuned circuits could only register fear.

A sizzling flame arched across the central viewport; a nasty crackling hiss filled the air. Emergency power flickered on and off, bathing the ship's bridge in a rich sepia gloom.

"We've no main power," muttered Bis.

"Flash bomb," Jordan grunted. "Knocked out our ship's main conduit." He bowed his head.

Goss swore. The crew would die when the ship's battery-power and life-support failed. That or Zikri sweepers would force their way in to salvage what survivors they could for the Mentera tanks. The Zikri must be desperate to attack in open space.

Goss signaled to Jordan and Bis. They and the three junior officers donned protective helmets with limited oxygen reserves. Wasting no time, they scrambled for weapons and armor in the kits strapped to the side walls. They sealed the door and barricaded it with instrument panels, seats, anything they could rip down; thus they blocked the bridge's only access point. While the ship floated lifelessly in space, thousands of miles from Rdelnar, the crew's darkest fears welled and their hopes died. The pale orange globe of Rdelnar swung obliviously below.

"We sent a distress signal planetside to Rdelnar's forces," Jordan said.

"It won't do any good," said Goss, "they'll never get to us in time."

Goss and Bis, Jordan, and the junior officers crouched grimly in the murk in full battle gear. They trained their blasters on what they knew would be coming soon through that door.

They did not have to wait long.

A crippling blast sent the double-door curling inward in a mass of tortured metal. Goss and his men braced themselves as they opened fire, leveling blasters at eye level on the sea of smoke that poured in. Writhing shapes jumped through.

Thrashing tentacles seized the first unlucky men before they could get a dozen clean shots off.

Some Zikri flesh fell charred and smoking to the floor. Goss's defenders fell too, screaming curses at the intruders' assaults.

Goss ripped at the slimy and strangling Zikri tentacles that flailed around his torso and buffeted the clammy bodies smacking into him. They expected to subdue him easily, not realizing what he was. Anguished shrieks and groans became one with the chitters.

As a cyborg Goss knew he was immune to the crushing force that would snap a human's spine and he ripped Zikri limbs from sockets, flinging them every which way, pummeling alien flesh with his unusual strength. But such an advantage was short-lived.

Krin appeared, a hulking brute of a Zikri, brimming with wrath at the human figure that was unleashing carnage on his soldiers. A useless waste of Zikri life. It was writ all over his polyped face. In three quick strides he glided forward and wrapped his muscled fore-tentacles around the synthetic's neck and gave a savage twist. Off popped Goss's head with its sparking wires and dangling components and thudded to a halt amid the wreckage and gore. The synthetic's headless body thrashed about the blood-drenched floor for several seconds before it lay still.

* * *

The Zikri invaders gaped in bewilderment and awe at the smoking heap of circuitry that they thought had been human.

"Pick up the pieces," Krin chittered. "Gather them and the humans, for Zrake."

* * *

On a signal from Bral, his personal backup, Krin boarded Mathias's N-Juen vessel and lifted a muscled tentacle to warn his soldiers to hold off on the torture instruments. His eyes strayed to the viewing terminal Mathias had been examining lying on the comfortable leather divan before he had been brutally apprehended. His polyp of a mouth rounded in a surprised exclamation. He would recognize that fierce and impassive face anywhere for as long as he lived. The killing machine aboard the Orb! But of course, no need now to torture the pitiful human lolling senseless at his feet. This advanced instrument enabled this human Mathias to track the man, evidently his hireling. He must have planted a homing device on him.

But how? It seemed impossible. Sewn into his armor? Why not take off the armor? Was the human not aware he was being tracked?

Krin stirred, pondering.

Remarkable. Easy enough with the receiver in hand to back-engineer this technology. A fiendish glint grew in Krin's eye. He would trace the signal.

Bral clicked a button on the interface and the human's facial profile spun in 3D on the console. Location: 692-V3 *Jorek* sector— the pirate sector, also known as the Dim Zone.

Krin gave a broad grin. His wavering tentacle wandered to the red button stationed on the monitor. Depressing it, he saw the life form depicted in yellow on the visual, pulse into hues of red and jerk spasmodically. A cold smile curled Krin's mouth. It seemed Mathias had an ingenious way of spurring his minion on. He motioned his soldiers to take the machine and the unconscious Mathias aboard the Orb.

    * * *

When Mathias came to, he found himself floating in a watery medium on an alien ship. He was upright in what appeared a telephone-booth-like chamber.

In fact, it was all a groggy blur, looking out of a glass prison, some sort of tank. Reeking tentacles had seized him with bone-breaking force...now there was Goss, his synthetic, ripped into several pieces, clumped in a glass container box before him, the gaping eyes and head lolling out.

This must be some hellish nightmare. Mathias cringed. He felt no pain, only a sense of vacuous non-existence, much more horrifying than any death he could imagine. The dispassionate Zikri leader and his entourage stared at him through the glass like judgment officers, a sort of vindictive triumph glinting in those pig-like eyes of theirs.

    * * *

Even subcommander Krin for all his fearlessness felt a frisson of anxiety as the Mentera Ring Station came into view. The double-torus craft was still undergoing repairs from the attack by the Jakru and their rogue general Zaul.

He had never liked dealing with the locusts. He believed the Zikri had become subordinate to the Mentera when the alliance had been signed. That they were doing all the insects' kidnapping for them, running all the risks. But he kept his polyp shut. It was not becoming of one of his rank to speak out against decisions made from higher up. Others would govern and effect policy, not him.

Krin's orders were simple: hunt down the escaped prisoners responsible for the Orb's demise and redeem his failure. That was his charge, that or die.

Some of the heat would be off his tentacles, now that the mastermind of the human expedition, the one called Mathias, had been caught and contained.

Summoned aboard Zrake's ship, Krin adopted a whole new persona: meek and deferential. He entered a roundish hall of barbaric splendor, dark and pillared with ribs like the innards of a gutted whale. The slick and gleaming curved walls displayed racks of their typical fiendish torture instruments of metal. He played a sensitive game here, sparring with Zrake who was a proven master several years his senior. A game where life and death were separated only by a thin thread.

"What happened to Vngbrug?" Zrake demanded, his grizzled face curdling in anger.

Krin recalled how he had slaughtered Zrake's *gurkuk* like a disobedient pup aboard Mathias's ship during the battle. "Alas, he did not make it." Krin reflected further, there could be only one commander, and Vngbrug was definitely not it.

Zrake's features contorted in new fury. "What do you mean 'alas', and how many Orbs did you lose?"

"Three, sir."

"I should kill you for that, Krin. On your knees!"

Without hesitation, Krin grovelled before his superior, splaying upper tentacles, white-side up before him, as was Zikri custom of kowtowing before a commanding lord.

Zrake gripped Krin's tentacles in his own, almost an intimate embrace, a visible display of power, dominance, hierarchy and strength. Krin showed just the proper hint of pressure, for it was an insult to squeeze back with full force, as it was likewise to meekly yield.

Zrake applied more pressure. It demonstrated he could rip off his underling's motilators at any time. That or damage the muscle beyond repair. Krin resisted enough to make Zrake feel powerful and respected, but not so much as to express an overt challenge. There were tremors of rage brewing there that were quite ready to tear Zrake's motilators off.

Zrake spoke at last: "As chief punisher, you know it is my duty to keep my immediate subordinates in place."

"Yes, lord." Krin remained prostrate, squinting at the racks of pain-inducing torture devices on Zrake's vine-draped walls. They were slicked with a gleaming gel. Three Zikri victims were currently in tentacle-manacles, in various degrees of anguish.

"So what happened out there?"

"Vngbrug was eager to prove himself. I counseled against bringing in more Orbs for reinforcements."

Zrake's grip pulsed with increased pressure. "True, but that does not exonerate you from blame."

Krin winced. "Your *gurkuk* bungled the job. Through his hubris and conceit, he foolishly engaged forces beyond his ability. An unnecessary risk. His only wish was to impress you with ripe spoils should his bold tactic succeed. He set me up to take the fall, should it fail. It did, with considerable loss of Zikri warriors and Orbs. I witnessed the savage robo-human thing. Tore your *gurkuk* and Kral apart like pups scrapping over a bone."

"So why have you come then?" snarled Zrake. "Do you have anything for me?"

Krin was about to divulge his famous prize, Mathias, but something stayed his tongue. A glimmer of ambition in the commander's eyes was enough of a signal for him. No, he would keep his treasure secret for now, until such treasure could bring advantages his way. If need be, he would trade the human's life for his own.

"I have—"

"What? What have you? What of the *druk* who ravaged the Orb on the dead moon?"

"We have a fix on him, lord. Our next mission awaits. I thought I'd report to you my spoils—in advance."

"An irregular procedure, but I'll allow it." Zrake lifted a tentacle, releasing its grip on his underling.

Krin gratefully lifted himself to his feet and massaged his numbed tentacles. "I have come to offer a dozen subjects and the remains of a human-like machine for study in our labs. Perhaps we can revive it and produce others like it."

Zrake twitched a motilator and chittered sullenly. "At worst, we can back-engineer the device and use it for our technical weapons' arsenal. Very good, Krin. Anything else to report?"

Krin licked his polyp of a mouth. He quivered a lower tentacle, indicative of a no. Lies like this spilled easily from his maw. He had told many of them during his rise to power. They came quite naturally now. But should he be caught in one by Zrake—Krin shuddered at the thought. He recalled Vngbrug choking in his own blood. He had hidden Mathias safely away in the hold, no chance that Zrake could readily get his greasy tentacles on him. Yet a quiver of doubt pricked his hide...

Krin's eye arched away from the torture devices, avoiding his commander's eye lest it find some way to detect his guilt.

"I will personally deliver the dozen specimens to Consul Jnedz aboard the Mentera station, as I have reason to curry favor with the First Commander. He's a prominent locust lord. You will accompany me."

Krin assented with a flick of an upper tentacle. He breathed a sigh of hidden relief. He was confident that he had disarmed Zrake.

Zrake turned his penetrating gaze toward one of the chittering, drooling prisoners suspended from manacles. "Vagul here was lax at his post and neglected to warn us of an invasion early in the Jakru attack. He left Zikri ships open to assault. Many deaths resulted. Five ships, can you believe it! The Jakru did that much damage to our fleet. *Treguk, Ak Gruilkaa!*" the Zikri cursed. "A hundred ships lost, and more from the Mentera's armada of lightfighters and Ring Stations."

It was news to Krin. He looked at Zrake with new respect. Zrake obviously had links higher up the chain than he imagined, perhaps even to admiral Nrog himself. He recalled snatches of the Jakru battle and knew they had flown in ships disguised as Mentera decoys. A clever plan, even if hatched by aliens. Even if it had failed to accomplish its goal. But only five ships? The paltry number appalled him. It did not, however, help his situation.

"Vagul is beyond redemption," Zrake chittered sadly. "He must be put to death for his carelessness. But not too quickly. You, however, are granted a chance at redemption, as we, the Zikri, are a forgiving race."

Krin bowed and watched the ends of Vagul's tentacles slowly being stretched to the max by metal pulleys and cables.

Zrake flicked a tentacle. A wall switch, activated by Zrake's motilator clicked, and Vagul's closest, most abused tentacle was drawn beyond its means of capacity. Krin heard a wrenching snap, then a ripping of flesh as the member was torn free from its socket and flopped onto the floor with a sickening thud. Vagul let out a screech that chilled Krin's innards. Horrific, beautiful torture—yet oddly, a sick fascination for all Zikri who witnessed it.

"He is nearing his hundredth round of torture," observed Zrake, "and will not last much longer. Pity. I quite enjoyed our sessions. Between the torturer and the tortured a sense of intimacy develops, Krin, if the victim lasts long enough. It's almost as painful for the torturer to let go of his charge as it is for the tortured to succumb to his pain."

Krin could understand something of this. He was just glad he had eluded Vagul's fate.

* * *

As Zrake and Krin approached the Mentera Ring Station in Zrake's personal shuttle, details became clearer. A Velasian starcruiser, one from the free colonies, enormous, gray, octagon-shaped, but fish-like at its fore, loomed disabled. This was a colony ship en route to Punara in the Bedjron sector. The hulk was being towed by a Zikri tug through the protective ranks of aphid ships toward the Mentera ring-torus. The locusts, Krin reflected, would take the starship's crew, which Krin estimated at a humble 3-5 thousand, and use the colonists for their vats. Quite a haul. The humans, trapped and wired up to the mesh like lab rats, would feed the locusts' power generators. The ship's technology would support the Zikri initiative and be incorporated into their own vessels. That, or they would use the craft as bait to orchestrate more ruses and heists.

Hundreds of warships prowled the vicinity like a swarm of bees: the hive being the hub centered around the partly ruined Mentera Ring Station and the Zikri megaorb *Vixlis*—the two like an eye of a swirling galaxy, a floating stronghold in space, an ark of terror. It had been centuries since the Zikri had centralized their power, otherwise they had operated as regional marauders ravishing their territory and collecting their spoils like the outlaw barons of old. United under a new leader—the upstart Nrog, a ruthless tyrant, if not an ambitious visionary who saw the Mentera as the springboard to the Zikri manifest destiny, ultimate rulers of the galaxy—they were a force to be reckoned with.

Krin had yet to meet this Nrog. Veteran Zikri had reported Nrog as being 'intimidating', 'indomitable', and they felt dwarfed, sucked dry in his presence, as if he absorbed their very energy through the air. The leader must be down there somewhere among those masses of ships, plotting, rousing Zikri to fight for him, Krin thought. How he would relish an audience with the warlord.

A forked formation of protector Orbs guarding the inner 'gate' parted now to allow Zrake's ship to pass through to the Mentera base station. No chances were being taken after the last ambush.

"Nrog has plans for us," Zrake said. "An invasion that will set the human colonies on their heels forever. We must be ready. Many opportunities are to be had."

* * *

On the Mentera space station, Krin and Zrake walked the long metal walkways through an impossibly high-ceilinged corridor. A guard detail of Zrake's ranged behind them, drawing their human spoils in tanks on wheeled carts. To the side gaped an empty blue-black space, plunging below into the bowels of the ship. To where those boundless gulfs led, hundreds of feet below, Krin could barely guess, but he had heard of some larger weave of trapped organisms in the vessel's core, and some sinister power that drove it. A soup bowl of souls. The same that drove the locusts' life support systems.

Much activity ranged around Krin and his lord. Broad, Zikri-sized locusts with wings long fused to their dark chitinous bodies walked on their hind legs or drove aphid-shaped carts filled with goods, supplies or members of their own kind to unknown destinations within the alien ship. Some clacked their way down dim side corridors, with their antennae twitching, or ascended to levels that spanned above. Krin saw other walkways and substructures arched across those vast spaces.

They came upon the rows of tanks spread to the sides. Krin peered curiously. Rows upon rows of transparent glass containers gleamed in the eerie light, resplendent in their greenish liquid and horrid living contents. While Zrake's servants ushered their haul forth on mechanized drays—a dozen more tanks with human occupants—Krin entertained little doubt that these victims of the Cybernetics Corp raid would slake the Mentera's lust for sustenance. Others would be used possibly to power their insidious amalgamators, a light drive system of its own, which allowed them to pop up anywhere between sets of parallel plates like ghouls. Perhaps such hapless souls powered their entire space station for all he knew.

Consul Jnedz approached with a translator box clutched in a pincered grip. With his insectoid face carved in an expressionless grin, he was a smallish specimen rising only neck high to Zrake, slightly lower on Krin, hunched on splayed hind legs like a repentant mantis, his left pincer glinting with impressive jewels. But the red eyes stared unblinking. Black antennae twitched, unnerving even the taller Zikri, his plated skull gleaming in the otherworldly light like a sinister beacon.

After a desultory introduction, Zrake conversed with Jnedz while Krin waited patiently off to the side, dutiful in his deference to his betters who discussed matters beyond his authority. He took time to study the tanks and their gape-eyed victims. Strange tubes extended from the stoppered plugs on the glass tops, which the locusts inserted in their navels to refuel. Several did so now, either kneeling or sitting next to a tank, hooked from navel to tank in symbiosis with a human or animal organism trapped within the greenish brine. The humans hunched within like toads, much to Krin's disgust. Everything pulsed with a sickening green glow. The storage and feeding chamber was enormous, a steel-plated dome that ran hundreds of feet upward into a plum-colored murk. He would be anxious to quit this living mausoleum and return to his own ship, there to resume his hunt for the renegade human.

Zrake glided over to Krin somewhat pleased. There was a flush to his gray cheeks, a buoyancy to his step.

"Your intuition was well-founded, Krin, in returning to the base. The prisoners were well-received by Consul Jnedz. Along with the timing of the delivery of the colonists, it has cemented positive relations between our two nations and given us more clout in our negotiations. The Mentera will go out of their way to support us and to expand our reach by tipping us off to more vessels and colonies. Easy prey to Zikri rapine."

Zrake reached out a tentacle to touch Krin's cheek. "You have done well, Krin. I will make note of this at your indenture hearing coming up before the Tribunal presided over by Admiral Nrog in the next moon."

Krin raised a tip of his own tentacle, suppressing a sly smirk.

"Nrog will make us strong," uttered Zrake. "The joint invasion will create a new order in the universe. One which will even set the Mentera reeling with trembling hearts!"

Zrake's communicator sounded and he grasped it in a tightly-coiled tentacle. He answered it with a chitter. His face turned grim. He hung up, turned a cold, reptilian glance upon Krin. "It seems a certain package was discovered on your ship. In a hidden place. The ship I loaned you. It was a human in a tank."

A knot of icy fear gripped Krin's guts. He jerked himself upright.

Zrake raised a tentacle upward, a signal for his escort to apprehend the subcommander.

Krin instinctively grabbed Zrake's two upper motilators. He pulled him in close, unleashed his most savage strength. Taken by surprise, Zrake lurched back, quivering in agony, fighting the unrelenting grip which threatened to tear him apart. His eyes bulged. Krin heard Zrake's upper cartilage snap as tendons ripped and what might have been bone. A dozen angry memories of being humiliated before his superior flooded his mind as he clutched his tormentor. Zrake's choking gasp was the last thing he heard spraying from his gullet before Krin hurled him into the abyss that dropped to the side. Krin watched the flailing body plunge below into the blue-blackness.

Zrake's Zikri escort paused stunned, then charged with wild chitterings. But Jnedz's locusts stepped forward and held them back, threatening them with their lumo-sticks. Two of the loyal Zikri were brave enough to charge the line, only to fall in sizzling, smoking heaps as the Consul's guards opened fire.

Jnedz clattered over, breathless, his clicking voice a blemish on the sudden silence. The locust instantly seemed to grasp the gist of what had happened. His beady red eyes narrowed on Krin. "Where is ambassador Zrake?" his voice rang over the translator. The eyes suddenly glinted. "Dear me, Subcommander, it seems as if you have done something rash. I think you are in serious trouble here."

Krin brainstormed ways of handling this predicament in a diplomatic way. A daring strategy began to form in his mind. "So are you, Consul. How do you think it will go for you when Admiral Nrog hears about this outrage, how Zrake died on your watch? Under your protection?" Krin paused, watching the Consul's reaction which was startled at best. "But it doesn't have to be like that."

Jnedz blinked, surprised but not cowed. "What do you propose?"

"Let me take command of Zrake's ship. I will cover this fiasco up, take his starship a hundred light years from here and dispose of his crew. These Zikri of Zrake's, your locusts can take to the tanks."

Three of Zrake's Zikri lunged and another fell to the lumo-sticks of the locusts. The others backed off, chittering.

The Consul considered the proposal. "It's not exactly a fair trade. The assassination of your superior is a treasonous offense. What else do you have to offer?"

Krin's mind spun. With a new ship, he had an unlimited reach. Let him sweeten the pot, as a safeguard—in case Jnedz backed out of the deal and doublecrossed him. An image formed in his mind: of the humans he could prey upon in the many cybernetic labs of the human Mathias. "I will lead you to a goldmine of human souls. Would that be a fair bargain?"

Chapter 7

The corridor arched through the gloom with service piping running across the ceiling, giving off a faint hum, as if carrying coolant or heating fluid. Perhaps oxygen? Yul stared, moving up the hall; Cloye was ahead of him. Black power cables ran alongside the pipes, thick enough to carry significant wattage. They were in some off-limits service area. Anything could happen.

Some minutes passed and they came to a large chamber, squarish in shape, dim of light.

A dead end? Only a heavy door with red bars blocked access to a chamber at the far wall. To reach that they must cross the chamber, but the room, while empty, seemed slightly suspicious to Yul's eye. He thought to make out a tiny pinprick of red light or a motion detector set on the wall to one side. Cloye moved toward the door, but Yul held her back, pointing to the sensor.

He stepped with care across the invisible line that cast a tight beam from left wall to right. He smiled, only to feel a ripple of pain course through his nerves from spine to toe.

Damn that Mathias! He had fired the nanoparticles in his blood again with his pain dispenser. Even as he lifted his foot to make the next step, he could not keep his balance or stop himself from triggering the alarm.

A sudden wallop of sound jolted from the leftmost wall,

machinery moving with a thumping electric whine. The wall pushed toward them, sweeping them aside into another dim chamber whose right wall to grant them access had vanished.

"Get back!" Yul cried, reaching for his weapon. But it was too late.

Rolling, he raised his blaster to take out two anthropomorphic shapes leaping out at him.

Mechnobots? They sported four wavering arms not dissimilar to Zikri invaders. But could it be? "What the hell—?"

He cursed Mathias's ill timing. The chamber had sealed itself. A row of the monsters with gruesome faces and mechno bodies glided forth to replace the others he had blasted.

Cloye let out a yell that sent echoes reverberating throughout the chamber as she loosed waves of blaster fire into the moving murk, severing heads from torsos.

Yul whirled about. From the smoking corpses emerged something hideous. Stringed masses propelled by mysterious means reached out wavering feelers. One of the glistening ropes whipped out and latched onto his blaster, to jerk it out of his grasp. He leaped aside, gaping as another tough cord coiled on to his mechanized wrist. He pulled free, found his weapon coated with a foul-smelling grease. Another jerked toward Cloye, tripping her.

No sooner had it descended upon her than she tore her arm free from the strangling creepers, to rake them with the side of her blaster. She clawed for the fire button. But it refused to function. Her weapon was now coated with more of the greasy substance to which Yul had fallen prey. That weapon too was wrenched out of her grip as a stringy mass pinioned her wrist.

The room was alive with the writhing shapes. Jellyfish-like streamers flowered from all angles. The last Zikri bots stood like wraiths, staring hollowly. Why didn't they kill them outright? Feeling he was fighting a hopeless battle, he broke from the oily masses and crashed his whole weight into the creature latched onto Cloye. Surprisingly, it went limp on contact and became a lifeless heap.

The floor fell through. He and Cloye thudded onto a hard surface. He looked up. The Zikri bots and stringed monsters were gone.

Yul stared in confusion. A trick? Some virtual reality mind bend? Glass partitions now came tumbling down from on high, trapping them in a maze. He saw Cloye's reflection mirrored in the glass— three of her, each staring glaze-eyed, her fingers pressed to the clear barrier. Yul snatched at his blaster which had fallen with him.

He raced toward her and smashed head-first into an invisible wall. He fell back, stunned, then turned left down another narrow passage. Another transparent wall came down, blocking his path.

With an angry grunt, he aimed his blaster and fired. The red flare from his gun ricocheted off the peculiar barrier, nearly taking his head off before he could duck.

"Shit! What is this house of horrors?"

The right wall disappeared. Then the opposite wall pushed him toward where the other wall had been. He blinked in amazement as he staggered out into a huge, fluorescent-lit chamber. The place was a beehive of activity. Fifty or more scientists, a mix of men and women, worked diligently at tables and workstations, garbed in lab coats. Cloye lay panting behind him. The moving wall which had pushed them out had stopped and merged seamlessly with the spacious chamber's wall.

A stocky man of middle age stood well back, regarding Yul with rising curiosity. There was a trace of admiration on his features, which quickly faded. The man had a dark complexion, curly brown hair and piercing gold eyes. He wore an immaculate, pressed blue lab coat, black shoes and thick glasses which he pushed high upon his nose as he hitched himself forward. Others, no less than eight who looked like hitmen, lingered at the sidelines of this huge room, hefting E1's.

"I see you ran afoul of my testing chamber," the man said. "It is a combination defense, security and testing entry to my lab. I get a little absorbed while making my observations. Your scores are high,

153

granted."

Yul wanted to reach out and strangle the man. "Test for what?" Blasters came up to his chest as he moved forward to seize the figure.

"The Zikri bots test your reflexes. The glass maze tests your loyalty to each other. The stringy horrors test your resistance to fear and willingness to engage repulsiveness. I have yet to test for stamina and creativity, but for now these suffice to assess potential recruits, or shall I say 'enemies', for weaknesses and strengths."

One of the security officers, a blond man with a scruffy beard, beckoned for their weapons.

Yul held on to his. He pondered a rash escape, a flurry of fire, but he suspected he and Cloye would be cut down.

"I sense you are irked about the Zikri counterparts," the man said. "Strikes a sensitive spot? I can explain." He sighed. "We captured a few Zikri on nearby worlds and I modeled some of my guardian bots on their unique physiology. They are prototypes only— it is fitting that we tested our machines on my obstacle course. It seems you have had the privilege of surviving them."

Yul glowered. Was this Hresh? When would he see the end of these nutcases?

"I forgot to introduce myself." The man eyed Cloye with interest, her chest heaving as she struggled to her feet. "I am Sigmund Hresh, chief roboticist and owner of Sybcore Technologies."

"Who the fuck cares?" muttered Cloye.

Hresh's brows rose, his forehead furrowed. He blinked through those thick glasses of his. "A hearty welcome to you too, Lady Kasan." He turned to Yul. "And you, Mr. Vrean. It is a pleasure."

Yul, startled, frowned. The man knew their last names too?

Hresh seemed to take delight in Yul's confusion. "I knew you were aboard my terraformer when the nano-particle detector sounded. I tracked you all the way from Namith." He pulled up a blinking image of a wire-frame figure on a nearby terminal. "Are you surprised? I designed the implant Mathias touts as his own and that he shoved into your blood stream. I can trace their signatures. A quick hack into his technical database and your name came up. Cloye, I know you are a well-known mercenary, a skilled assassin."

She dipped her head in a mocking bow. "Now that we've cleared all that up, how about a little lighter on the artillery, Hresh?" She jerked an elbow at the men with the unsmiling faces and the automatic rifles.

"I think not," murmured the scientist. He motioned to his security team and they took Yul's weapon and reached to bind his wrists behind his back. But Hresh shook his head.

"Don't I get special treatment too?" mocked Cloye.

"For now, no. Weapon, please." He held out a hand.

Yul studied his surroundings. On a long, low metal dais rested a large glass case shaped like a submarine. Floating bulbs the size of potatoes bobbed inside the space, a sealed vacuum, Yul guessed. The light, brownish objects seemed to be flying around of their own accord, without stimulus or provocation. The whole exhibit looked like something out of an eerie science center display, or some fiendish school science fair exhibit.

The visual monitor connected with wires and electrodes attached to the glass's surface lit up in strange colors. A spike appeared on a 3D graph whenever any of the objects touched or even glanced off the sides.

"You seem interested in my showcase," Hresh said amusedly.

"Let me guess, the *Biogron*?" said Yul.

Hresh clapped his hands. "You are informed. And I thought you were just some boorish bully boy. Only a handful of people in the galaxy have heard that name."

Yul shrugged. "Thank Mathias."

Hresh croaked out the word, as if it were a hated thing. "*Mathias*. It seems he and I see different futures for my invention. After all, I built it. Why should I not govern its fate?"

"Mathias trusted you to finish the job while on payroll," said Yul.

Hresh chortled out a cruel laugh. "Trusted? What does that mean in today's world? A trusted friend, a talking head that says good morning, hope you are having a nice day, all the expected pleasantries, then sinks his fangs in. If you knew what ruthless deals Mathias masterminded, how he bulled his way to the top, you would be not be as sympathetic to his cause."

"Trust me, you're preaching to the choir, Hresh. I'm only a hired gun. On a mission that went bad."

"So I gather. How much did he pay you? 1000 credits? Cheap bastard. Whatever he paid you, I will double it."

Yul shook his head. "I'm sure you can, Mr. Hresh, but for the record, 10k is what he paid me and it's a moot point when my head is on the block."

"Come, Mr. Vrean, let's be realists. You are human like any other. Everyone has a price. Mathias bought you cheaply. I can offer you more, and what do you do? Quibble, try to do a morality check on me. Have you never been swayed by the highest bidder?"

Yul's lip twitched as a brief memory stirred: the time he had betrayed Bedraltr, the smuggler on Maven for certain privileged information. He was still fleeing from that cock-up. Of course, Hresh probably knew all of that with his computer wizardry.

"Spare us the violins, Hresh," Cloye growled. "What do you want? How do we get off this planet?"

"You're welcome to leave at any time." Hresh motioned. "There's the door. But the atmosphere outside is unbreathable. Like most of the uncharted worlds in these sectors. When I came here over a year ago, this was an uninhabited wasteland. Perfect for my needs. Now it's a fully operational research facility. Out of sight and mind of opportunistic eyes."

The man's words seemed to enter Yul's brain but not register. His eyes drifted to the glass case with the pulsing balls, jumping around randomly as if by magic. He stared transfixed, as if there was untethered power there which chilled him.

Hresh gestured at his prized experiment and put on a boyish grin. "Your expression tells it all, Yul. This is the first positive proof I've had in months that the *Biogron* can actually interface with life to drive an avatar." His words were excited, his cheeks fevered. "Those objects you see flying about are *andorphs*, a lifeform native to *Sigren*, one of the remote planets in the Dim Zone. I did some research on historic missions to the outer realms and discovered some puffballs, or subspecies, that were reported to roll of their own accord across the sands, classified as neither plant nor animal. Probably a wives' tale of some sort, spun by a drunken explorer, but I hunted them down all the same to satiate my curiosity. To my joy, I discovered they actually exist."

Yul shrugged. "So? I don't see how puffballs are going to help you build cyborgs."

"I can sympathize with that sentiment." He peaked fingers on his nose. "At first glance, they seemed no more than roving planetary epiphytes, things that could self nourish from the soil and air, yet could manage to survive the harsh climates where other organisms died. We gathered numerous specimens for their compact size and ability to counter predators. Most impressive was the fact that they required neither brain nor central nervous system. The organism is miraculous in that sense. It has a hive-mind mentality that can rally its peers to protect itself against threats. Thus the difficulty in interfacing a complex brain to a machine is voided, a problem for which modern science may never find a solution."

Yul shook his head. "That makes no sense to me. Mechnobots? Living freaks melded together in some Frankensteinian soup? Why not just hook up an earthworm?"

Hresh gave an exasperated sigh. "It can't be just any random organism. All you people do is criticize! So linear of thought, so myopic. The scientific mind is based on curiosity and imagination, Vrean. The search for the unknown, the impossible. Unfortunately it seems not many are gifted with those talents. My *Biogron* makes the leap. It can pick up the resonant frequency of an organism's actions and synthesize that signature into useful energy, without electrodes, implants or the like. This initial discovery led to others, in harnessing a controllable intelligence. I proposed the idea of an *Imagron*, a vessel that could contain the motive force of any given lifeform and use it for constructive ends. Channeled in my controlled environment, the implication is staggering. In fields too numerous to name. Imagine an avatar able to solve problems and construct things that challenge even humans. Things that we tell it to: unbreachable collapsible bridges, colony ships and shielded star highways. Who knows? Even curtail the depravities of the Zikri and Mentera. Hypothetically beyond our means of science today, but possible in the near future. I did find some short cuts to cut the gap down by an estimated one hundred years."

He motioned to a lab tech to add more solution to an intravenous line that connected to the *Biogron*. "Mathias practically screamed at me to speed up my work, trying to get more inside information." The scientist gave an unsettling but throaty chuckle. "I had him by the neck and he knew it. I gave him a cursory sweep of the concept, the rest remained locked in my brain. He begged me for details. He promised me all the resources I needed to finish the project, however long that might be. I quizzed him about his plans. With that Machiavellian gleam in his eye, he dropped hints regarding a use of my innovation that caused my hackles to rise. My suspicions were confirmed. We did not share the same vision."

Yul frowned. He was going to ask him how those 'visions' differed, but Hresh was oblivious. "When his pleas grew to threats, I knew I had no option but to disappear. Especially when blackmail entered the equation. I am a smarter man by far. That's why I am on Remus, deep in the Dim Zone, creating revolutionary things, miraculous things, while Mathias and his lapdogs are struggling to find what they will never find..."

Yul chewed his lip. He was in danger and Hresh was a threat. He and Cloye could have easily been killed by the Zikri bots in the obstacle course. It would not pay for him to be on Hresh's bad side. It could be them next plunged into the *Biogron*. Hresh, though, would not be easy to outwit.

Yul winced. That he had let Cloye gull him into exploring this restricted area had been stupid. Better to humor the man. There might be a way out...

The corners of Hresh's lips quivered. "I see where your devious mind is going, Yul. I advise against it. You will fail badly at whatever scheme you're cooking up."

Yul drew a soft breath. "What do you want? We're at an impasse here."

"I want everything!" Hresh croaked. "It is you who are at an impasse."

Cloye began to scratch at her shoulder. She was sweating profusely now. Cold drops of liquid beaded her brow and dripped down her olive-colored cheeks.

The security leader took the movement as a sign of aggression and he moved over to frisk her, for a possibly concealed weapon.

The man's eyes widened when he caught sight of something animated near the base of her throat. He grabbed at her hair and tore the fabric loose from her left shoulder. "What's this?" He gazed over at Hresh. "Sir, you'd better take a look at this." He thrust back the woman's head, exposing her bare neck to reveal a bright orange, leech-like frond that had coiled about her collar bone.

Yul hastened forward, his face pale.

Hresh clumped over, annoyed at the interruption to his train of thought. His eyes rounded at what he saw. Beckoning one of his assistants to bring tongs, he peered more closely. A man in a white lab coat hastened over with an assortment of instruments to extract the creature. But the more he tugged, the more Cloye wailed, the creature clinging tenaciously to her flesh.

"What the hell is it?" The technician perspired.

Cloye whimpered. "I d-don't know. It wasn't there before."

Yul gazed in alarm. His jaw dropped. The woman was infected by one of the pods! Shit, he had kissed her! It must have grown in the time they had flown to Remus and stalked Hresh's complex. His eyes drilled into her. "You said you were down in Mathias's lab? Something about a moth?"

"Y-yes. Mathias showed me the tank in the lab, said to be on the lookout for similar ones in Hresh's compounds. The place was all helter-skelter, as if a fire had gone through."

Yul swore. "The thing must have latched onto you down there. How?"

"I don't know!"

Hresh stroked his chin, his gaze faraway. "Remarkable. Transmitted by airborne spores?"

"No, from the moth!" rasped Yul.

Cloye writhed, pulling at the thing, but it only wound tighter. "Get it off me!" she cried. The plant ring coiled more securely about her shoulder.

"Calm down, relax," reassured Yul. He looked anything but reassured. "The plant just wants a place of stasis. It doesn't want to harm its host."

"I don't care what it wants! Get it the fuck off!"

"What's this about a moth?" Hresh moved in, regarding Cloye intently.

Yul cringed. He recalled the creature back in the Orb's tank room. He could relate to Cloye's horror. "I curse the day Mathias sent us out to collect specimens on Xeses," he mumbled.

Hresh gazed at him, examining the thing closer. "There appear to be small nodules growing from its tips."

"They're pods," grunted Yul.

"They demand study."

"Screw the studies!" Yul cried. "Get it off her." He looked about desperately. If Cloye were down in Mathias's lab and got infected, what did that say about him? He pawed fingers over his body, but felt nothing. Hresh moved in, staring at him. "What's this about a damn moth, you say?"

Seeing Yul's look of dismay, Cloye snuffled out a sob. "I told you, Mathias brought me down to show me what kind of tech to watch out for."

Yul's mouth sagged.

"Mathias sent you—to this place Xeses?" Hresh asked matter-of-factly. "To search for plants?"

Yul nodded, not liking the piercing look in the man's eyes.

Hresh seemed to ponder, as if a million variables coursed through that mind of his. "Mathias must have picked up on my idea long ago. A search for the perfect host. Did I jot it down in a journal? Pity." With an impatient grunt, he seized the assistant's tongs and forcibly ripped the thing clean from Cloye's shoulder. She screamed in agony. She fell to her knees, an angry red welt where the suckers had been extracted, dragging the skin with them.

"What the hell did you do that for?" Yul cried, arching toward Hresh. "You hurt her."

Hresh ignored him. He moved toward the *Biogron*.

"Wait." Yul lifted an arm to stop the man.

"Stay back!" cried Hresh. One of his security guards took hold of Yul. Yul brushed him aside as Hresh twisted away from Yul's metal fingers. Three men restrained the mercenary. Yul struggled to fight them while Cloye slung the torn flap of her assassin's suit over her naked shoulder, glaring at the ogling men.

Hresh paid no heed and dropped the pod into a pressurized tube that ran from the table to the top of the glass case, the *Biogron*. He quickly resealed the pressurized cap, then flicked a switch on the machine. The pod was instantly sucked into the vacuum, floating in free space with the other puffballs. It dangled there for several moments before the white bouncing puffballs seemed to notice anything untoward. Then they began to speed up.

"You see, Vrean," chuckled Hresh, "electronic circuitry, third generation cyborgs, they have no intelligence. But the life force does! These bots are just buckets of bolts clambering around, running clever algorithms. Stiff as starched sheets. But life is an altogether different entity. The magic of consciousness... Every thinker, scientist, philosopher, spiritualist has pondered over that intangible mystery of the universe, the essence of the unknown. I took the search a step further. To tap the energy of the creatures in this box, through this box, and infuse the neural-net of a mechanical avatar with their wisdom. Their intelligence!"

He strode over to a covered mass, flush to the nearby wall. It rose head height over anything else in the lab. He pulled off a silver gleaming tarp.

Yul gazed at Cloye who stared back at him with unease. Together they looked upon the metallic exoskeleton of some elder beast. Raised on its hind legs and shortened forelimbs, it glistened in the bright light. On its back, curled a metallic shield, some kind of spiked dome, spreading as a peacock might fan its tail. The avatar sported an armadillo-like look to it, though with a head of plated steel, sporting a great horn like a triceratops.

Hresh smiled proudly. "What is it that causes the neuron to fire? To make new pathways? We don't know. We just observe it happening in the human brain and formulate clever theories about it. In the same way, we don't know why one mass attracts another, like the orbiting planets tugged toward their sun. We call it gravity but it's just a word. We can only observe it, not understand 'why'."

The puffballs swirled furiously in their contained environment, as if sensing an invasive force. They surrounded the foreign pod with brutal tenacity thus fused to its surface like barnacles. Yul likened the scene to white blood cells swarming foreign particles to attack pathogens in the blood.

The pod flared and surged red. It formed spikes on its surface. The barbs punctured the invading gray masses which quivered and folded like cards and which bled out a white, syrupy liquid. It floated like smoke wisps in the vacuum.

"Fascinating!" Hresh mused in his erudite tone.

More came to replace their skewered brothers. The pod grew larger, shivering with wrath like a rattlesnake as if to warn its attackers to stay away. The puffballs paid no heed. They swarmed in numbers and the pod shivered and jerked every which way like a jelly bean in a deep-fryer. How, Yul had no clue. He saw no means of locomotion for the pod: no legs, cilia or jets of propulsion. He simply watched the spectacle through the filmy glass with an awed and chilled expression. Whatever it was, it shucked off each invader. The other puffballs, seemingly too programmed to get the dire message, melted when the pod oozed a thin vapor which withered their outer flesh, much as it had the men's faces back in Mathias's lab.

"Wondrous! Fascinating!" cried Hresh, clapping his hands. "It's beyond belief."

Cloye clenched a fist. "Let's hear you say that when one of them is clamped on your shoulder."

Hresh appeared not to hear. He mumbled words to himself, as if in the grip of some poignant memory. "Mathias was solely in it for the money. How can we use the *Biogron* as a military weapon? How can we drive prices higher. How fast can we sell it to the highest bidder? Whole armies exhibiting invincible forces! He made my blood turn cold. An entity such as this, with its adaptive intelligence, could go much further. What I propose could aid civilization on levels beyond human imagination: to explore new worlds and inhabit them without threat. To figure out new ways of designing and engineering systems, organizing our living environment and settlements in dynamic, futuristic ways."

Yul scowled. Somehow he doubted such miracles, considering what he saw before him—this sprawled mass of teeth, horn, sharp edges, and titanium steel. "What you crazies seem to forget, is how are you going to control these things?"

Hresh moved slowly back toward his glass case. He studied the pod's fight against the puffballs with renewed fervor. "We can introduce override controls. Enhanced circuitry, monitoring algorithms."

"The hell you can!" Yul scoffed. "What if it adapts beyond your plated playtoy's restraints?"

Hresh gave a shrill laugh. "You think the thing's cleverer than me?"

Now it was Yul's turn to laugh. So thought Mathias and Dez when they were scrambling about in efforts to contain the butterfly when it hatched.

Hresh frowned, stroking his thick black hair moodily. "The thing is almost functional, but not quite. It lacks motility, impetus. A sprawling spider, a freak, a primitive dinosaur, no more. My avatar has much potential, but not a significant wellspring of intelligence to drive it. The *puffshrooms*, as I call them, don't have enough life-power. They are intelligent, but lack the depth needed for the capabilities I dream of. Look at them die now fighting against this one organism. Pah! I have sent my aide, senior researcher Leam out to collect more of them. But it may be futile. If I have a high enough concentration, maybe it's the first step. But, my suspicion is that any number of them won't be enough to power the entity for what I want."

"You will never accomplish what you set out to do, Hresh," warned Yul.

"Failing that," mused Hresh, hearing nothing, "I will try human counterparts, as illegal as that may be. I'm open to volunteers—Are you up for it?" He stared whimsically at Yul, who shuddered. "No?" He laughed aloud, shot a suggestive glance at Cloye. "Perhaps your lady friend—"

Yul looked at him as if he were insane.

"Of course, the two of you could have an unfortunate accident in my lab. Then I wouldn't have to ask you."

Yul clenched his fists, ready to pound Hresh's muscle-men with his bare hands if need be.

"Just jesting, friends! I have a macabre, if not flamboyant imagination that startles people sometimes. I would not coerce anyone into jumping into the *Biogron*. I'm not like Mathias."

A distant boom like a ruptured oil drum came from somewhere overhead. Yul looked up as a massive light fixture fell and shattered on a nearby worktable, sending glass and electrical equipment everywhere. A communicator beeped in the blond security officer's hand. He passed it to Hresh.

Hresh listened scowling, annoyed at the interruption. Yul, standing nearby, caught the words: "Sir, looks like Zikri Orbs are in the air, but I can't be sure. There are other ships out there too—they look like bloated aphid-shaped blimps."

Hresh gave a disinterested sniff. "Deal with it, Gustav. Use our automated defensive weaponry." He closed the circuit. He turned back to his guests and the puffballs. "Ah, where was I?" He mumbled praise for the pod that now was clear of any foes. "Classic protection mechanism, ingenious."

Yul blinked. "That's all you can say, 'ingenious'? Meanwhile bombs drop on your crib? The Zikri are here...Think, man! More will come. Or Mathias."

"Let them come. Let Mathias come with his starships!" Hresh waved a dismissive hand. "My ground forces will take care of them."

"You will not ward off a fleet."

"We've got surface-to-air cannon that can take out invaders. My supply ships come out of light drive for only a small moment of vulnerability. If they've picked up tails, we blast them out of the sky. So far we've only needed to use it once. A freelance outfit out of Ujax. Space bullies, no common sense in their heads."

Yul shook his head. "The Zikri are a deal more violent than a few moronic thugs looking for trouble and excitement. You're lucky the Zikri haven't blown this hatch and dragged you away in their tanks."

Hresh shrugged. "You must have led them here, you idiot—despite your musculature and high test scores. These are the risks of doing business. I should have known." He chewed his lip. His eyes remained glued to the containing vessel.

The pod had cracked open to give birth to a large dragonfly with a mushroom-like body. Not dissimilar to the dragonfly Yul had witnessed in the Orb. Frenzied, knife-edged wings now sheared off the puffball's flesh like saws. The dragonfly smashed its eyeless face against the glass, but the shock-proof glass held, containing the creature's repeated assaults.

"This is more important than any puny attack on my complex. Look at it!" he marveled. "Incredible!" He stared at the indicator needle on a nearby device pointing off the scale. "This shows intelligence beyond any recorded species...immediate extermination of enemies while evolving into a hybrid to escape its cage. The discovery of the century. Do you realize—" He shook his head. "No, it's impossible. I know what to do. I'll put it through a battery of tests. Employ everything we've got. No more nuts and bolts and circuits and prosthetics, but a new breed of AI!" He danced a small jig.

Yul's mouth worked. The man was insane. If he thought Mathias was way off, this lab rat was degrees beyond.

Hresh gave curt orders to his tech team. A man plodded over to a crane and picked up the Biogron receptacle to insert it into the bowels of the armadillo avatar. Hresh directed him with a flushed face. "Now—a heart for a heart!"

Chapter 8

Hresh ordered the steel portal to the 'obstacle course' raised. He motioned the utility crane forward. Without pause, the operator clamped forks on the shiny dino-armadillo hide and dragged the hulk into the spacious chamber where Yul and Cloye had undergone their tests. The place seemed more massive than Yul remembered it. As if Hresh had changed its size and configuration.

The crane whirred closer and Yul pictured the dragonfly knocking against the Biogron's glass container inside the avatar, fluttering about in confusion. Various members of Hresh's science team drifted over to watch in curiosity. Meanwhile, his personal commandos stood by, blasters on the ready, awaiting any further development. Several flashed eyes on the ceiling as more booms echoed.

The crane deposited the mechanical creature inside the obstacle room, backed up, and the doors slammed shut. Hresh and the others gathered around a terminal observing the beast, as it hunched on all fours in the dimly-lit room.

The blond security guard frowned. "The mechno's unresponsive."

"Give it time, Nonas," Hresh purred. His lips curled upward as if he had complete confidence in his creation.

Yul recalled the improbability of the thing surviving in the glass case and he scowled. "How do you expect the alien pod to control whatever outer shell you've given it?"

Hresh steepled his fingers. He responded without looking at him. "The Biogron is the ultimate feedback loop. The hardware reports whatever impulse signal is sent from inside, to the outside, namely the outer shell. Vice versa, it forwards all stimuli from what's on the outside to whatever's inside. So, our dragonfly can move the avatar's body as well as perceive what is happening outside its metallic body."

"Impossible." Yul stared at the screen. "What about this obstacle course? Is it real, or some VR trick?"

Hresh sighed. "It's a combination VR and 'real' robot test bench. To hammer test our new models for real-world application. Your questions are tiresome, Vrean. Save them for later."

Hresh's communicator buzzed. "Gustav, talk to me."

"Sir, not looking good. We've got enemies incoming and they're not going away. Two down, but two are hot in the air. We smoked one, but they blasted a hole in the hangar's dome. They mean to dock."

Hresh's left cheek twitched. "Stay on it, Gustav. Enforce emergency backups as necessary. Do your job." He hung up.

Hresh frowned and worked his lip. He checked figures on a monitor. His beady eyes searched the inert hulk vainly for any signs of life.

Yul tilted his head in amazement. The man was either a nitwit or completely oblivious to the danger. Did he have some other line of defense? His ground forces—Gustav and crew—were taking a beating.

"So you kill a few of them?" grunted Yul. "What then? You going to ignore the army they'll bring to avenge their losses?"

Hresh appeared not to hear. He flapped his hand at his assistant. "Arm the radon penetrators. And observe."

A dozen crimson dots appeared from eyelets in the ceiling and trained ruby energy lines down on the hulking monstrosity. Pulses of light streamed down from the eyelets to strike the plated back.

The titanium hide flashed red hot. It appeared to quiver.

"Just little love taps," explained Hresh. "Up the juice, Ahmid."

The technician paused, pushed a red, stiff lever. The laser-like fire increased in intensity. Heat waves and coils of smoke rose from the shiny back...it seemed to jerk and twist now with spasmodic intensity.

Yul's skin tingled. He knew what fury the creature was capable of when provoked.

The metal creaked and sizzled at the heat. More laser fire stabbed down from the ceiling.

The dino-armadillo, powered by the Biogron, leaped like a spider out of the line of fire. It formed a shield around its now luminous body. Barbs like arrows shot out from small orifices in its shell to pierce the laser weapons one by one, incapacitating them.

Hresh watched in stunned silence.

Yul looked over to see Cloye still squirming from the pain of her excision.

"Test #2," cried Hresh. "Fill the chamber, Ahmid. Bring in the *aquamons!*"

Massive sprays of fluid began to jet down from the ceiling, splashing the mechno's back. Hot metal sizzled. Before long the armadillo shape was covered mid-thigh in water which quickly swirled over its spiked hide.

The camera switched to underwater filter viewing. The visual showed a sepia tint. Four of Hresh's mechnobots shaped like giant pike dropped down with a splash from a secret opening in the ceiling. Tails thrust them toward the armadillo. Their beaked snouts glinted in the tinted light and lifted to reveal massive incisors which hooked on the armadillo's limbs, two to a side.

Two more aquamons dropped into the water. That made six.

"Is that real, or VR?" demanded Cloye.

"This is quite real," affirmed Hresh.

The aquamons flapped tails and shook their grouper-like heads back and forth like pack dogs, yanking at the metallic limbs.

Hresh's creation curled into a ball, quivering much like it had in

Hresh's Biogron earlier as a pod when attacked by the puffballs. The mechnobot sea marauders tugged at the intruder, threatening to pull the legs from its body.

Yul stared with doubtful expression, thinking maybe Hresh had pushed his experiment too far.

Yet the impossible happened.

The legs extended, slitted sideways, formed rounded paddles. With a forceful lunge, the avatar propelled itself upward through the churning water, dragging the four predators with it.

Hresh's lips parted. His creation was performing a miracle. It banked right and smashed its horn into one of the free-floating predators, plowing it straight into the wall. The mechno crumpled, sending electric sparks into the turbulent water.

"Brilliant! Amazing! The alien's reaching out to its new hardware. It's modifying what's already there."

The armadillo turned and crashed again into the other free-floating predator, mashing it into the wall. It slid down in a sparking heap.

Forelegs and hindlegs flailed. The armadillo whipped off its aggressors, ridding itself of its pesky enemies before it paddled on and systematically annihilated them one by one.

Hresh grinned ear to ear. "I name you A13!" He gave vent to a mad shout of glee. "My thirteenth attempt at a successful working miracle. On to test #3."

Nonas tapped him on the shoulder. "Sir. I don't think there's time for more tests." He handed his employer the receiver. Hresh snarled and snatched it. "What? What is it?"

Gustav's agitated voice rasped over the com. "Orbs, sir! They've stormed the hangar. I can't hold them off much longer—" His voice cut out. The connection went dead.

Hresh stared for several seconds at the device His lips curled as if struggling with a gnawing doubt. He briskly turned back to the monitor, clicking his tongue in annoyance.

"I told you—you're in over your head," cried Yul.

Thuds came from above. Plaster and metal cracked and crashed down. It was only a matter of time before the lab was breached.

Hresh mumbled, "Very well, open the containment door."

Ahmid, his aide, stared. "Sir, it's not properly tested yet."

"All the more interesting for us." Hresh's face curled in a sinister grin.

Yul and Cloye watched in dismay as Ahmid's fingers reached for the control. Sweat beaded Cloye's brow.

Before the gate slid up though, something large within smashed through the titanium and tore the metal apart with its forehorn. Water gushed out, flooding the lab in a deluge. Desks were swamped, tables, lab equipment, occupants. Yul felt the water swirling past his knees. A menacing shape lumbered out, robot eyes flashing on either side of a glistening horn, trained upon the feeble humans before it.

Hresh's mouth gaped. "How? The A13's exoshell is not capable of force that strong!"

Cloye backed away through the water. Bright fear showed in her eyes.

"Idiot!" hissed Yul. "It somehow figured out how."

"Impossible," Hresh muttered. "My calculations show—"

"Your calculations mean nothing here!" Yul shook him like a doll. "You've bred a monster."

The dino-armadillo loosed a low, guttural roar that filled the lab with spine-chilling fear and that rocked metal walls and workstations.

The thing advanced, eyes sighting on possible enemies. Just before it lurched toward Hresh's security men.

In panic, they lifted their weapons. They locked through their sites on the Biogron casing at chest level—its vitals.

Yul cried, "Don't shoot, you fools! I know these plant aliens! They attack only forms that threaten it. Don't fire or show any aggression."

Hresh gave a quick nod. His men stood down. The armadillo paused with wary reflection. In spite of the seriousness of the situation, Hresh relaxed his bedraggled frame, pink fingers smoothing out his lab coat.

It should have been obvious from the pod's ability to kill the mechnobots that the thing was in defensive mode and an aggressive danger. But these men didn't know what they were up against. Neither did Hresh.

But that might have been a good thing, Yul thought.

The main door to the lab curled outward in a melt of flames. A flood of lumo fire poured out of the smoking gap. Green trails belched forth, lashing at tables, benches, cutting into nearby human figures.

The scientists cried out. They fell sprawling, noses to the water, as it began to gush out now that the door had been blasted to shards. Yul ducked a spraying blast as hideous, human-size locusts streamed through. Nonas's commandos opened fire, taking out the shoulder-high invaders that hopped through like large grasshoppers.

It all made sense now as Yul's stunned mind gained full awareness. Zikri invaders came gliding in after the locusts, weaponless but wearing body armor on both chest and head. Glistening tentacles probed like octopi feelers. Yul knew that the tanks would soon be filled with human hosts, and it made his skin crawl.

"Give me that," he snarled, snatching his blaster back from Nonas.

Nonas trained his E1 on Yul.

"Give them their weapons!" cried Hresh. "They're trained for combat."

Nonas grunted. He ordered his man to toss Cloye her compact E6.

Yul saw that the Mentera beams were not calculated to kill their human prey, just stun them. The lack of blood on the bodies slumped all around him in the pooling water was evidence enough.

He quickly struggled for cover behind an overturned bench. He dragged Cloye beside him.

The clicking locusts advanced. Perceiving the monstrous

armadillo shape as a threat, they opened fire, turning their green lumo fire into lethal, crimson blasts. Rays of destruction pelted the armadillo's titanium hide. Most deflected off it, the sheer force driving the creature back.

"No!" shrilled Hresh, despaired.

"Happy now?" cried Yul.

Hresh crawled like a worm beside Yul. "Quick—duck into the obstacle course!"

Yul and Cloye wasted no time. They followed Hresh who dipped behind the hulking A13's legs through the twisted gap into the dripping chamber. Others followed. Several of the scientists halted, doubting Hresh's strategy. Locust rays soon immobilized them. The rest ran shrieking for cover, only to be gunned downed by more locusts that quickly surrounded them. They hoisted the limp forms on their chitinous backs and shuttled them back through the exit. Hresh's commandos, signaled by Nonas, did not hesitate, although half of them were already down by Mentera fire.

Only six of the scientists managed to escape into the chamber before being stunned. Two of Nonas's men yet lived.

Yul turned and blasted the locusts clacking after them. They needed to distract the enemy! Whatever Hresh was planning, it had better work.

Hresh led them past the ruined aquamons toward the end of the chamber, touching several buttons on a wall console. A door slid open. Yul caught ghosts of movement behind them, the smell of scorched metal.

The armadillo curled into a ball upon the enemy fire. It shielded its horned head and stumps of limbs, its most vulnerable spots.

What the invaders did not realize was their blaster fire was destroying the creature's environment, the worst possible affront against the alien plant-turned-dragonfly. Its first call of duty was to protect its habitat. In a fit of rage, it sprang forward.

The armadillo crouched before its adversaries, arched its back and five foot spikes sprouted along its glistening hide. These glinted like swords under the lab lights. Its eyes glittered like black pearls, sighting on its enemies. Strange insectoid whines echoed from beneath its tusked snout, as if the Biogron's neural link were reaching out to the dragonfly's speech centers.

Tucked into a ball, the thing rolled—a raging fiend, steamrolling Zikri and locusts alike that came to meet it. It stormed the lab, mowing down anything that moved, reaping a ghastly harvest of alien flesh. In that few seconds Yul could see that even encaged in its ghastly armature, the thing was adapting at an alarming rate. No surprise, given the almost unlimited power of Hresh's mechno-wizardry.

Hresh beckoned them all down a hall through another door and into an adjoining chamber. Much like the previous room, it led the chittering Zikri and Mentera into a trap.

No sooner had he sealed the door when jets of water pounded on the trapped aliens. Yul peeked through the glass; he saw squids and locusts floundering in waist-high water, firing useless rounds off the fire-proof walls. The fishy mechnobots began dropping down on them with vicious intent. Behind thick steel walls, the screams and cries of the Zikri and Mentera went unheard.

Hresh pressed another button then entered a code into a wall console. The fugitives surged through an opening door. An alarm rang in the adjoining hall—the scuffle of feet, the burst of enemy fire. Then the booms and explosions of Zikri assaults echoing with it down the hall.

"What about that thing back there?" cried Cloye.

A crazed smirk passed over Hresh's haggard face. With age circles under his black eyes and his matted hair lying flat, he looked like a bedraggled raccoon. "They will not be able to withstand it. I would love to watch, but pressing business awaits...Hurry! To my ship."

Yul laughed. "The locusts'll blast your protégé to pieces."

Hresh shook his head. "It has the adaptive intelligence of ten geniuses. The aliens may at best subdue it but with huge costs to themselves. Nonas, take the lead! Get us out of this rat-trap!"

"Where's your ship?" growled Yul.

"The hangar, where else?"

Yul quivered in disbelief. "Didn't you hear?" he grunted. "Your depot is toasted, compromised."

That panicked the scientists—four men and two women. One woman whimpered. Another man began to tremble, his eyes darting around the blood-strewn halls. "I don't want to die, stuffed in a tank. Did you see those insectoids carrying them away?"

Hresh roared, "The only way out of here is by ship. They're all out there for the taking, including the terraformers. Do you have any other ideas?"

Nonas stared. His fierce gaze defied Yul or any other to contradict his employer. Yul kept his mouth shut. Creating more hysteria with these civilian-scientists was unwise. But surely rash stupidity was even worse. He couldn't think of any other plan, except engaging the attackers full on or hiding out in one of the labs like rats in a cellar.

They crept down the halls. Nonas led with his two security men, weapons raised. Hresh followed with the other petrified scientists. Yul and Cloye took the rear, crouching, training blasters, scanning any cross corridors for unexpected activity.

One of the scientists cried out, "Even if you get us to a ship, Hresh, what's to stop us from getting blown out of the sky by Zikri? Gustav has said—"

Nonas flapped his hand for the woman to be silent.

The diversion was costly.

The rush came so quickly that none of the party had time to react.

One minute an empty corridor, the next a door flying off its hinges. It was melted and a wall of pincered flesh and slimy tentacled monsters surged against them. Nonas's two security agents were taken down and dragged off in a writhing mass. The six cowering scientists were bowled over, engulfed in similar walls of flesh.

Yul batted aside tentacles, lifting blaster to wreak carnage. Reeking flesh swarmed before his face. Digits, claws, tentacles, all were everywhere in his line of sight, kicking, clawing, and coiling about. He fought savagely to keep himself and Cloye from being overwhelmed by the slimy tentacles and sharp claws. He jammed an elbow into a locust face, heard it crack, pivoting to spray rounds of blaster fire into an advancing wall of Zikri flesh. Then he ducked a wheeling slash, knelt and blasted the legs off three attacking Zikri. This saved Nonas's skin. But two more locusts jammed in tight and Cloye whirled a round-house kick into the insects' necks in a blur of motion. She blasted the others and jerked back to avoid being snatched by Zikri tentacles.

Hresh, in pure terror, backed away, the farthest from the melee, his eyes bulging and teeth chattering.

"For crap's sake, they're everywhere!" rasped Yul. "Quick, in here!" He motioned to a side chamber, a steel door marked with red, no-access bars.

Hresh grimaced, clutched at Yul's muscled arm. "No, this way. Try another bay!"

"Why, you miserable shit? You hiding something? You want us to get cut down? Inside!" Using his massive strength, he ripped the bar free and shoved the protesting scientist through. Nonas followed with a grunt. He pushed the door shut, shouldering Cloye aside. Blood streamed from a wound on his brow. The man was limping from a crippling shot that had penetrated his leg armor.

Yul's mouth sagged at what he saw.

"I told you not to come in here," said Hresh.

Yul's blinking eyes adjusted to the murk and he caught a glimpse of many bathtub-shaped vessels containing deformed heads, twisted limbs, dismembered appendages and naked body parts, all floating in cloudy water—monsters, dwarfs, human, subhuman. It made no difference. The blur was indistinguishable. Bits of metal—racks or plates—were sewn into some of the skulls, and upon reptilian-spined backs: circuit control boards or implants, from what Yul could ascertain. His mind gave up trying to understand. He clenched his fists, then seized Hresh by the shoulders and pulled him close with his iron fingers.

"You miserable hunk of filth. What the hell have you been doing here?"

Hresh, wincing in pain, spewed spittle. "You think it's easy, Vrean? All these ideas? The dead ends I hit, the swamps I wade through everyday?"

"Spare us the violins," Cloye snapped. "You're a deranged psychopath."

"Call it what you will." Hresh panted. "There's darkness to the places I go. Any visionary must make the plunge, take the risks."

"No shit," Cloye cried, slapping his face hard and boxing his ears. She hip-checked him to the ground.

Yul pulled her off him. He sucked in a deep breath and cast many uneasy looks around at the cages off to the sides. They contained live specimens. "Easy, Cloye, the damage is already done."

"Don't care! This reptile should be put down. He obviously used live humans to test drive his horror show."

The figures in the cages rattled their bars. Yul caught ripples of movements: of human eyes, bare patches of skin, furred fingers, bodies crawling on all fours.

"They were willing subjects and signed waivers," said Hresh. He wiped his bloody lip, as he regained his feet.

Cloye tossed her hair. "No fool is going to sign a waiver for this."

"We only used their DNA," Hresh objected. "To build clones for studies. They're not real—These weren't real humans."

"Says who?" snorted Cloye. "I'm sure they had feelings too, breathed, laughed, thought and shat like anyone else."

"That's a matter of opinion. Bold experiments...all failed. Preliminary research to the Biogron, prototyping the neural net to flesh route. I had to be sure. It didn't work."

"I should kick your smug ass for what you've done, Hresh."

Nonas looked on in amusement. He enjoyed the spectacle.

"Listen up, children. We've got precious minutes to find a way out of here before those hostiles swarm in here through that mangled door."

Hresh glowered in silence. Yul turned on him, "Where's the exit?"

Hresh lifted a finger. "There." He indicated a darkened alcove at the back of the lab.

Metallic thuds boomed on the door. Cloye and Nonas pushed through the murk.

Yul blasted the locks off the cages of beasts to either side as he passed by. The monsters, raw-fleshed, furred and nightmarishly hued, flowed out of their cages as one, cringing at the flashes of movement that came bursting through the door. Now they peered in venom, alerted to their new circumstance.

Some cut into the locust attackers that appeared, with teeth, nails and claws; others went wild and scattered in every direction. Yul was last to reach the exit. He was not sad to leave the locusts behind to contend with the panicked brood.

He caught a glimpse of Nonas's bewildered expression. The man, blinking and muttering, seemed ignorant of Hresh's whole secret sordid operation. Lucky for him or he would have wasted him along with Hresh right there.

Yul slammed the door shut and pulled down the bar. The exit was secured and his chest heaved at the thought of abandoning those who were inside as human fodder for the locusts. "How did the locusts track us so quickly?"

"Who knows?" Nonas panted. "The bloodsuckers must be swarming all over this warren. The place is infested with their reek. Why? Does it matter?"

"This is bullshit," cried Cloye. She smacked her blaster against the wall. Tinny echoes rebounded up the hall.

"Quiet, or you'll alert the squids," said Nonas.

"Let them come. I'll fucking kill them all!"

"Control your wild bird, Vrean, or I'll clip her wings."

"Try it," Cloye grunted.

They scrambled up the corridor, Hresh wheezing and trailing behind. They went skidding left at a T junction.

But they didn't get far.

Three hulking Zikri stormed out of a side hallway. Hresh groaned in dismay. Like a babbling lunatic, he backpedaled to stay away from them, knocking over a water dispenser. Nonas, E1 trained, jerked the man to his feet. Hresh scrabbled up the corridor. Nonas got a shot in, blasted one of their heads off. He hurried to catch up to Hresh.

Yul and Cloye stumbled after, but the two remaining Zikri cut them off. Yul squeezed off a blast, which ricocheted off the first squid's armor, stunning it momentarily. But their backs were to the wall and they were forced into an abandoned lab room, desperately backcrabbing to avoid those deadly tentacles. Beakers spilled and lab equipment clattered to the floor as they blundered in.

The second Zikri ducked Cloye's fire and charged her. She fell crashing into a table full of electrical equipment. Circuits and glass carboys went flying.

A tentacle whipped out, smacked her in the head. She sagged, fell limp.

Yul roared in fury. He kicked out a leg at the questing tentacles and with a chitter of triumph, the larger Zikri, a hulking brute with gray, wavering tentacles, charged him and bore him back.

Yul swore he could sense a glint of recognition in those pig-like eyes. But that was crazy! This Zikri seemed to target him almost instinctively, as if its chitters were profane announcements of a score to settle.

Yul's second blast shimmied off the Zikri's chest armor as the scuttling creature jerked crab-like and set Yul spinning back.

Stupid! He should have aimed for the thing's legs!

His mechanical fingers caught a whipping tentacle before it surrounded his throat. Another slimy appendage looped around his torso, threatening to crush his midsection. The air whooshed out of his lungs. Yul gave a dismayed groan. Damn, the thing was far stronger than anything he had ever experienced before. It was going to rip his body apart!

He twisted left, caught a second motilator that quested to wrap around his head. He tore, wrenched the flapping limb with an unrepressed fury, mashed it to pulp. A grunt from the ugly mouth came burbling out and the member hung limp. Yul's ribcage was near bursting. The Zikri, in pain and rage, whipped a lower motilator around Yul's throat, choking him.

Yul pulled it off with his strong left hand. He gasped for air.

The second Zikri skittered closer and was almost on him, reaching slimy motilators to ravage him from behind.

Cloye, coming out of her daze, jumped in to savage the Zikri's back with a powerful kick. She snapped the thing's neck with a second kick. It gave Yul time to fall backward, pulling the first hulking Zikri with him. He flipped the monster over his shoulders to crack on a piece of shattered metal with pointy edges. The Zikri chittered in anguish, its hide punctured by several metal prongs.

Yul grabbed the flailing tentacle and looped it with triumph over the overhanging bars of the lab table. He pulled the thrashing member down and tied it around the Zikri's neck in a crooked knot, choking the creature with its own flesh. Yul loosed a savage roar of vindication. The squid twitched, gurgling out noxious fluid from its butt hole of a mouth. Yul grabbed Cloye and his slimed weapon and staggered for the exit, eager to leave the dead and dying Zikri to their last moments. But a glint of metal beside the choking Zikri caused him to pause.

A queer expression crawled over his face. One of doubt and astonishment. The gun at the dying Zikri's side: it was the same as the pain dispenser that Goss had held on him back on Phallanor. How the fuck—? He shook his head in bafflement. There was no way that it could have gotten in the hands of a Zikri. Unless... The implication was staggering. It could explain how the Zikri had tracked them here. These squid-lowlifes got hold of Mathias's pain distributor. But what about the Mentera?

Yul's head swam with the possibilities. They only made his head hurt. He took his boot heel to the weapon, smashing it to bits.

The voice came over the loudspeaker: "*Danger. Air breach. Lockdown in progress. Contamination warning.*" The female emergency recording droned on. Red lights flashed in the corridor, bathing the white-washed halls in a blood-pulsing glow.

"Are you okay?" Yul rasped.

"I'll live." She gripped her elbow with trembling fingers. A welter of bruises covered the space from throat to mid collarbone where the plant ring had gripped her. "Let's catch up to those cowards, teach them a lesson."

"Forget them. We're on our own now."

"Your head's all banged up," she whispered, reaching up a hand to his forehead where it was all red and raw.

Yul winced. A goose egg was forming nicely on his left temple. His right leg was gashed and swollen and his hip throbbed. "A rib or two feels cracked. Otherwise I'll live."

"How do we get out of here?" Cloye murmured. "I've lost track of direction. Hresh and his bodyguard are the only ones who know this place."

Her eyes traveled to the tiled floor. Yul admired what he saw, the round curve of her full breasts, her slender waist, firm bulge of hips. "Well, there's one of their blood trails. If we really want to find our weasels then we follow this, catch up with them and get out of this rat's maze." She whipped back her tawny hair like a defiant cat. Clenching blaster in blood-caked fingers, she whirled to face him, studying the keen interest in his dark eyes. A fierce light shone in her own.

Yul smiled and slapped a fist in his palm. "I'm up for some more ball-busting, if you are."

Chapter 9

Yul and Cloye slunk like wolves down the hall. Blasters were gripped in both hands. They passed broken bodies of Zikri and Mentera, tentacles burnt, or with claws and heads singed. Some were smoking or sheared off. A fine job of trailblazing, Nonas, thought Yul. The man had skill.

They caught up with Hresh and his bodyguard at the air lock to the hangar. Hresh, rubbing his temples, pacing in tight circles, looked out from a blackened face, his bare arms scored with burns. Nonas peered miserably through the glass that provided a view of the parked ships and an open hole blasted in the domed roof. Yul bored eyes into him.

Nonas turned to glare in turn. "I had to look after Hresh."

"Sure. It makes perfect sense."

"Look, he was scrambling up the tunnel. Lucky I came after him, otherwise he would have been rat bait, wouldn't you, Hresh?"

Hresh looked away with a sullen gaze.

"Three of those squids were up there skulking like bloodhounds. They're in squidy heaven now. Always moving in packs of three, these squid-slugs."

"Makes perfect sense," Yul repeated, his face deadpan.

"Let's shut the small talk, you dull fucks," growled Cloye. "We need to find a way out of this mess."

Yul smiled and bowed. "After you, Cloye. Spoken like a true princess."

Nonas smirked. "Wish you two had have been here. Couple of roughnecks like you would have made short work of these squids."

"Yeah, what's your story?" muttered Yul, looking on the man's wounds and blackened, blood-streaked face.

"The Zikri started throwing pressure caps at us. I managed to chuck back one at them. As for the other, I was a little late." He grinned, a wide gap showing where two of his front teeth were missing.

"Tough break. Some people just don't have any luck."

"Yeah, I thought so too."

"How is that all the halls aren't flooded with toxic air?" demanded Cloye.

Hresh waved a hand. "There's an automated airlock in section E that seals the lab areas in case of accidental breach."

"But the squids don't seem to have blown those yet," Nonas observed.

The recorded voice droned on, "*Danger. Hangar 1 is flooded with high sulfur dioxide levels. Repeat, danger! All personnel in the vicinity report to evacuation chambers. This is not a drill. Repeat. Not a drill.*"

"Shut up, you stupid—" groaned Cloye.

The robotized female voice continued to drone on and Yul grinned.

"Great, now what are we going to do?" Cloye hefted her E6.

Yul pushed Nonas aside and looked through the glass. Locust ships amassed in the air, slipping through the cracked dome. Wrecked ships and mechnobots, dead bodies, human and various types of alien, lay strewn across the tarmac. A massive Orb had landed in the middle of the hangar and several Mentera craft ranged beside it. A smaller one with beams lit up the air, and a medium-sized Orb lay ruined beside it. A gaping hole lay in its side. Hresh's terraformers and three other lighter ships lay to the side, seeming as of yet undamaged. Locusts milled about in black pressure suits, pincers outstretched while the Zikri roamed, garbed in their light air masks, leaving the rest of their ropy masses of skin exposed.

"Well, the ships are good news," said Yul, eyeing the intact vessels.

Hresh hitched himself forward. He lifted an excited finger. "That's my V6 lightcraft over there. If we can make it—"

"We've got to suit up first." Yul pushed him aside. "Make for your ship, or one of the others."

"It's a battleground out there," murmured Nonas. "Are you up for it?"

"Any better ideas? It'll be a battleground here pretty soon too."

They grabbed suits from the emergency dispenser to the side of the airlock. Yul checked Cloye's oxygen level after she had suited up. It was at 90%. They tuned their radio frequencies to each other. As it was, it would be a challenge to get across the gap.

Hresh entered the security code override in the wall monitor and Yul pulled open the air lock and fingered his blaster. A flood of poisonous air whooshed into the chamber, nearly knocking Cloye and the others off their feet.

Yul wasted no time. He herded the three toward Hresh's light craft and ran ahead with Nonas to engage the enemy.

Mentera scouts stirred at the first glint of movement. They lifted their lumo sticks. Green flares arched their way and Yul ducked low, blasting Zikri stragglers that glided by as he ran. The aliens exploded in splatters of blood, air masks disintegrating. He plunged on, scrambling past the landed Orb, ducking stray locust fire.

Tentacled figures clutched captured humans, the remnants of Hresh's research team, and headed to the open cargo bay of the landed Orb. Locusts with lumo sticks oversaw the operation. The gruesome scene brought chills to Yul's body. The victims were herded in with slimy appendages. Lost. No way to rescue them. To storm that stronghold was suicide. One or two against hundreds, with armed ships about, was a dead man's mission. As much as he would have loved to blast those aliens to atoms, he had others to think about.

It would take them two plus minutes to reach Hresh's V6, he calculated. Should it be a seamless entry, they could be airborne in as little as a minute or less. Hope flared in Yul's chest.

A whirring sound whined overhead.

Yul craned his neck. What the hell was that? Hresh's invention? No, it couldn't be! The A13. How the hell did it get in the air?

Like the butterfly in the lab on Phallanor, the A13's outerbody had formed wings, which now flapped with purpose to propel it airborne. Much like the hybrids Yul remembered back on the Orb on Phebis, this one was equally disturbing.

Yul gazed on it with awe; Hresh, no less. He halted to grunt at his brainchild. Not without pride.

The landed Orb, distracted by the mechnobot's sudden appearance in the air, trained its guns on the A13.

Yul cursed. He ran across the debris-littered tarmac. "Hurry, you idiot," he called after Hresh through the com, "more Orbs and aphid fighters will be coming any second."

Hresh's sudden euphoria vaporized as he gazed on with tear-filled eyes at the ruin of his enterprise. "What a stupid waste!"

"Quit your bellyaching." Cloye clipped him on the back of his helmet and shuttled him along. "You've got the entry codes to the ship, or I'd leave your miserable hide behind."

Two of the Mentera ships, the ones shaped like bloated mantises, took to the air, treating the A13 as a visible threat. The landed Orb rocked upward. It was powering up its ion cannons. The aphid ships loosed fire, but the flying A13 deflected the blasts off its titanium exterior.

How it survived that battery of assaults, Yul could not fathom. A massive torpedo launched from the Orb trailed a red flare. It burst through the armadillo's armor, penetrating the Biogron, cracking the glass and releasing the vacuum. The avatar collapsed with a sizzle, and Hresh groaned as his magnificent machine crashed down from the sky into the litter of bodies and debris.

Almost as quickly, Hresh's dreams faded to dust as his precious escape ship erupted in a ball of flames before his eyes. The concussion knocked him backward.

Crawling on his hands and knees, Hresh sobbed. "No, no! It wasn't meant to be like this!" He pounded fists on the ground.

Looking over to the other ruin, Yul gave a caustic scowl. If the dragonfly creature hadn't been confined in Hresh's *Biogron*, it would have survived the onslaught. "Up, you!" he cried at Hresh, turning back to gather up the distraught man. "This is far from over. We may need you to fly one of the alien craft. You're a scientist, you should know something of technology."

Hresh's eyes rounded like saucers. They mirrored resentment at the sardonic remark. "Why not fly one of the terraformers?"

"Too slow, too obvious," grunted Yul. "One of those gets in the air and the Orb'll gun it down in a second."

"This ship here then," Nonas cried, motioning to the last aphid lightfighter parked a stone's throw away.

The commando sped up the locust ramp and smashed the butt end of his E1 on the access control panel. The door jerked open and Yul and Cloye scrambled aboard, dragging Hresh. Obviously the locusts kept no security here, expecting no resistance to their clear occupation of the hangar.

The foursome crouched low, crawling ahead in the dimness.

Nonas motioned them to the sidelines with his weapon. The whites of his eyes betrayed no sign of hostile movement. His lips moved as if to utter a reassuring word, then suddenly his head and helmet exploded in a crimson mash. Yul and Cloye ducked, staggering back, faceplates coated with Nonas's brains.

Yul cursed. "Shit!" So a guard had been posted.

He ran full tilt through the murk. Bending low, a blood-crazed yell on his lips, he slammed hard into a weapon-bearing locust with its lumo disruptor clutched in its pincer. He knocked the weapon aside and sent the insect flying. He crashed on top of its crusty carapace, his full weight straddling it like a gorilla, then he smashed his gloved fist into its chitinous face. It lay there, stunned. Yul's mechanical fist arched back for a killing strike, but he stayed his hand. It took all his willpower to temper that iron hammer from smashing through its gullet and into the back of its skull.

No, another time. They would need this verminous creature to fly this piece of shit out of here.

The thing was still conscious as Yul dragged the insect into the pilot's chair.

The locust played dumb, its head lolling. Yul twisted its claw with painful effect. The locust chattered out a cricket-like sound through its bleeding mouth. Yul grinned with satisfaction.

The locust set pincers to tapping the key console. It got the message, Yul saw. The engines roared to life.

The creature twisted and turned more sticks and toggles that looked like insect antennae. Cloye and Hresh stared at the ship's surroundings in horror. Each ruminated on the dire situation and their chances. Cloye prowled around like a caged lioness, wincing at the murky tanks off to the side. These were replete with gape-eyed human occupants. She dragged Nonas's headless corpse off to the side, gagging at the carnage.

Hresh stood mute, like an unmoving statue. His eyes glazed over.

"We're all dead," he mumbled.

"Make yourself useful," growled Yul. "See if you can figure out these controls. We could use some weapons right now."

"Forget about their weapon systems," Hresh sighed. "This panel's covered with alien script. How do you expect me to decipher it?"

"The same way you rig up a mechanical monster out of a butterfly. Figure out their crapbox weaponry," he rasped. "This grasshopper here—" he motioned to the dazed locust "—doesn't look as if it's going to be much use with weapons, even if it's capable. I'm thinking at best, it's a pilot."

Hresh grunted without enthusiasm. He clomped over to sit before the adjacent console.

With Yul's and Hresh's assistance, the ship lifted into the air, then passed easily through the crack in the dome.

Alien chatter came over the com in garbled bursts.

Yul lifted a finger, cut it across the insect's neck. "Don't answer that, freak. Show me the map, the star map." His quiet command hissed in the insect's ear.

Though the thing could understand no human tongue, Yul's suggestive and mimed coercion was of such ominous simplicity that the creature brought up a clear map of immediate space.

"Zoom out... Alpha sector! There." Yul stabbed a finger at a luminous area 18 parsecs away. He pushed his blaster to the thing's head. "Now. Set it!"

Cloye sucked in a breath. "That's far, Yul. Does this ship have the capacity for it?"

"It better, or we're dead. The farther we're away from this alien nightmare, the better."

The locust tapped in the coordinates with haste, fearing the intruder's threatened punishment. Bright fear danced in its crimson eyes.

"Do you think it understands?" asked Cloye.

"It understands well enough. If it tries to double cross us—" Yul sliced a hand across his neck. "That head comes off."

Cloye shrugged. She wrapped her arms around her midsection. "I'm itchy and cold, Yul. I'm taking this suit off. The suit sensors show the cabin air's breathable."

"No! Keep it on. We don't know what tricks this bug may be up to. It could poison us for all we know with a flick of a switch."

Ion blasts rocked the ship at her stern. Aphid lightfighters ravaged the shields. They had clued into the hijacking, but it was too late. Yul felt the tug of the light drive hit his gut as the ship entered the light highways. The forward viewports glowed with blurred lines and triangles, then the ship entered the zone of impossibility, a singularity to nowhere, and everywhere.

Yul breathed a gasp of relief. They had left behind Remus.

While he and Cloye were conversing, the locust made motions to lift itself from the chair, reaching for a side panel.

In three strides, Yul was at its side and stuck the weapon in its ear. "Fly this thing!" He waved his mechanical fist dangerously close to the locust's head, pointing to the star map. "To the free colonies—"

The locust seemed to understand that its life was otherwise forfeit, and settled back in its chair.

Yul hated the sight of the tanks that glowed off to the sides— Hresh seemed to be examining one now with macabre fascination. "Get away from there," Yul ordered.

"You're strung too tight, Yul," said Cloye. "Take a break, I'll watch the bug."

"Perhaps you're right." Yul frowned. He looked around and found some tough cord or adhesive like rope, probably what these bugs used on their victims during their raids. It was in the supply kits by the tanks, which he promptly wrapped around the locust's chest, securing it firmly to its seat. He wrapped several more loops about its pincers to reduce its mobility so it couldn't try anything covert. He took several strides aft, stooped, pocketed the lumo disruptor which he had kicked away earlier from the locust's pincer.

A reek emanating from Nonas's rapidly decomposing body forced him to find a large enough compartment to stash the body in. He recalled, grimacing, that the air units in their suits were drawing oxygen they could obtain from the cabin...he also recalled that the slightly alien air mix was somehow contributing to the fetid stench and accelerated body deterioration of Nonas.

This unpleasant task done, he glimpsed an escape pod aft which could prove useful. Nearby, two small bays with raiding gear and supplies: hooks, grapples, carts, equipment he assumed convenient for the locusts' kidnapping missions. On closer scrutiny, Yul saw this pod was more an EV vessel, complete with locust tail and wings, perfect for the locusts transporting captured humans.

"I'm burning up," Cloye gasped. She scratched at her neck and shoulder.

Yul frowned. "Fever." He uttered a worried sigh. "Probably from the toxins when those plants stuck to your skin."

He eased himself with a grunt into a sitting position beside the command post near the tanks, his fingers pressing the bridge of his nose. His eyes were closed, chasing pain and exhaustion away from his aching limbs and wounds. His mind traveled to the nightmarish memory of the squids as they dragged Hresh's scientists to their doom aboard the Orb.

"Those poor bastards," he muttered, "they didn't have much of a chance, did they, Hresh? Your scientists."

Hresh shook his head in gloomy affirmation and remained silent.

No matter. What was done, was done. Yul's eyes fluttered closed. Cloye would have the first watch...

* * *

Yul awoke with a start to find Cloye's olive-skinned body curled around him, practically naked. She had taken off her suit. What was she thinking? He growled out a curse, lurching to his feet, jolting her awake. She blinked, wiping sleep from her eyes.

Hresh was sitting with his back against the nearby wall, like a bag of potatoes. His head lolled, his mouth sagged open. He snored, feet pushed out in front of him like a clown.

The delinquent locust was still strapped to its wire-meshed chair, but the adhesive bands seemed looser than what he recalled. Yul grunted a sour oath. It looked as if it had enough wiggle room to reach one of the side control panels.

"Fuck! That was stupid, Cloye."

"Sorry, I—must have dozed off."

"The damage's done. Get back in your suit."

"Well, aren't you a spoil sport?" She pressed closer, her lips drooping in a sultry pout. Her breasts heaved with each rise of breath.

"I am when I'm thinking that I could have had my throat cut."

"Relax," she purred. She eased into her suit, taking her sweet time. "Our grasshopper's as harmless as a lamb."

"Is he?" Yul regarded the locust through slitted eyes. "Don't trust that thing farther than I can throw a shoe." The thing glared back at him, silent as a mouse, still as a statue. Something was not right about the creature. He could sense it in his bones.

Its red eyes gleamed with a hatred that looked like speculation. Yul breathed a quiet breath. "This bug's fucked us somehow. I can feel it."

He stalked over to the console and tried to pull up the star map, remembering the sequences the locust had tapped before. The 3D hologram came up, but vastly different than before. Yul blinked in confusion. "What? Wait, did I? What the—"

"We're still in the Dim Zone," hissed Cloye.

"It can't be, we've been flying for what, hours now?" cried Yul.

Hresh blinked, half asleep, "It must have changed the course."

"It couldn't have. Its pincers are strapped to the chair," said Yul.

"It must have tricked you before you strapped it in," muttered Cloye. "Set a faulty course. So don't blame me."

Yul tensed in hollow rage.

The ship came out of light drive as if of its own accord.

Yul whirled and caught his breath. He gasped at the panorama revealed on the viewport.

Toruses, Orbs everywhere. Ring Stations, odd-shaped ships. A firefly swarm of them, like nothing he had ever seen before. "It's a world of warships..." he murmured.

Mentera heavy vessels, L-16's, destroyers with massive artillery guns, conning towers a hundred feet high and insect-like superstructures, outstretched wings like grasshoppers. They were coming for them.

"What in the holy shades of hell—" Yul smashed his fist into the locust's plated face. "You double-crossing piece of—"

"Those are Mentera ships!" cried Cloye. "Why are there so many? Where'd they come from?"

"It's the Zikri and Mentera alliance," Yul croaked. "So, it's real. I see Zikri Orbs here." And there was more: a gray planet a thousand miles below them, gleaming like a pale beacon.

With nothing to lose, the locust whipped its left claw free of the tape. It snatched at a toggle on the console, doubtless the hailing frequency.

"He's warning the bug fleet!" Cloye yelled. "Control the thing. Fucking cricket!"

Yul smashed the insect on the side of the head. It chittered and tore its way out of its straps which it must have been working loose while they dozed.

The creature bore Yul backwards, ramming him hard into a nearby tank. The locust's strength was not insignificant. Yul felt sharp pincers pricking at his suit. He grasped both clacking claws before they could rip the lining and wrenched the pincers completely off. He whipped the thing off him and stomped a boot on its throat, breaking the wind pipe. The thing jerked spasmodically before it gave a final twitch and lay still. A viscid green fluid dripped from its cracked skull and mangled throat, spreading over its hard carapace.

"That was a stupid thing to do," groaned Hresh. "Now it can't fly us out of this mess."

"There's no flying out of here." Yul flicked a hand at the viewport. "There's a thousand enemy ships around us. Don't you see? Quick! Into the escape pod. We'll have to brave the planet below."

Hresh stared in fascination upon the locusts' ring-torus-shaped vessels.

The hailing frequencies were open. Alien chatter sputtered across the air waves, filling the cabin with clicks and clacks like the frenzied buzz of insects from a faraway rain forest.

Yul blocked it all out. He had to think. Damn it! He thunked a fist on the control board.

"Hresh, get over here. Turn your attention away from the shipfest. I want you to fly this thing right into the center of that destroyer." He stabbed a finger at the insect-shaped L-16 on the viewport.

"Are you nuts?"

"Do it! We're dead meat anyway. Our only hope is to escape in the pod. Cloye, you think you can work it?"

"I have a basic training in evac. Part of my assassin's training."

"Good! To the pod then."

"We're sitting ducks," Hresh gloomed, still shaking his head.

"No kidding, anything else you'd like to add?" Yul glared at him.

Yul kicked the locust corpse aside. He cast a fierce glance from the controls to the oncoming mass of ships.

"Hresh, you hear me? Move your ass. Help me figure out these guidance systems!"

The scientist gazed at the controls with owl-like eyes, passing tentative fingers over the maze of toggles, switches, and lights. "That looks like impulse, thrust, and stabilizers here, I think."

"Faster! Shit, man, are you a paraplegic? We've no time!"

Hresh started pressing buttons at random, pulling sticks and knobs.

The ship gunned itself erratically toward the fleet, in a direction 30 degrees closer to the destroyer. The crew was thrown back with the sudden acceleration. Hresh, twisting sideways, smashed his faceplate against a nearby console. The ship lurched like a lab specimen under electric shock therapy. The locust corpse slid across the cabin, slamming hard against the four tanks.

Cloye, recovering her balance, yelled from her station down the hall. "I've almost got this launcher working, you clods. Careful. I don't want to fuck it up."

Yul leaned in toward the controls, squinting through the viewport at the dim planet looming below. His lip curled in a vindictive grimace. "Aim closer to the destroyer."

"They'll nuke us as soon as we near it!" Hresh objected.

"That's the point. Do it." Yul saw the ship launch ion torpedoes at them.

Hresh flipped the alien controls. The ship wobbled on a jerky approach toward the fully-armed L-16. No less than a dozen cannons looked their way. The radio chatter grew in intensity. Yul scowled. He pulled Hresh away from the controls and shuttled him toward the pod. Cloye yelled at them to hurry. Yul slammed shut the hatch.

He and Hresh plunked themselves into the bucket seats and pulled the straps over their shoulders. They locked themselves in tight.

Cloye engaged the launch lock. The pod, a bullet-shaped four-seater with two port windows and rear double thrusters, burst from the launch bay.

Just in time.

The enemy torpedo struck and a raging fireball exploded behind them. Their aphid lightfighter, now blown to dust, rocked the escape pod with a jarring force. Cloye was wrenched forward, straining against her straps. Hresh howled in pure fright. Through the viewport Yul caught a gory glimpse of red hot shrapnel swirling in oblivion: scorched metal that flew through the emptiness and splattered against the destroyer's gray flanks. Random fires burst out on its spiked hull, hitting some sensitive areas: glass, metal fans, conning towers, penetrating the shields. Another concussion rocked the pod. Yul's look of dismay changed to triumph as he saw the destroyer momentarily distracted.

The escape pod plummeted toward the murky gray planet below. Rolling and bucking like a horse, it corkscrewed through the blacks of space. Yul glimpsed another bright flare to the port bow. The pod rocked side to side. A deafening roar filled his ears as it entered the atmosphere.

Cloye wrestled with the controls, guiding the alien craft down as best she could. Enemy fire swept after it, slick trails sliding by the port windows like sheet lightning. A blast grazed the pod, sending it into a crazy tailspin. "Hold on!" She jerked hard on an anti-roll stick, or what looked like one.

Hresh's eyes tilted up toward the pursuing ships. The man looked ready to vomit into his helmet.

Lights flashed on Cloye's console. The ship was tumbling wide on a crash course for the planet. The enemy ships—four aphid aggressors—whipped up and over the yawing pod, turning back to the Mentera station, a bright patch many miles in the distance. Their job was over. The pod and its occupants were doomed.

Cloye's teeth clenched in a show of white. Her tight-knuckled grip never left the controls. Hresh, pale as a ghost, gripped his arm restraints with one hand; two of his fingers trembled on the straps across his chest. Yul braced himself for impact. His mechanical fingers twitched and released. His mind was angry with the knowledge that there was nothing he could do. The ship's nose was up. Cloye launched the first of deceleration sequences. The high G's had them sagging into their straps, skin pulling away from their cheeks.

The landscape loomed closer: vague shapes of dormant volcanoes, dusty plateaus, rocky headlands from long-dried up seas.

Blinking against the massive force, Cloye kicked in the main stabilizers. Her cheeks and brow were oozing with sweat. Liquid practically dripped from her pores, but a determined gleam rested in her eye.

Yul recognized that level of tenacity...it could be the difference between life and death. The pod's navigation system seemed much simpler to operate than the aphid fighter's with its reduced number of controls. Fortunate for them, otherwise they would have been ripped apart.

Cloye released what reverse impulse power remained before impact in an effort to halt the pod's descent as much as possible.

Their breaths caught in their throats. The drab features of the landscape flashed by at alarming speed and Yul's jaw sagged. Hresh's eyes pinched shut.

The ship tore in on a shallow angle. The pod's tail glanced off a patch of sandy landscape, dragging like an anchor. The nose kicked upward. While the hull bucked and rocked, skimming many times on the sandy surface, it finally came to a skidding halt before two rounded boulders.

Silence. The rush of air, escaping gas from somewhere within. The drip of liquids, internal fluids. A fine dust billowed around the windows.

Yul struggled to rise from his seat. He blinked his eyes, coughed. Groggily, he loosened the straps. He kicked off the light aluminum panel that had fallen from above. No broken bones. He staggered to his feet and loosed Cloye from her straps. She seemed dazed but was breathing normally. He pushed debris and air bag parts out of her way while Hresh murmured at her side delirious words.

Yul helped her up and wondered if he were in some fantastic dream. The ship's functions seemed miraculously intact. Lights still powered the console and the cabin air seemed breathable. But no hull breaches, audible or visible. And yet the hiss of air implied the cabin's life support system had been compromised.

He stumbled over to gaze out of the viewport. The pod had flipped partially on its side. All he could see through the filmy glass was a grayish brown featureless plain and some daylight.

"Good work, Cloye," he croaked. "You saved our asses."

"But for how long?" She coughed into her helmet.

Bloody hell, she looked rough. Sweating like a pig, with dark circles under her eyes. "We need to get out of here, investigate our surroundings."

"Ship's functions are minimal," she remarked. "Not enough juice to lift us. Too much exterior damage." She coughed again.

"Why not stay here?" Hresh suggested. "We have air." He crinkled his nose at the bleak glimpse through the dust-caked glass.

"Ship's sensors show life at twenty miles distance," Cloye mused. "Wait. Some closer, three miles."

The ship's sensors beeped. Cloye frowned, her eyes glistening.

A cause for concern? Yul did not know.

"There are life readings?" he asked, tossing Cloye her weapon.

Hresh gave a skeptical grunt. "Or as easily, death. One of the locust or squid colonies. I don't doubt this world is a home planet."

Yul ignored him. He reached for the air lock ring which was tilted up at 45 degrees at shoulder level. The depressurization chamber was fortunately above them, rather than under. When the ship had come to a rocking halt, it had settled one side up, otherwise they would be in a bad way right now.

One by one, they climbed up into the air lock chamber and Yul locked the seal behind them then forced open the outer hatch. He slid down the shiny, gray fuselage. Cloye and Hresh were right behind him. An arid landscape spread before him. Scattered rocks dotted the plain; also what looked like mesas not far away. A crater lurked in the distance like a blasted off mountain top. It was about eight miles off. The sun's pale white light gleamed on the southern horizon. Mid morning or late afternoon? Yul was undecided. Air was thin here, less than 50% human-breathable oxygen content. A slight breeze wisped from the northwest. He guessed it had warmed here recently, for his suit's climate sensors reported the subzero temperatures now hovered just under zero.

He knelt and grabbed a handful of the sand at his feet, letting it trail through his fingers. A fine, colorless loess. The softness of it had saved their lives.

"I don't like this place," Hresh muttered, casting anxious glances around the inhospitable terrain.

"I'm guessing it doesn't like you either," Cloye grumbled.

Yul examined the boulders pressed to the ship's starboard reach where one of the pod's wings lay sheared. The long shadows draped over the hull's stern like phantom fingers. Goliaths—probably eroded long ago, carried by melting glaciers during a distant ice age, thought Yul. The ghostly landscape left a hollow pit in his stomach, a chalky feeling in his mouth.

"I'm figuring the lifeforms the sensors picked up are in that hollow over there," Cloye pointed out. "About three to four miles away. Guess we could hike over and investigate."

Yul registered a slight breeze on his suit monitor. Wind had picked up from the northwest. His suit air was at 72%.

"Well, we'll all die here without food, shelter and oxygen. We seem to have no choice. Let's go."

* * *

Soft gray shadows fell over the dusty soil. Everything was too quiet, not even a breath of wind now stirred or whistled around the few peglike rock forms they passed. Their footfalls fell in dull thuds across an endless plain.

The dusty crater loomed ahead, a dipping blemish among a vaster expanse of others like itself. As they approached, Yul halted, knelt, scrutinized what looked like tracks, three-toed ones, neither Zikri nor locust, but perhaps a mix of both. Reptilian? The creature's stride was short, whatever it was. Sometimes it appeared to crawl, obliterating its own tracks.

Yul frowned. Possibly more than one organism. The trail wound off toward the flat-topped mountain much closer now. He did not have a good feeling about that place, nor the one they were heading toward. His metal fist closed tighter on his blaster.

They loped more easily in the lighter gravity than walking in full G. But it was dangerous. One slip and one could smash his faceplate on a rock.

They approached the lip of the first crater and Yul slowed, reflecting on the macabre events of the recent past. The destruction of Hresh's research installation had probably set back cybernetics decades, but better than letting those damn butterflies rove free about the galaxy. A part of him knew that the plant pods were never meant to leave Xeses.

If he had been granted knowledge of the past, he would be appalled at the reality that worlds like Xeses and Sigren with their territorial puffballs and pods were only one of the thousands of worlds that the Masters had seeded eons ago...The Masters, long vanished from the stars, that mysterious race which had created the Mentera and the Zikri in their fiendish vats in bygone eras. They seeded lifeforms on worlds in the Dim Zone and beyond: the puffballs of Sigren, the Xesian plant-pod butterflies, a thousand other species hidden away on remote worlds, far from human eyes. Even they could not have envisaged the strange, exotic and brutal universe they had spawned out of sheer, idle curiosity—or in an attempt to answer the question, what if...?

Yul felt the changing ground crumble underfoot as he stepped closer to the crater. Below spread a gentle sloping hollow of gray sand sprinkled with brown boulders and flat gray rock. The basin was roughly circular, and the lip continued on to the other side where it rose in rockier formation, about a half mile away. A small meteorite had struck here. Yul reasoned, perhaps hundreds, if not thousands of years ago.

Cloye snorted at the visible lack of any lifeforms. She bent sideways to make her way down. But Yul held back. Three-toed creatures lurked about, or had been here. Many clawed prints lay etched upon the crumbling slopes and in the dusty soil on the plain. "Cloye, hold up," he warned her.

She turned him a carefree grin. "There's nothing here, Yul. The sensors must be whacked or something. Either that or the lifeforms are farther on, perhaps on the outer edge by those rock formations. Let's get a move on, Yul. We don't know how much daylight is left on this weird planet."

Yul said nothing. While he couldn't disagree with her assumption, he was not all for running recklessly into danger. Cloye was a magnet for trouble. Even as he formulated the thought, a wild shape hopped out at Cloye, from behind a flat rock. His warning came too late. She whipped out her blaster, but the thing was almost on her. A weird half-bug, half-octopus creature. Human-size.

It grazed her hip with a set of rippling appendages, raising a chitinous snout and gargling out an otherworldly cry. Not a familiar animal cry or even an insectoid chitter. Yul aimed his weapon low as he scrambled down to help her. How to blast the creature without killing her? Hresh stared, frozen-faced.

Regaining her balance, Cloye blasted the thing as it squirmed back on all four motilators, tentacles rippling like an octopus's. It fell, writhing in a smoking heap, charred beyond recognition.

Yul caught up with her and knelt beside her, gasping. "You okay?"

She nodded, recoiling at the alien monstrosity smoking a few feet from her. She kicked at it. While they darted wary glances about, she croaked, "More of them about? Are they scouts?" She wrinkled her nose.

"Others might be around," Yul admitted. He looked about with uneasy suspicion but he could see no sign. "What is this weird place? Doesn't look like a colony."

Hresh half-slid over to halt and study the crisped body with curious horror. "It's alien, but nothing like I've seen before. Can't say whether it's Zikri or Mentera."

"Both, is my guess," Cloye said. She was unable to mask the disgust in her voice.

A glint of light caught Yul's eye. It was several paces away toward the edge of the crater. "Over there," he motioned.

Hresh and Cloye's eyes narrowed. Hresh stepped back, swallowing a gulp of air.

Yul went to investigate. As he came closer to where he spied the gleam, he paused. The shiny reflection appeared to be a small pool of dark water. Three other pools were nearby, no less black or limpid. A body of a spaceman lay beside the first one; his suit was torn apart and the man within frozen. A dull glaze of horror gripped the man's ashen face. Ice crystals clung to a thin mustache.

Yul turned in sorrow to the foremost pool. A human figure lay trapped beneath a filmy surface, like a glass medium. The murky material showed brownish water below. Yul stepped back a pace. He tried to make sense of the scene. The figure seemed aware of the movement above him and feebly raised an arm, beckoning with a finger.

Yul did a double take, blinking in confusion. Through the gloom of the water he saw that the figure wore a space suit, like his dead peer. But the face—it was so white and withered—

Yul stared on grimly. "We have to get him out of there."

Hresh came panting beside him. "Wait, Yul, we don't know what's down there or what he could be carrying."

Cloye pushed between the two. "Back off, Hresh! Are you going to leave the poor bastard there?"

"I'm not saying—"

"Move back!" Yul shouldered Hresh aside. Cloye, clicking her tongue, hopped away to grab some rocks to crack the glassy surface that entombed the victim.

When she returned, Cloye pushed a large stone into Yul's gloved hand. He knelt, arching high a downward strike, shattering what appeared to be some synthetic material.

The thin layer spider-veined like a split egg as Yul peeled away the pieces. The water rippled below. The spaceman struggled weakly out of the water and Yul and Cloye grabbed him, hauled him to the chalky soil while Hresh hitched in closer to gawk.

Almost instantly, a multi-legged thing jumped out of the water, a knee-high crab-like squid. It hooked onto Hresh's leg and cut a hole into his suit with its proboscis. The thin cold atmosphere of the planet whooshed into his suit.

Hresh screamed, backpedaled, kicking to get the shelled mutant off him, as it struggled to burrow into his suit to get to his flesh.

Yul fired at it, sizzling its coral-like carapace. The creature gave a whistling screech then scuttled away toward the boulders. Cloye aimed a series of blasts which nipped at its legs, crablike and spindly as they grazed off its gleaming white shell. The creature strayed off its course—tracing slow circles now as it scuttled to find a hidey-hole out of range.

Hresh was howling a high-pitched wail. He slapped hands over the tattered liner at his knee. Yul swore. He fiddled with his emergency pack, trying to tear off a great length of adhesive from the suit repair roll to slap the polyethylene over Hresh's rip. He covered the fluttering fabric and heard air begin to return to Hresh's suit. But would it be fast enough? The man's face was contorted, blueish.

"What the fuck was that?" Cloye cried.

"I d-don't know," gasped Hresh, his teeth chattering. "I'm not waiting around to find out." His breath fogged his faceplate.

"What about this guy?"

"What about him?" Hresh wheezed. He looked at the prone man who convulsed and whose eyes now bulged as he was out of his protective cocoon. "The man can't be saved. Some primitive colony, as I said." His eyes rolled as if even in his delirium he were analyzing a weird science experiment. "That thing was more crab-squid than insect."

"Whatever," grunted Cloye. "What about our pale-faced diver?"

Yul turned his attention back to the convulsing man. With speed, he twisted off the cracked helmet. "Help me pry his jaws open. Quick! I don't want the man choking on his own tongue."

Water had gushed into the victim's suit. What had put him there? Yul reeled at the possibilities. How was he alive? Like those freaks on the Orb? This man would freeze, if the temperature got lower. He guessed it would within the hour, as the sun sank. The man's suit luckily seemed intact, with the exception of the filmy faceplate which remained spidered with cracks and sported a large hole in the center. The man's dead comrade near the other pool was not so lucky.

The suited man went into deeper convulsions, choking out mouthfuls of foul water. Yul pushed palms on the victim's chest. He applied CPR, giving him a chance at life. The man began to gulp the thin air, his chest heaving.

Yul cursed, fumbled for the extra outtake valve on his own suit. He forced open the frozen lips, shoving the valve into the man's mouth. He adjusted it to allow a graduated stream of oxygen to flow out and the man's eyes dilated, rolled in wild abandon. His face was utterly drained of color, pure white with an even whiter sucker mark arching from cheek to cheek. It was the same color as the crab-like thing that had raced off to the rocks.

Yul shuddered. The man's nose looked flattened, as well as his left ear mangled, as if something had half chewed it off—no doubt that crab thing that had scuttled away.

The figure began to shiver uncontrollably.

"Quick," snarled Yul, "the man's freezing on contact with the air. He's going into shock. We've have to drain his suit, otherwise he'll die of exposure."

Why the water didn't freeze earlier Yul could not guess, but with the Mentera and Zikri around anything was possible. He'd seen enough weirdness to last a lifetime. The locust tanks, Hresh's horrors... He didn't doubt these pools were something of the same order.

Yul barked a command to Hresh and Hresh switched his own extra regulator with Yul's. Yul and Cloye lifted the shivering man by the heels and let the water drain past his neck.

They set him down. Yul motioned a hand to Cloye. She hopped over and twisted the helmet off the dead astronaut, which seemed intact. She gave it to Yul, who screwed it onto the gasping man's suit. Yul flicked the regulators at the back. A green light came to life. There came the familiar whish of oxygen in the pipes and a slight bulge to the suit. The man roused. He blinked his eyes in rapid succession.

"Who are you?" whispered Yul. He brought his ear close to the man's receiver.

The man's pale tongue slipped between parted lips. He gave a weak hiss. "I'm F-Fenli. F-First officer...against the Jakru invasion. Reporting for duty, sir!" He managed the last words with a crooked grin, then passed out.

Chapter 10

Back in the abandoned lab room, Krin managed to chew through his tentacle where the human had looped and tied it around the bar. He slumped with a thud onto the wreckage and bloody ruin of his comrade's body.

Bral gazed out from sightless eyes. His polyp of a mouth gaped open, dripping pungent black fluid, now pooling at Krin's side. How lucky the warrior was to have met his death in honorable combat, as it should be for a warrior of his caste, Krin thought. Death soon would be his release as well. His hours were coming to a close.

His main motilator had been mutilated beyond repair and he was barely able to drag himself out of the lab along the mirror-smooth corridor. The sucker pads on his working appendage allowed that agonizing locomotion at least. The rest of his body was smashed in multiple places. Four tentacles trailed behind, crushed or severed beyond repair. Before his primary motilator had been rendered useless by the human, he had caught a glimpse of metal peeking up from under the skin of the terrible fingers of the devil that had ripped a chunk of his flesh out. The human must have been one of those machine men, like the one he had torn to pieces on Mathias's ship. But what did that matter? Now he was dying, bleeding out, and he had lost the most important fight of his life.

Krin's breath rasped out of his chest in slobbery gasps. He

coughed out a gob of black blood onto his mask, which dangled askew, not quite covering his nasal orifices. He almost retched as he dragged himself with torment down the corridors.

The human had fought well, like the dervish he was, and had won. A salute to him. As a warrior, Krin could respect that and not feel bitter toward him, only applaud him, and honor the creature in his own death in accordance with the warrior code that he served. He was prepared to die peacefully and alone on this alien world. A death he could have met earlier. Many times he had escaped doom, but not this time.

Krin's polyp of a mouth curled into an ironic grimace. He had saved the human Mathias by plunging him into a tank. What irony that the human with that pup's grin was still somewhere on his ship, had been granted near immortality, one who would stare glaze-eyed out of his glass prison forever. The human would bear the ravages of time until the elements corroded his container and spilled his innards out in death. No one would venture to this world ever. Most of the Zikri here were dead, as were the crafty locusts, and their ships destroyed or flown away.

How Krin dragged himself those hundreds of yards through the human corridors was beyond any who could have observed him. His emergency mask dangled even further from his cheek, only half covering his bruised mouth, as he chittered in anguish in various stages of delirium. At last he was at the hangar and through the damaged air lock. The erstwhile Zrake's Orb had gone, taken away by the Mentera with their trove of humans from the research facility. His smaller Orb lay on its side with a gaping hole, defunct, shot down by the research team's counter-defenses.

Where the human machine that had crippled him was, he did not know, nor did he care. He crawled with grief among the wreckage of bodies closer to his ship, his mausoleum. No time to get to the Mentera tanks that could rejuvenate his ravaged and broken body. He was bleeding out too fast.

The last thing Krin saw was the mechanical juggernaut looming over him, gazing with certain curiosity. Twitching bodies of Mentera lay crushed under its mechanical feet as it staggered closer. Just as suddenly came a sound of fluttering over his shoulder. A dragonfly. The pod-birthed-creature flew through a jagged gap in the avatar's metallic breast and Krin glimpsed through the smoking hole in his ship's side, Mathias's tank, and he understood...

That three beings from far-off worlds were inextricably linked by fate, all brought to a tragic end.

* * *

The dragonfly observed all this as it flew out of its breach in the *Biogron's* glass. The atmosphere of this strange world did not seem to affect its peculiar physiology. Its bodily functions were made for adapting to constantly changing situations and conditions of its existence: atmospheric, climatic, physical. That and chemical shock or physical imprisonment were its banes and strength-givers. Such was the nature of the alien's survival mechanisms. As its mechanical avatar smoked and sizzled in the blood and flesh of Zikri at its feet, the dragonfly adapted again. An insight dawned in its agile brain. Flying with fervor back into its armadillo shell, it reached out to state-of-the-art circuits made available by the Biogron. The avatar twitched its metallic ears, lowered its horn in response, while the dragonfly continued to send more pulses to heal its mechno-circuits and outer wounds and urge its ravaged, plated form forward across the ruin of bodies closer to the Zikri ship that held Mathias.

The dragonfly realized it could fly free of its glass case at will, or it could fly back into the Biogron casing and use its protective armadillo armor when it needed to—like a virtual mechanical god.

As the mechnobot of Hresh's creation lay there smoking in the sallow murk now lightening before the alien dawn, its robot eyes sighted on the multiple forms of Mentera and Zikri corpses, the sizzling clumps of jagged metal and twisted wreckage, and it sensed a perfect Utopian stasis: a harvest of corpses in a peaceful graveyard of eternity, its for the taking, and it, the dragonfly, the sole lord of its domain.

Chapter 11

Life had taken an unfortunate turn for Regers—if such euphemism could be applied. Left to his own resources, he was to die in the most lonely, hellish manner possible, abandoned by his crew to the tentacles of the Zikri.

As he lay choking in the cold, oxygen-deprived air pouring in from the desolate moon through the Orb's breached hull, it was the dead bodies of the marines that saved him. Several of their suits were nearly intact. The adhesive that Yul had 'kindly' left behind had served to repair one he had exchanged for his own. Regers had used Hurd's oxygen mask during that grim melee, knowing the sod wouldn't mind, suffering while he sucked air and jerked about, freezing in the cold as the room slowly warmed up. By the time he had loped back to the hold, *Lander* was gone. Mathias's mop-up crew had left without him. *The fuckers.*

Regers had slumped on his knees, praying for death, with the big eerie dragonfly following him everywhere about like a mariner's albatross. Now the thing was more a dragonfly than butterfly since it had grown: a thing of horror and majesty with its tapered, chitinous body and lethal wings.

Regers would never forget that Yul had left him to die here in a swamp pool of scum. Of body parts, feral aliens and the cuckoo bird-butterfly. In the end, the creature had been his savior. It considered him part of its environment, a necessary fixture to protect. It would protect him at all costs, even against the ruthless Zikri.

Regers worked the muscles of his disfigured cheeks, arms, and his left hand mauled horribly by the heptadoria. His warped soul was cut even deeper. He knew he was a survivor. He had not gotten to where he was by luck alone. Where all had died, he had survived. He had outlived team members, gang members, friends, foes, family, even Salma... poor Salma, his vibrant young wife who had died much younger than she should have. His body ached beyond words after spilling out of that locust tank, even though the greenish water had supplied a healing power which he could not explain. His body had been repaired—to a degree. In the unlikely case he made it to a medical bay, a prosthetic unit could replace most of his former hand. Maybe he could appeal to his cybernetics freak Mathias, for some new limbs. This was a dark irony, one not wasted upon Regers.

Scrubbing furiously, Regers had only partially succeeded in removing the white chalky substance that caked his skin. It appeared to be some sort of resin or effluvia the heptadoria had jetted out as excrement, or some foul ejaculation of fluid to defend itself much as an octopus would, squirting ink in times of trouble.

Regers would hunt the bastard Yul down until the debt was paid... This one savory thought had kept him alive during his hellish trials and would continue to while his plan gathered momentum...

None had come to investigate the Orb until now. He had self-nourished, jumping back in an unoccupied tank to heal in the magic liquid. Everything had healed except his left hand. That was beyond repair, gone forever. No infection, no fever, just a throbbing agony as the cells multiplied and the ragged skin layers knit together. Angry raw scabbed flesh where normally his wrist would have been, formed at an unprecedented rate. It ached like a bitch, but he'd live.

The dragonfly had protected him; it had followed him wherever he went as he nosed his way around the ship. Once, twice, before self-nourishing he had managed to secure the door to the tank room before the thing could slip through. Then, he could hear it banging its iron-hard head against the metal, trying to get out, to get to him. It was as if the thing couldn't stand the possibility of being without him. Regers cringed, shivering at the memory of the thing. Birthed with him in the Mentera tank, its place of entry into the world, it had seemingly identified him as a 'guardian', a stable force in its habitat. He guessed he was something of a father to it. In the end he had had to trap it in the adjoining chamber. But soon enough he would have to return to that hellish room containing the bodies to get nourishment.

The starship *Albatross* was crippled. One of the captured lightfighters in the Zikri hold might have given him passage off this loathsome world—if the main drive hadn't been blown out by a uro bomb. The other...well, at best it could operate with some repair and maybe his rudimentary flying skills. But a big if. The Orb—forget it—it was breached and crawling with Zikri once again: guards he guessed to protect it from scavengers. Even if he took off on impulse power, it would be tracked or flagged by other warships and gunned down.

Regers had explored the seemingly endless adjoining rooms and found hundreds of victims in the gruesome tanks. The resultant spoils of countless raids; they floated and bobbed in their greenish aquaria. The eerie ghastliness sent chills up Regers' spine. The machine parts of the raids were probably shipped to Zikri bases around the galaxy. This explained the hold's relative emptiness at this time, whereas the humans had not been passed to the Mentera—yet. For this reason the ship would still be important to the Zikri. They would return with even more squids...and soon enough. With this in mind, Regers worked hard and fast. He'd been spared an agonizing demise thus far by perverse fate alone. He did not want to push that luck. Freedom was his...for the moment...and there would be hell to pay when he was mobile...starting with that fucker Yul who had left him to die in the tank room. Mathias would also be due a reckoning.

Regers had managed to seal himself off from the Zikri invaders by working the self-locking control to the door of the main Zikri tank room bordering the hall. The dragonfly had provided the rest of his backup. It had been fascinating to watch. The insect sprayed toxic stuff more deadly than acid on the tentacled guards sent to protect the valuable cargo from looters. In a daydream reverie, he had recalled it cutting them to shreds with its fabulous wings. Such a wild instrument of death! Beauty in motion!

Regers named it 'Shredder', his pet dragonfly. He could hear it banging now against the sheeted metal, trapped in the adjoining room where he had last lured it.

In his requisitioned suit, Regers prowled about a new room of tanks, a hundred, maybe two hundred telephone-booth-like tanks, whistling happily, moodily to himself... The time was ripe for action and he was the maverick who would pull it off.

At last, something of a large enough pool for his purpose. He had managed to seal the chamber, all monstrously dark and dripping, and the Orb's working systems brought breathable air back into the room. This was something he had experimented with earlier. For backup, he had dragged in ten suits by the leg, with painstaking effort given his chewed off hand, suits formerly occupied by Mathias's dead, 'mop-up' mission crew, the sods. Well, five to be exact. The other five he could not separate from their gray garb, they were so badly mangled.

He picked several fresh tanks with human figures and marked them with some of the white stuff that still coated his skin. He had to be sure; nothing like good old intuition for picking subjects which he had in spades. There were some women too, choice pieces of ass, but practically he must allow utility to prevail over pleasure, and they looked too traumatized for the use he had in mind. He used his E1 like a sledgehammer to smash the tanks he had chosen. Glass shattered; green water spilled out, the victims flowing with it.

While he whipped about smashing tanks, he conducted mock colloquy with himself, calling out the attributes of the men he had chosen, brawny physique, defiant looks, glares of roguish cunning.

"Regers, Regers, why not just pull the trigger and blast these poor wretches out of their jars? Do it the easy way?"

In answer, he jumped over to the spot of the imaginary figure he just talked to. "As a matter of fact, Mister-Poo-in-the-Tank, it's more fun this way."

He moved on past one of the tanks previously marked with white chalk. He peered with a frown at one who looked too pedantic, easily intimidated. He skipped it, moved on to another. Yes, he liked this one. The man had a perpetual leer.

He took his time, smashed the glass of the second last tank, and sat back with a smirk of satisfaction. He amused himself, eyeing the goggling antics of figures coming out of their watery hibernation: groans, retches, pitiful jerks and convulsions like mannequins. Some were recovering too slowly for his tastes. "Get up, you shivering fuckwad," he called.

The dazed man in the dripping slime grunted as Regers' foot met his midriff. Viscous fluid spewed from his mouth. "There, probably did you a favor."

He shook another with one hand, till his teeth rattled. "Time for you lotus dreamers to wake up, and your happy nightmare to begin."

The other he booted with the back of his heel.

One refused to respond. He flipped this wretch over and slapped his face. "Get up, you!" Still nothing. Grabbing a handful of putrid water from a half-shattered tank, he dashed it into the man's face. That didn't work either. He grabbed another handful and forced it down the man's throat.

Gagging, clawing at his throat, the man loosed a spiel of gibbering protests.

"There, you'll be fine. Just a little mouthwash."

The man retched and rubbing his temples, garbled out curses.

Regers slapped his thighs with laughter, a gleeful hyena sound that had the rousing men blinking in confusion. "You're all fine specimens."

"Who the hell are you?" croaked one, a lank-haired marine who looked like an officer. "Where the hell am I?"

"You're in hell and I'm your Uncle Regers," said Regers with a happy grin. "You're in the middle of funland, call it a 'squidy Orb'."

The ten men looked at each other, as if assessing the state of Regers' sanity.

"Don't give me that prissy look!" Regers stomped over to thrust his blaster in one man's mouth hard enough to make his gums bleed.

The man's muffled groan echoed weirdly in the creepy gloom.

"That's better," Regers chuckled. The crooked smile returned. "Now listen up, bitches! We're going to take this hold, that's about 800 feet down those filthy halls, through black, slimy corridors. Problem is, we've several squids just waiting to squeeze the love out of us and put us in those ever-loving tanks. Get it?"

They stiffened and remained silent. Each peered around the high-ceilinged hall shrouded in gloom. The disgust and apprehension lighting up their faces was not feigned. The gleaming resin on the walls slicked with a rank shellac was real enough, no less the off-putting, squid-like forms with gruesome heads and questing tentacles sculpted in low-relief on the walls.

Regers caught their disturbed glances and allowed himself a chuckle. "I've scouted out the hall already, along with my friend, Shredder. In case you didn't know, Shredder is my dragonfly-pet. He's in the next room. That's him hammering against the wall. Looks as if there's one ship, a lightfighter, intact in the hold. That's our target. Any one of you engineers?"

One man crowed, "Name's Jennings. Mechanical engineer."

"Guess my lucky picks were right on the nose then. Figured one of you boys would be the mechanical type. Question is, can you fix it?" He lanced Jennings an intense glare. The man stared back wide-eyed. "It's got a big bash in its side. I fooled around with the panel box on-board, even pulled up the diagnostics boot sequence. It was showing a 'multi phase' yellow disorder on grid RC2, whatever the shit that means?"

"My guess is it's one of the rear stabilizer cells. Must be fried."

"And? Can you fix it?"

The engineer shrugged. "I can try. Maybe patch in series one of the working cells with the blown one."

"Atta spirit, Jenner."

"The name's Jennings."

"Whatever the fuck, *Jennings, Jenner, Jiminy Cricket*, I could care less..." He lifted his E1. "Gather weapons from these stiffs. These dead fucks won't need them. There's enough firepower here to raise Lazarus from the grave, praise the Lord!"

A meaty man with a fleshy jowl stared at him in awe. "You a religious man, Regers?"

"You betcha, now get your ass moving! We have work to do."

The ten men groped about, arming rounds in their rifles, testing weapons.

Industrious. Just like he liked them. That fat fuck who had asked him about Jesus wouldn't last long, but the others? A shit-eating grin had begun to curl on Regers' face again. He had that look a lot, ever since that pansy-ass Yul had abandoned him. Why couldn't it have been like this aboard the *Albatross*?

He snorted. Well, maybe there'll be a homecoming yet. "Yul, baby, I'm coming to getchya!" He piked his rifle in the air, saluting the idea. One last flight aboard the good ole *Albatross*, God rest her soul!

The men nearby frowned, thinking Regers a complete lunatic. Regers laughed, the men having no inkling of the depth of his lunacy.

The recruits fanned out, rifling through the suits Regers had brought, looking over the arsenal of weapons. Some fingered knives and explosives, others E1's. The more sensible ones examined their knives and tested them on the stubborn corpses that stuck in rigor mortis to their suits. He recalled the blood, sweat and tears it had taken to get those fully-suited men into the tank room and the luck that he had Shredder to run interference on any curious squids.

Regers curled his lip with approval. The dark man with the balding head, Deakes, or so his name conveniently labeled on his uniform said, scrutinized everything. He tested his mobility in his suit, practicing mock maneuvers with another marine, Vincent, a wiry youth with straight black hair. He prodded about, studying the surroundings with a careful eye. They would be rising stars, these two. He knew it.

One man, blinking like a toad, frowned at the dozens of vacant-eyed figures floating upright in the tanks. His pale tongue flicked out to lick his lips. "We have to set them all free, Regers. Every last one of these men and women."

"No, we don't," intoned Regers. "The minute we open those doors, they'll all die. We don't have suits for them. Unless you think they can breathe ammonia."

The man's mouth worked and a hot flush reddened his ears. "Well, we've got to figure out a way, damn it!"

Regers made a buzzer sound with tongue and teeth. A cold grin surfaced on his haggard, fish-white face. "The lightfighter will take only a handful of men. And I don't want to be shitting, eating and breathing recycled air with a bunch of turds like you."

"That's a cold-blooded way to—"

Regers whirled and with all his strength laid into the man's skull with his E1, cracking it like an egg. The man fell like a log, blood oozing from the wound. The others peered on in stunned wonder. "Anyone else with a brilliant suggestion?" Regers growled.

The men exchanged wary glances, teeth clenched.

"Then listen up, you fucks. You're the chosen ones! My knights of the round table, for lack of better words. Risen from the grave! Jenner, I give you the privilege of choosing a replacement for this misguided soul. Pick a man, any man!" He laughed, a ribald chuckle. "Not the women though. I see that bulge in your pants, you sneaky bastard. Keep it on a leash."

Jennings shook off his displeasure. His look mirrored the question *what had he done to deserve Regers?* Grimacing, he blasted a nearby tank that contained a glaze-eyed Jakru inside.

"Oh, you like the horned ones, do you?" Regers sneered. "Well, sure, Jenner, whatever. Come here! I dub thee 'Sir Knight of the

Horned One'." He guffawed, made a sweeping bow before Jennings and touched left and right shoulders with his E1, knighting him on the spot.

Sniggers drifted from a few.

"Anyone else have skills to bring to the table? Like piloting a ship?"

The rough-looking Deakes and the fresh-faced Vincent grudgingly offered up their names.

"Listen, I've picked you well. None of you surviving pansies are to free any of the women or our poor little froggy-floaters in their brine. You realize we have to save your own skins here, don't you?"

There came some muted rumblings and Regers smiled.

"Then suit up, bitches! Don't fail me. There's a shitload of ammonia out there. The hull's breached. It's freezing out there. In case I didn't mention it."

Three of the men grunted. "Here, here!"

Quick to recover and to size up the situation, the hawk-nosed Jakru with the horns stepped forward, dripping and expressing his gratitude. "I am Ramra. Grateful for this second chance at life." He bowed low before Regers.

Regers thrust his weapon in the air again, acknowledging the tribute.

* * *

After they were all suited and had used Yul's adhesive to repair any tears, they engaged in a full check of their oxygen levels and ensured that all their feeds were working. Vincent had a defective air line in his back pack and had to sub in from one of the spare suits. Thinking ahead, Regers had dragged an extra one in to be sure.

Some of the Cyber Corp rescue team's corpses were looking pretty hacked up and in advanced rigor by the time they had dragged them out of their suits. Acid burns on their faces and caked blood in gruesome places brought grimaces to the faces of even these hardened men. Regers shook his head, reckoned them as cargo haulers, miners, marines, security men, engineers, pilots, the like.

All in all, it had taken Regers longer than expected to prep a decent working team. Even then he wasn't sure. There was no guarantee that these hacks with their hack-job suit exchanges would work, or that their makeshift patches would bear up in the alien air before they could get to the lightfighter and safety. Well, they would find out either way...

Regers released the door. The men leveled their rifles as a wash of toxic air whooshed in.

He resealed the door. With stealthy stride they marched through three more tank rooms before they reached the main hallway.

Regers motioned. "Down this way. A straight haul to the hold. Watch the sides and corridors. They're sneaky bastards, these squids. Don't look back."

Eight men ran two to a shoulder down the dim corridors, with rifles ready.

Regers took up the rear, watching the steam issue from their helms. Better that a few of the eager pups die first should they encounter enemies in an ambush. A highly likely scenario.

The low throb of machinery or something more sinister came to Regers' ears. The interior, like the insides of a rotting whale, appalled him; it reeked of danger, casting in every corner unnerving shadows in a murky sepia hue.

But he set such distaste aside. He and his crew passed like wraiths, stepping over scattered Zikri corpses. Regers began to grin. The remains were in various stages of decay, mutilated bodies beyond recognition, the work of Yul or someone like himself. The cold air had decelerated the decomposition. The arriving Zikri forces obviously weren't capable housemaids. Regers snickered.

They rounded a bend and it was another 300 feet to the hold. Wait, what was that? A flicker?

Regers strained his eyes in the dimness. Nothing. Then he saw a slithering movement.

"Incoming! Stay alert!" he howled.

The ambushing squids wore masks but no suits. They seemed

able to handle the cold internally and on their skin, damn them.

A tentacle came out to wrap around Regers' faceplate. The grisly member joggled his helmet and he could feel toxic air flooding his suit. He screamed, hacking with his E1. The barrel sprayed useless fire. The thing locked him in an unbreakable grip. Out of the corner of his eye, he caught the movement of a familiar shape. A colored flying thing. *Shredder.* The creature swooped.

Never before had he been happier to see the monster. The crafty git must have figured a way out of its prison. But how? No way it could have busted its way through those walls of steel. One of the squids must have let the thing out by accident.

Regers could feel his shoulders on the verge of crumbling. He couldn't fight, compromised as he was with the use of only one hand and the effort needed to hold his breath. The squid's ugly warted face pressed close to his. The squid suddenly went limp. A razor-edged fin of a wing had cut through the corded Zikri sinew, and a spurt of black fluid sprayed across his faceplate.

Regers reeled back in disgust, letting the terrifying mass slide to the floor.

He dropped his blaster and knelt, lungs bursting for lack of air. A trembling hand and rigid stub efforted to screw back on his helmet.

"Forward!" he croaked. Air began to flow once again in his suit. Staggering on like a drunken man, he dodged tentacle-flailing squids. "Get to the hold, you idiots!"

Deakes bulled his way through, blasting squid flesh and tentacles. Head parts flew. The fiends that slipped through the knot, he slashed with his bowie knife until the gleaming blade was dripping with black-goo. The youth Vincent was right on the man's heels, picking off rippling targets.

Four of Regers' men scrambled ahead, spraying fire into the clot of writhing shapes. Regers snatched up his rifle, blazing rounds into the fray.

Two of his men were down in a quivering mass of flesh and gripping tentacles. Regers didn't expect them to survive. It seemed this batch of squids was not intending to take prisoners, having learned the hard way from their past mistakes. Bully for them, he thought. The fat fuck, as he had predicted, was joining the roll call of the dead, his arm twisted on a backward angle, his mouth arching in what he'd call an agonized cry. Zikri lashed at his defenseless body and punctured his suit.

More of the enemy would have followed had not the dragonfly kept them busy, slashing out at them, its colored, knife-edged wings slicing down at their gruesome hides. It dive-bombed them with merciless flair and feral skill. Swooping and rolling like some alien bomber, the thing was an iridescent queen, multi-colored wings whirring like propellers, darting about the cramped corridor with hummingbird swiftness. It lay ruin to anything with tentacles that moved forward to threaten its guardian.

Regers snorted. Damn it to bloody hell. The Zikri must have posted sensors in this hall. How else had they snuck up on them so easily? Didn't matter. The corridor opened up into a dim, cavernous space—the hold. No time to lose.

Regers bolted toward the *Albatross*. Panting for breath, he motioned what few of his men were left, toward the chained lightfighter whose faded decal read 'Xaromar'. The ship was a Daulk model. Simple, efficient, no bells or whistles. A compact, sleek, smooth-lined craft, capable of serious horsepower, armed with ion disruptors strapped to port and starboard. Chains with keyed locks securely anchored the landing gear struts to the plated Orb's side.

Regers counted Deakes, Jennings, Vincent, Creib, the horned Jakru and one other among the survivors. "Saw off those chains," he ordered. "You three. I saw cutting tools back there on that workbench."

As soon as Jennings tweaked the circuit to force an entry and open the hatch, Regers and Deakes both clambered aboard. Regers stood at the foot of the craft, on the lookout for enemies, knowing that Shredder would be a capable back-up. He was pleased to note that the Jakru had discovered plasma cutters, or what passed for them. All were busy firing them up. The loops of chains on the first of the four landing gear struts, blackened and weakened from blaster fire, were melting under the ministrations of the men.

Regers gnawed his lip. The fact that the squids would leave such tools lying about implied they were not worried about security. The chains here were used more for anchorage. He massaged the raw ache in his neck where the tentacle had nearly snapped off his head. The right knuckles of his blaster hand barely made an impression on the wound, even while pressing firmly on the liner of the suit. The tentacle would have wrenched his head off, if not for his helmet.

Of course, a moot point, given the timely appearance of the dragonfly. How many times had Shredder saved him? Hard to discount that it'd be profitable to carry the insect aboard in a sealed container. He could sell it to the highest bidder—inevitably some eccentric billionaire or rich research company that would pay dearly for it. But the memory of the feral thing jetting about his watery prison, peering on him with almost human feelings, savaging the heptadoria, caused him to shiver and he swept the idiotic thought out of his mind. No fucking way was he going to mess with the damn thing. It scared the hell out of him.

This blowtorching was taking too long. He hitched himself forward, squinting down at the nearest imbecile who had almost burned off his gloved thumb in his nervous haste to get the job done quickly. Who knew when Zikri would slither out of the murk like serpents...

"Ramp it up!" he yelled. He drew back in dismay. "Shit, there they are now!" Above the Zikri shapes swooped the dragonfly, whizzing out of the dim corridor like some mutant wasp.

The sounds of the lightfighter's whirring engine filled his earpiece. Regers jerked to action. The pilot lights flashed green on the transom. He made for the hatch, catching a dark glimpse of Deakes and Vincent through the thick glass fiddling with the light drive controls on the bridge.

Creib melted the last of the chains and the Jakru, Regers and a black-bearded man clambered aboard, securing the hatch tightly behind them.

Regers stepped over the dried blood staining the floor of the bridge. Likely the aftermath of an uncooperative crew member under Zikri assault. Jennings scanned diagnostics while Vincent and Deakes toiled at the control console. They guided the ship toward the Zikri tractor pad and the jagged hole of shredded metal in the Orb's side. Regers saw the squids had still not repaired it.

A murky twilight bathed the bleak landscape in an otherworldly hue. Stars glinted in the alien sky.

Regers reeled as the dragonfly smashed its iron-hard, bullet head against the glass. "Hyperdrive out of here, Deakes. I'm sick of this fucking place."

Another jarring blow hit their moving ship broadside, strong enough to take them off their course. Regers shuddered. "Get this shitbox out of here!"

Creib started forward, his muscles tensed. "We'll burn up, Regers. Initiating light drive so close to a gravitational field like this moon is too risky."

Jennings concurred. "She can ride rough on impulse power with her rear stabilizer blown, but better not risk sudden warp in high grav."

"Quit squawking, you chicken shits," muttered Regers. "A little risk isn't going to kill us at this point in time. Besides, Shredder is looking a little pissed right now."

Deakes and Vincent grinned. They continued flicking dials on the upper consoles, as if to start up the light drive sequence.

Regers muttered, "Better too, than facing a squid ambush in the air."

Creib shook his head. "It's foolish, Regers. Warp sequence magnifies gravitational pressure on the hull. Superstructure overload will likely crumple it. It's common knowledge. All ship manufacturers caution against it." Shredder smashed its head against the glass again, and the ship shuddered.

"Well, well, my foolishness then," said Regers with a mock trembling hand covering his mouth. "I should check with Captain Kirk on this one. What do you say, Vincent? You okay with it?"

"Captain Kirk is okay with it."

"Then—!"

A blip came over the digital viewer. A yellow light flashed on the 3D hologram, cutting Regers off in mid-sentence.

Jennings pointed to the image on the viewport with a creased brow. "Looks like we're in for some more heat, Regers."

Regers mouthed a curse. He gaped at the massive, spiked hull hurtling toward them. "Fucking squids. Can't believe it. Just our bad luck."

Vincent growled, "One of them must have radioed ahead before we could cut it down."

"More than likely. Man the weapons! Jenner, make yourself useful. We're in for a dogfight."

Ramra gazed at him incredulously "Why not hyperdrive out of here, Regers, like you were going to do?"

"Well, Creib here, thinks it's a 'gravitational risk'. 'Causes severe stresses to hull superstructure, against regulation code', that kind of shit."

"Well, it's true," defended Creib.

Ramra threw his hands in the air. "You're all going to get us killed!"

Deakes shrugged, as if it were all one to him. "Death is death, Ramra."

"Get those shields up!" Jennings yelled.

Deakes looked at him as if he were a genius. "Uh, why didn't I think of that?"

Regers laughed. "You boys are larks." His smile faded when Shredder veered in for another assault.

Ramra reached down to scratch furiously at his right leg. Sweat pooled on his throat. His suit lining was frayed where he itched and rubbed. "I say we nuke them all, the bug too."

"Yeah, I appreciate your input," said Regers. "But it's a dumb plan. As Creib said, the flux generated by a large gravitational body or for that matter, any large weapon, will convolute our light drive exit... We can't fire and enter light drive at the same time."

Uro bombs came pounding at the stern against the *Xaromar's* shields; more star pricks of orange fire glinted from the Orb's looming cannon.

"Won't matter now," grumbled Regers. "Fire on those damn squids!"

Jennings and Deakes plied the weapons' controls. Flaring ion streams torpedoed out of the lightfighter's twin cannon to smash against the spiked hull.

The Orb easily absorbed the shock with its shields and maneuvered to launch more bombs.

"Fuck it!" Regers hit the hyperdrive activation switch.

The hull creaked. The torturous groan of a thousand metal plates racked the air as a suspension bridge would under hurricane forces. Eyes peered up at the paneled ceiling. Unfathomable tidal stresses bulged the metal which was threatening to cave in on them. The cabin went dark.

Regers felt as if time had gone still. it effectively had. There was a flash of yellow light. A soundless, hair-splitting moment passed when each man thought he was caught in the floating limbo of hyperspace, from which there was no return. Research papers had been written on the experience of singularity, attempting to describe such a bone-chilling dimensional rift. That *place* of absolute incomprehensibility where one's spirit roamed bodiless through the ethers, the place of human souls in eternal transit.

Creib closed his eyes. Ramra gasped; white spittle dripped from his mouth.

Regers saw the man's face suddenly stretch like a horrible pumpkin, and the others' bodies reformed and stretched too, then morphed and reformed again, pulled like putty men. Then they were tall stick-like caricatures spinning like tops, shaking violently, blurred at the edges. Regers looked down at his own hands, saw his own limbs stretched as if viewed through a distorted lens.

Then they were normal. He relaxed as the ship lurched into the light highways and their forms became whole and still again.

Regers roared, "Woohoo! Hot damn! We have liftoff, boys!"

Creib loosed a moan of relief. His bulk swayed against the console, his trembling hands clutching for support.

Deakes laughed and Ramra slapped Creib on the shoulder. "See that? Creiby here almost shat his pants."

Creib retorted, "If you knew what danger—"

"Can it, Creiby," Regers croaked. "This is no time for morose reminisces; methinks celebratory acts are in order."

The ship slipped along the lightstream on a general course for Perseus. Deakes had programmed an auto vector into the smart nav leaving the Dim Zone only a memory. Nothing less than complete engine failure, or the wrath of the Almighty could stop them now.

The men were significantly lighter of spirit after the successful jump. They flopped on padded seats in the bridge or prowled around the ship.

Jennings continued to study the navigational charts while Vincent and the others raided the larders, ravenous as wolves. Deakes found shelves of bagged coffee, packaged meals, protein liquids, nutrient pastes in twelve assorted flavors.

They also found booze. Only mild spirits by Regers' standard, but gallons of it. The Daulks sure knew how to stock a ship, even if they were donkey-eared anthromorphs from faraway *Gfand*, laughed Regers.

The lightfighter purred along like a kitten through the ethers despite her banged up hull. Regers wondered where the squids had captured her. He didn't recall many Daulks down in the tank rooms. Perhaps the squids had blasted them? Or eaten them?

Regers shrugged.

The rabble of men he'd recruited was not ideal, but exceeded expectations. Deakes was probably the most useful of the lot. The man had a good head on him, especially in times of danger, as proven by the way he had hewed down those squids with his knife and blaster. Best of all, he didn't flash any priggish looks behind his back like that smug fuck Jennings. Likewise, Vincent had performed well, racking up an impressive tally of squids, doing the old feint and blast while watching Deakes' back. Jennings, he grudgingly admitted, was a close third, though he would have to lose that stodgy, passive-aggressive personality. Ramra, while devoted, was a bit of a whiny bitch who'd get his horn and tongue clipped in the near future if he wasn't careful. Creib, he could take or leave. A bit of a mamma's boy in his opinion. Surprised the stocky fuck had made it out of that corridor with tentacles taking men's heads off. But then again, if Deakes and Vincent hadn't been paving the way... He shook his head with a grim smile at the memory.

Jennings approached the drive console, motioning to the com. "We'd better fly this thing to civilized territory, Regers. Some port in the free colonies will suffice where we can make a full report. A proper intelligence report of what we know to New Order Alliance base on the outer peripheries, to the Jakru, the Daulk."

Regers stared at him as if he were a talking fish. "They'll want ship's identification papers, credentials, the whole kaboodle. Then they'll take away our ship. Ever think of that, Jenner? Even accuse us of stealing the craft. Interrogation."

"We can swap information for exoneration," Jennings grunted.

"I say we can't," sneered Regers. "I say we keep flying this pretty little ship to Alastra station, as I intended. It's a gift from above, and I don't plan on losing it."

Deakes and Vincent muttered agreement.

Ramra croaked his own wish to alert some of the authorities. He licked his lips, a fine sweat beading on his throat. "At least tell somebody the coordinates of those people down there."

"And have it traced?" Vincent queried.

Jennings hesitated, seeing he was outnumbered. "I mean—"

"Jennings, when did you get so righteous?" Regers rounded on him. "Get all goody-goody pansy-ass on me? I didn't peg you as the do-gooder type."

Jennings purpled. "Maybe since I fell victim to those brutes—being on that Aldebaran freighter and getting pulled out of my bunk by one of them. Then bobbing in that freak-tank. I wouldn't wish that on anyone. Call me sentimental, but if I could save anyone from—"

"Oh, so you're a savior type? We're all supposed to sit back and pay the piper while you get a bleeding heart for some philanthropic mission? You going up against the squids, solo?"

"Just a simple anonymous call."

Regers swept out an arm toward the com. "Be my guest."

Jennings jerked away like a marionette. He made the call. Ramra and Creib who had said little or nothing, looked away noncommittally.

Regers turned back to the others who gathered at the stand-up table and stared back with sober, sullen looks. "Jenner over there thinks he's the martyr to carry the torch of some damn galactic war. But it'll never end. There'll never be any winners in this war. Bloodshed maybe. One side trying to dominate the other. I say, let them eat each other's balls for breakfast. Stuff each other in tanks, same deal."

"Calm down, Regers," soothed Deakes. "Sounds as if you're the one getting sentimental on us."

Regers winced and shook his head. He peered down at the leftovers on the table. "Yeah, maybe you're right, Deakes. But I don't want to hear any more whining or squabbling about those floaters down there on the Orb. What's done is done. On a happier note, I'm proud to have you boys as my fellow knights. A toast—to the motliest band of rogues of the times. One ship today, rulers of the galaxy tomorrow!"

Vincent lifted his glass. "Here, here!" he cheered, getting into the spirit of Regers' madness. A broad grin split his boyish face.

The Daulk ale had started to do its work and Regers reeled to his feet. "We're the Robin Hoods of the new age. Stealing from the poor and giving to the rich!"

Deakes laughed, choking on his drink. "That's rich." The men were warming to the idea, encouraged by Regers' no-holds-barred sense of wild adventure, or insanity, depending on which way one looked at it. Each hardly dared to believe that they were free from the oppression and macabre reality of the locust tanks.

"How be steal from the poor *and* rich and enrich ourselves!" Deakes suggested.

"Not bad, Deakes. There may be a place in my fleet for you yet."

Deakes gave a cawing laugh, drunker than ever. He swayed in his seat, his eyes blurring over. "Not if our horned-headed Jakru here doesn't wash himself. The man reeks of that locust piss water."

Ramra sneered. "Hardee har har. You think you smell any rosier?"

Regers leaned back in relaxed comfort. He and his merry band would get along fine. So they enjoyed their jests and insults, and for the moment, their loose-knit alliance, formed in a most improbable place, had gotten off to a good start. He figured they were beyond the edge of the Dim Zone, between the pirate belt and Perseus Major, somewhere in the haze of hyperdrive.

Regers looked around, pleased with the proceedings, but he grew wary. There were too many details to work out. Too many risks and perils lay ahead.

Deakes snapped Regers out of his reverie. "So, what you got planned for us, boss? Trolling the dives on *Thieves World* for some choice wenches?"

Regers grunted and waved his hand. "That's kid stuff. I got my sights set on bigger fish, Deakes. Right after I get this hand looked after. Kinda getting used to it though. Could plate it up with some tempered steel." Regers mused. On a sudden impulse he scrambled on the table, did a cakewalk, wiggling his ass. "I'm your Captain Hook, your baddest, meanest, bloodthirstiest Bligh! Shiver me timbers!" He lifted his stump and play-chopped at Creib's neck.

Deakes snorted out a laugh. Ramra, having drunk too much, fell nose-first in his packaged mash of half-finished shepherd's pie.

Deakes probed. "So what's so important in Perseus, Regers? You got a boyfriend out there?"

Vincent laughed.

"We could as easily land in Taurus, or jump over to Betelgeuse," growled Deakes. "Thieves World, like I said."

"Nearest hub to Phallanor," said Regers. "There's a guy I have a score to settle with. But first that fucker, Mathias." He jumped down from the table, jarred out of his jocular mood.

"Mathias?" Vincent queried, "as in the CEO Mathias of Cyber Core, or whatever it's called? You got to be mad."

"Keep the course set for Phallanor, Vincent," Regers said grimly. "There's going to be hell to pay..."

OTHER BOOKS IN THE ALIEN ALLIANCE SERIES:

FRONTIER
XARES: FINAL COUNTDOWN
AUDRA
THE TIMELOST

https://innersky.ca/alliance

ABOUT THE AUTHOR

Chris is a prolific author of fantasy, adventure, and science fiction. His writing spans many genres: heroic fantasy, sword and sorcery and speculative fiction.

Browse Chris's books at:

https://innersky.ca/books